PUFFIN BOOKS
Editor: Kaye Webb

D1098732

The Bright and Morning Star

One great tragedy has overshadowed Reuben
and Thamar's perfect happiness – the affliction
of their second son, Sadhi. Deaf and dumb since
early childhood, Sadhi has grown ever more
vicious and, by refusing to eat, has put his life in
great danger. 'He is dying of his unhappiness,'
weeps Thamar. In despair, she heeds the words
of an ancient prophet and, seeking for a cure,
takes Sadhi to the land of Kemi.

Her friend, the great King Merenkere, puts Sadhi
under the care of his Royal Architect-Physician,
Hekhti. But Thamar and Sadhi have reached the
Court at a moment of upheaval. The King's
daughter is to marry her brother Sinuhe, the
Royal Heir, who has fallen under the influence
of a sinister Priest of Set.

When Apep, the great serpent in the Nile, rises
to swallow the Sun – throwing Kemi into darkness –
the Priest's plans become grimly clear. Merenkere's
throne is endangered, and the courage and loyalty
of Reuben and Hekhti are tested to the full.

Funny, exciting and perceptive, this story makes
a fitting completion to the adventures that began
with *The Moon in the Cloud* and continued through
The Shadow on the Sun.

Rosemary Harris

The Bright
and Morning Star

Puffin Books
In association with Faber & Faber

Puffin Books, Penguin Books Ltd, Harmondsworth,
Middlesex, England
Penguin Books, 625 Madison Avenue,
New York, New York 10022, U.S.A.
Penguin Books Australia Ltd, Ringwood,
Victoria, Australia
Penguin Books Canada Ltd, 2801 John Street,
Markham, Ontario, Canada L3R 1B4
Penguin Books (N.Z.) Ltd, 182–190 Wairau Road,
Auckland 10, New Zealand

First published by Faber and Faber 1972
Published in Puffin Books 1978

Made and printed in Great Britain by
C. Nicholls & Company Ltd
The Phillips Park Press, Manchester
Set in Linotype Pilgrim

For Bruce and John

Contents

8 *Contents*

Author's Note

The Bright and Morning Star is the last book in a trilogy which began with *The Moon in the Cloud*. Some years have passed since the adventures described in *The Shadow on the Sun*, and Thamar goes down to Kemi with an afflicted son, Sadhi, in search of cure. The children of the Royal House and Reuben's children, the cat Cefalu and his descendants, are drawn together in the pattern that began when Reuben, alone in Kemi, became Merenkere's musician and his slave.

Inheritance in Egypt was through the female line, and the Throne itself was no exception : the King's daughter, if he had one, was his heiress, and anyone who married her — or his widow — automatically became the next Lord of the Two Lands. For this reason the royal princesses were almost always married to their brothers, so that the succession should be assured.

Imhotep was one of the greatest human beings this world has ever seen. He was a contemporary of the Third Dynasty King Zoser, and was Vizier, architect, and Chief Ritualist. He was also a scribe, astronomer, and poet, and the most famous physician of his age. Veneration of him started within two centuries of his death, and the Graeco-Roman world identified him with their own god of medicine, Asklepios, and worshipped them together. From early times the sick would spend all night at his tomb, hoping to be cured, and to the ancient world it became the equivalent of Lourdes. Its probable position at Saqqara, near to the immense Step Pyramid that Imhotep designed for his king, has only lately been discovered during the excavations led by Professor Walter Emery.

Prologue

The Firedrake

The Firedrake

Cefalu was sitting by a small dung fire outside the Palace walls. He loved to sit there, dreaming of his past. The triangular lids fell over his eyes as he half snoozed, thinking of things that would never come again but were as vivid to him in old age as the present sunlight, and the sound of Reuben's children playing nearby in the olive grove.

Dung smoke rose towards the sky in a twirl of blue vapour. He opened his green slits of eyes which were still brilliant as jade although the fur around his whiskers was grey and, in some places, white. A swallow flew just above the smoke, and Cefalu's muscles automatically tensed, and twinged with rheumatism. His extremely long tail was kinked with it. Again he shut his eyes and sat bolt upright, his paws correctly placed together, his head a little forward, neat and scarred. Once more he dozed. His eyelids were like wrinkled paper, his whiskers stiff but scant.

Three kittens came romping towards him and fell irreverently on his tail. They patted it, rolled on it, and generally pushed it about. One of Cefalu's eyes opened thoughtfully, and then closed again. A stern father, he was a fairly indulgent great-great-great-great-great grandparent. He and his offspring had taken the command 'be fruitful and multiply' with thoroughness, and the resulting kittens were very much in everyone's way.

'They tease you, Cefalu,' Thamar often said. 'You mustn't let them.'

'Spirited little things,' he would reply, tolerantly feeling his tail. Old age was sad, but to have lived so hard and so knowingly, and to have produced so much life to pass the matter on, what more could any cat ask?

One of the kittens nipped too sharply, and Cefalu hurriedly moved his tail. 'Words from that Pearl of Wisdom, Meluseth,' he said sternly. '" Enough is enough."'

The wisdom of Meluseth was a tradition here in Canaan. Her retorts spiritual and advice material were quoted in all places where Cefalu's descendants dwelt. The homespun excellence of every pithy saying was laid at her door, or rather, at her tomb, and it was said that if all Meluseth's wisdom could have been recorded it would have taken ten wise scribes a lifetime to write it down. By words attributed to his first, fluffy, long-dead mate, Cefalu had felicitously ruled his later mates and offspring. In the Palace of Canaan it was known as the Way of Meluseth, and Cefalu's neat black velvet favourites went much in awe of it.

'You really should settle down again, Cefalu,' said Reuben often, as he chased several she cats off his and Thamar's bed.

'Settle?' Cefalu would respond, licking his tail, and with a glint in his eye old as the glint in Adam's. 'As one grows older youth grows increasingly attractive but, alas, exhausting. One could not settle with it.' And he would roll himself into a furry ball on Thamar's pillow, and sleep.

He had many dreams – of life before the Flood, of the great king's palace down in Kemi, of the wicked land of Punt. Joys and sorrows had been mingled. Everybody who had shared Cefalu's past adventures had had a share, too, of joy and sorrow. Reuben, who had been a penniless animal-trainer and musician, a king's slave, an honoured king's servant, and was now the Prince of Canaan, was no exception; nor was Thamar, his lovely wife.

Their home in Canaan owed its existence to Reuben's integrity and the King of Kemi's wealth. It was like a jewel, a rich gift from heaven. The Palace, part fort, part dwelling-place, covered a large space of what had once been mud. Now ochre-coloured flat-roofed towers rose above lush groves and pasturage. Reuben's rule of his princedom was tactful though firm. His children were to be inheritors of this land, but to bring it to blossom from a muddy waste while they were still young must be the task of settlers from lands beyond the devastation caused by the Flood. Reuben had wondered if he should exclude them, but Thamar had been firm.

'The wicked tribes have gone, haven't they? If these other, gentle people had been meant to go as well, the Flood would have stretched farther, wouldn't it? What's wrong with making a muddy waste blossom like the rose, if it's not for one's own glory or tinkling anklets or the love of gold? What's wrong with making the infertile fertile?'

'What indeed?' asked Cefalu, opening one eye and shutting it again.

'You must let old Ashrat ben Josept have the land he wants, Reuben, really you must. The Lord wouldn't wish you to starve your neighbours, when the mud could teem with life so quickly. *He* sent us servants and maidservants from Kemi, by the hand of Merenkere, didn't he? That's what I'd call a tactful suggestion.'

'A very convenient one,' replied Reuben. He had done what she told him, for she was often right, but at the back of his mind was a slight sense of unease. Perhaps it was this doubt that made him work for his people and his country as he had never worked before.

Fruit and flowers and children; the placid bleat of sheep and goats; great rosy pomegranates hung like lamps among their dark glossy leaves; figs and vines; storks flying in from the Unknown to perch on the crenellated towers, and swallows swooping overhead : all these were part of his heritage. Here, the land was so fertile you had only to look at it and something grew, though farther east it was hard to grow scanty blades of grass – until sudden rain caused the ground to blossom with lilies of the field. All this, amazingly, was for him and Thamar.

Most important of all, there were the children.

Five of them already. Joshu, the eldest, would be Canaan : handsome, and apparently solemn till his long lids opened wide to show wicked laughter. Sarah and Miriam, the two small girls, huge-eyed and sleepy looking, but given to fits of gaiety which made Thamar thankful for her Kemi maidservants. Five-year-old Phut, the youngest boy. And there was Misraim, called Sadhi, who was the second boy – and one sorrow in this paradise. Sadhi, when he was Phut's age, had suffered calamity.

The hand of the Lord, cackled the old women, eager to lay the blame on masculinity even in heaven. Thamar, crooning to her stricken child, knew only that it would be arrogance to go through the world and expect no trouble. Reuben, dark in spirit, searched for his own shortcomings, and remembered his unease at having invited strangers to share his land. But whatever – whoever – had invited trouble, it was Sadhi who suffered the result.

It had seemed at first like an ordinary childish illness. High fever, delirium. A small boy who stared about him, demanding why the strangers he saw everywhere wouldn't play with him. Then there were convulsions, and terrible black days when he lay cramped with pain, and when his terrified gaze sought his father and mother, silently begging them to relieve him, to comfort him, to find, at any cost, a cure. Then had come worse days when it was only by a responsive movement in his hand as Thamar held it that they knew he still realized her presence; and then there had been paralysis, and they had waited hopelessly for death.

Frequently since that dreadful time Thamar had found herself wondering if death wouldn't have been more merciful than what happened to her child. For when Sadhi at last turned the corner towards recovery it was found that he had suffered a grim change : he could neither hear nor speak. As his body grew stronger but nervous shock or damage kept him dumb and unhearing he grew frantic. He would try miserably to communicate, and would then hit about him in desperation, flailing at his bed, at Cefalu, at his little sisters, his father and mother – even at Joshu, whom up till now he had loved best of all.

Neither Reuben nor Thamar could bring themselves to firmness with a child who had suffered such grievous hurt. His affliction was theirs. Their endless tenderness and attempts at teaching had no effect, and gradually the spoiling he received turned Sadhi into a pathetic tyrant. No one could tame him, unless they cared to break him by brutality, which neither of his parents would allow. He was spiteful, sly, and the cruelty of his fate made him cruel to everybody else – when Phut was born a constant guard had to be kept on his cradle, or Sadhi would have damaged him.

Cefalu was the only living creature in the Palace who withstood the tyranny. Early on, after a few blows and tail-twistings, he had summed up the future accurately, and scratched Sadhi so fiercely from knee to ankle that thereafter he was left alone. The ancient herd dog Benoni, now stiff with age beneath his heavy coat, had expressed himself as scandalized. *He* allowed himself to be buffeted from head to tail, and made no reproach.

'The wise will consider the time and the action suited

thereto; and layeth up for himself a fount of fortune,' responded Cefalu tartly – and added 'Wisdom of Meluseth,' as an afterthought.

By the time Sadhi was eleven Reuben and Thamar had tried everything they could think of : prayer; herbs; visiting foreigners from far lands who said they knew effective cures, but didn't; even a rare charm from Sumeria. (This last attempt caused Reuben a twinge of conscience, which he stifled for Sadhi's sake.) And in the end it was all useless – Sadhi remained as cut-off as he had ever been. Then Reuben and Thamar tried to resign themselves. They had a gracious inheritance and everything to make them happy except – a reminder that they were small and human and fallible – one stricken son.

The other children learned to deal adroitly with the situation. When Sadhi was in his better moods they would include him in their games, pushing him kindly in the way they wanted him to go, until he lost his temper, when they would holler loudly 'Caltah !' and hold Sadhi till his own servant came running to control him in a bear-like hug. (Even Phut learned to hold Sadhi's feet in a way which made it impossible for him to kick.) As he grew older his moods had grown more vicious, but they were now interspersed with lengthy bouts of melancholy which would keep him sitting alone and cross-legged day after day, motionless except to slap away an encroaching fly. His dark eyes looked out suspiciously at the world under brows twisted into a perpetual scowl. Tall though he was for his age, his suffering seemed to make it impossible for him to put on weight. His face developed the immobility of a more Eastern child's, and his appetite began to fail and his ribs to show.

'He is starting to die of his unhappiness,' wept Thamar to Reuben.

'Beloved, perhaps we have to face that it may be better so.'

'Oh never, never,' wept Thamar. '*Someone* might cure him still.'

Reuben sighed. They had been over this before. Over and over it. Sadhi would never be cured, and Thamar wouldn't give up hope. In a way he wanted her to give up hope, so that he could have some peace. Resignation is a sort of peace – and Thamar could never seem resigned for long. Just when she declared she was, she would start talking of a cure, as though it could exist. The only hope Reuben still clung to was in prayer. But so far, during seven years, no still small voice had spoken to him, as it had once spoken to him in Punt for King Merenkere's sake, and told him what to do. Now he looked at Thamar so tragically that she felt she mustn't worry him again. She tried to smile, and pressed his hand, and went away leaving him to his musical instruments, and to await a young astronomer who was coming to instruct him in the art. Men could escape from reality by burying themselves in things like that, but women couldn't. While Sadhi lived Thamar was tied to a constant sharing of his sadness and despair.

It was almost time for her to find Sadhi and try to make him eat, but for once she put off her duty a little longer and went instead towards her groves and gardens. They were very lush, and still. It was past midday, and the scorching white shield of sun stood high in the heavens, subjecting the land to blazing light. The daytime scents were heavy on the air, and fountains shot their sprays of clear water towards the sky, arrogantly, as though challenging the sun to dry them up.

Thamar went with her light step to her favourite grove. In its shelter she paused to look about her. Leaves above her, against that tremendous light, were shadowed to black-green. Pomegranates were ripe, luscious and rosy-orange. She pulled one down against her face and held it there, wondering if she could make Sadhi eat it. While she wondered, a voice fell on her ears : 'Go with God, Princess,' it said on a reedy sigh.

Thamar started, so that she plucked the pomegranate by mistake. She held it heavy in her hand, and turned. A very old man leaned against the next tree. His beard was grey and his dingy robe almost the same colour. Against his meagre chest he had folded several pomegranates into his garment so that they bulged there in a peculiar way, betraying themselves by an edge of colour. He made Thamar an inclination of the head and smiled at her courteously with his rheumy eyes. He was a beggar, and robbing her, but so graciously that Thamar knew she couldn't even scold him.

'Go with God,' she responded shyly. 'You know me?'

'Who does not know the Princess?' demanded the old man. He peered round him wildly. When he was not being gracious he looked distinctly half-witted.

'I wanted a pomegranate for my son,' explained Thamar, somehow feeling that she must calm him down. 'He – he is not well.' She looked at the fruit, and tears stole down her face and dripped on to the bright surface like drops of dew.

'Ah, *that* son.' Now the old man didn't look mad at all but infinitely knowledgeable. 'That son of yours, lady, will not cure, no matter what fruit you give him in this land of yours – no, nor what tears you shed for him. He will not cure,' he reiterated, and emphasized his words by quickly plucking three more pomegranates and stuffing them down inside his robe.

Thamar gave a loud sob and dropped her pomegranate,

which rolled to the old man's feet and stayed there like an offering. He scooped it to him, and then looked at her more kindly. She was wondering dismally if he were a prophet: they weren't always the most likely people, look at – well, look at Noah! (Though there's nothing wrong with Noah, she told herself hastily.)

She took a step closer. 'If I can't cure him here, where *can* I cure him?'

He had been hoping she might give him something. The ancient eyes clouded, and his mouth opened in a snicker of discontent. He turned, his dirty robe fluttering about him, and began to make off between the trees. Seized by a sense of surprising urgency, Thamar ran after him crying, 'Stop! You can have any fruit you choose – figs and grapes too – only say where I can cure him?'

But the old man wouldn't stay or say. He was flitting off between the trees like a bat, now whitened by sunlight, now black beneath the boughs. At last, hearing Thamar's insistent calling, he turned once and cried over his shoulder, 'Don't ask me, Princess, where to cure him. Ask it of the firedrake –' and with another twist and turn and flutter he was gone.

'– and then he said to ask it of the firedrake! Reuben, what *is* a firedrake? Is it something very knowledgeable?'

There was such hope in her voice that Reuben couldn't bear to look at her. 'I – I'm afraid,' he said hesitantly, 'the old man was cruelly jesting.' He saw the pitiful fall of her face, and added quickly, 'or perhaps he was just half-witted, as you first thought. A firedrake is another name for a shooting star.'

'I hadn't heard that,' she said in a wondering voice, and sat staring into space, so that presently he asked her for her thoughts.

'I was remembering that the old women in the desert used to say that someone who was – well, afflicted, had a missing star at birth.'

'A missing star?' Reuben looked startled.

'It was just the way women gossip,' she explained, 'when they're being superstitious, and don't want men to hear. They meant, I think, that the heavens rule us when we're born, and someone like Sadhi had a star eclipsed at birth.'

'A poetic explanation for a very nasty thing,' said Reuben drily, and rose. He had to see his shepherd. 'Please don't let that old man upset you, Thamar.'

'I will not,' she said – and there was an obstinate tilt to her chin that Reuben hadn't noticed for some time. Usually it meant that she had set her mind on something, and wouldn't speak of it till it was done. What she was thinking of this time, he couldn't guess.

Thamar thought: That old beggar wasn't really a very nice old man, but people can still be *used*, for prophecy. No still small voice has spoken to Reuben, and yet –

That night she stood upon the flat roof, all alone. She faced north – the direction in which the old man had gone – and stared toward the sky's depths of dark, rich blue. As she looked at them the stars seemed to grow and burn and colour and dim – no : it was her eyesight that dimmed, after staring at them. She blinked, and looked again. She saw the firedrake fall out of the sky and flash on its way downward like a thrown diamond, and disappear almost before she realized what she saw. What message could something so ephemeral hold for her? So brief a passage, and so quickly over . . . It seemed a heavy omen for Sadhi's marred young life, and it was with a heavy heart that she left the roof and went to bed.

But the next night something drew her back again, and again a firedrake fell. This time it was an even smaller chip of light, and its path was shorter. And the third night the same thing happened, though this time the star was a mere flicker of light which vanished into a paler sky. Then, convinced the old man had been a prophet after all, Thamar guessed her son must die.

After sundown next day Caltah came to her grievingly to say that Sadhi would eat nothing, had attacked him viciously, and now lay kicking on the floor. Thamar hurried to her child, but he only glared at her, and made his single gobbling sound when she tried uselessly to calm him. Unable to bear it longer, Thamar fled. She wandered disconsolately through the Palace, searching for Reuben. Her little girls and Phut were sleepily waiting for her to say good night, and when she left them she felt as though something once more drew her towards the roof.

This time she turned her back upon the north, and stared south-west instead, gazing into the night sky as though daring it to do its worst. Nothing happened, and she began to think of going in; but the air was warm and scented, and it was pleasant here where no one would look for her and call her back to Sadhi, who might stare at her with sick hate as though she could have cured him if she would. She wandered the length of the rooftop, and then stared into the southern sky again. As it darkened the stars shone brighter still. In the direction of Kemi hung a jewel of a star: enormous, pulsing with a harmony of coloured light. She thought of King Merenkere and his Great Royal Wife, Meri-Mekhmet, in the Palace of White Walls at Men-nofer, and wondered if they saw the star as well. It was exceedingly beautiful. She didn't know which star it was, nor how Reuben and his gentle young astronomer would have named it. She stared and stared, unable to look away.

Then again she saw a firedrake fall – above Kemi, and above that exceptional bright star. It fell in a lengthy arc pointing towards the star, and instead of dwindling rapidly away seemed to grow larger before it vanished. The huge star pulsed with almost orange light, as though extra brilliance had been added to it.

Thamar hurried from the Palace roof in search of Reuben.

'That old man *was* a prophet, after all – and we must take Sadhi down to Kemi !'

'Take him where ? Thamar – ' She was so excited that she was dancing up and down as one of her children might have done. To her present optimism Sadhi was already cured. Reuben anxiously loomed closer. '*Gently* – ' (She had danced on his foot.) 'No – stop it, Thamar ! Let me feel your forehead, you're very flushed – ow !'

Instead of dancing on his foot she had lightly stamped on it. 'Reuben, *listen* ! Three nights I looked northward, and there were weak little falling stars – hopeless, they kept dying and –'

'They do.' Reuben rubbed his foot.

'Yes – but tonight I saw another one, over Kemi. It fell above an enormous star, which seemed to grow brighter – I mean, it took on an *astounding* life. So, don't you see, it's plain we must take Sadhi down to Kemi ?'

Her husband simply looked at her. Thamar felt some of her glorious certainty die. 'Don't you see ?' she repeated pleadingly.

'Because the omens of the firedrake were better in the south-west than in the north ?'

'Yes – yes !' she was ready to dance again. Reuben held her by the arms and looked at her gravely. 'But Thamar, are we superstitious children to believe in omens ? You think we should drag our poor child all that way, when he is sick – and for what? What do you expect to find for him in far-off Kemi that we cannot give him here?'

Her face fell, and she shook her head. She couldn't say. She only knew that briefly, superstition or no superstition, she had believed that Sadhi would be cured.

'Surely, if one's as miserable as Sadhi, it's better to die in one's own country and one's home?' he asked her sadly.

Thamar didn't want to hurt him, but replied almost inaudibly: 'He hates his home, he hates *here*; he hates – us.'

'No, Thamar!' Reuben turned pale.

'Yes, Reuben – you've never faced the truth. He hates us – he has hated us for years, because we're his mother and his father and we cannot help him.'

'I didn't know,' said Reuben, dumbfounded.

'And I never told you. But now you *must* know that it will make no difference to Sadhi where he dies – if he dies as he is now he will die hating, wherever he may be.'

There was a lengthy silence, which at last she broke.

'Listen, Reuben: you think me irreligious because I say it was an omen – but who are we to say what are pointers to truth, and what are not? You think only that the still small voice would have spoken – but I say that perhaps it has spoken, in a different way. Or perhaps I'm a silly and deluded woman. All the same – let's take Sadhi down to Kemi! Even if – if he dies there. The King at least will be glad to see us. Though you're a Prince in Canaan, aren't you still officially his musician? You should repay his kindness to us.'

'I've returned to visit him three times – and played for him. You know that.'

'Without me. And never told him why I wouldn't come.'

'How could I bear to tell him and the Queen what had happened to my son?' asked Reuben.

'Yet he must surely guess.'

'Guess? How could he?'

'Oh Reuben, my sweet simple husband – how could he not? When you don't take your children down to Kemi, and never talk of the second one, and your wife always stays behind – ! And then there's the flood of talk that follows travellers from one place to the other until it grows into monstrous lies – I daresay Merenkere has heard our son's an imbecile, or deformed, and that's why he never mentions him. As for Meri-Mekhmet – she's been so discreet about not asking me why I never joined you on your journeys, that I know she understands. If she thought I didn't want to go, she would have been most hurt, and said so.'

Reuben agitatedly took a turn or two about the room.

'Thamar, you're right! Now I see why the King took me last time to visit one of his chamberlains who has a crippled son – and spoke of how one should always share such troubles.'

'Oh really, Reuben! The King said *that*, and you never told me?' In spite of her distress for Sadhi, she began to laugh. 'It's not an imbecile son I have, but a simpleton husband. The King must have given you up as hopelessly obtuse, I fear!'

When Reuben had finished chastising her slightly, he said, 'Now please remember you're a princess, and have a grave and much respected person for your husband.'

'Oh Reuben, I do – except sometimes, when you're silly. And we will go to Kemi, won't we?'

'In two or three moons' time – when the annual feasting and tributes, and the fastings and, most of all, the thanksgivings are over.'

'In two or –' she looked downcast. 'But that will be too late! It will be too late for Sadhi.'

'Be reasonable, beloved! If there's any meaning in your seeing that firedrake, then nothing can defeat the meaning.'

Thamar's eyes were huge with reproach. 'What would have happened to Noah – and to us – if he hadn't built the Ark at once?'

'But you forget my responsibilities! Haven't I enough burdens without your making me feel so –'

'Yes, you have enough. Forgive me, Reuben – for I do understand your duties, as well as I understand my own. Since you cannot come now, let me take Sadhi by myself?'

She waited breathlessly for his response. They both hated being parted from each other, and she was in two minds about what she hoped for in his answer. At last he said painfully and very slowly, 'I shall be miserable without you – but if you must go, you must.' Then she flung herself into his arms and burst into tears.

'You'll have the other children to comfort you,' she wept, 'until you can bring them with you and follow me!'

Reuben held her in silence, and then said, 'But you must take Phut, Thamar – or he will die of grief.'

She nodded dismally, and clutched her husband to her, and sighed, 'He's very young for such a journey ... It will be hard in any case, and may be difficult with Sadhi – though Caltah will come too.'

Just then they were luckily distracted by a sense of twining and twirling that seemed to be going on around their legs. After it had stopped, Cefalu sat down on Thamar's toes and panted, before making the traditional cleaning of one paw. His twining was not quite so deft as it used to be, and he looked faintly put out.

'I assume,' he said testily, 'you will have the grace not to leave me long in doubt as to which kitten we shall take with us as tribute to the Sovereign?'

'Oh Cefalu! Are you coming too? I would hardly have thought – I mean, you're not quite so –'

'We are none of us that, but youth or no youth your appearance at the King's court would hardly be acceptable without *mine.*' Cefalu dealt so fiercely with one whisker that it snapped back into place with an audible 'snsst!'

'I'm not taking Benoni,' said Thamar hurriedly.

'Naturally not. There's no link between a herd dog, however reputable, and the ancient worship of the kings of Kemi, so far as I have heard. I say nothing against an elephant such as M'tuska – since it's his proper task to carry things, and a cat like myself would scarcely enter Kemi without porterage. You will recall that I am still Lord of the Waterfront Cats in Men-nofer, even now.'

'*No*, Cefalu – we shall be taking Sadhi, and –'

But Cefalu merely loosened his claws, and sat looking at them thoughtfully. 'Ah yes – young Sadhi. Perhaps he'll sit quieter if I am on his knee, who knows? And I've decided which kitten we shall take to see the King: Casper. He will benefit from visiting the tomb of Meluseth.'

In the event, Thamar set out one morning just as the sun had sprung above the horizon like a god of light, and before the freshness of night had been dissipated by the day's stupendous heat. Reuben had sent messengers ahead of her to the King of Kemi, begging the Sovereign's hospitality and help – although he still couldn't bring himself to write openly of Sadhi. Thamar had M'tuska as baggage animal, and he carried Caltah too. She had as well a company of spearmen to act as protection against bedouin robbers who might attack a small caravan on the great trade route to Kemi before it could reach a point where the King's arm was all-powerful. She herself, Sadhi, Phut and the cats travelled in a large litter with heavy hangings to keep out the sun.

One side of the litter was left open, so that she could wave good-bye. Phut sat on her knees, while Sadhi crouched beside her and didn't wave. A belt laced tightly round his waist kept him on the seat, and made him as sullen as a captured animal. The three other children stood close to Reuben, and waved and waved. The little girls were crying, but Joshu was only gulping and determined not to show it. Already he thought himself a man – so he stood very straight, and managed to look very like his father. Thamar's eyes blurred as she saw Reuben put an arm around his shoulders. She felt sure that girls would fall in love with Joshu soon, for his gay and generous smile.

She was borne away with Phut wriggling in her lap, and Sadhi sullenly defensive. She tried to make him sit more comfortably, but his only response was to hit at her and scowl. In the last few days he had grown even thinner than before. Suddenly she felt an awful stab of fear – what a mad journey to embark on, with this sick child ! It was only because Reuben couldn't bear to refuse her anything that he had let them come . . .

At that moment the litter gave a violent lurch. Sadhi was precipitated into her arms and lay there, his skinny form pressed against her and Phut in a parody of lovingness. She could feel his dry heat, his emaciation. Whatever had been done for him in Canaan, nothing had been of any use at all. If he were to die during the journey she would simply have to endure it – his death at home would have seemed certain too. Gently stroking her child's head – which was soon jerked away – Thamar stalwartly resolved to think only of the great star that had brightened over Kemi.

Part One

Hekhti

Heirs to Kemi

Ta-Thata, the King's daughter, carefully pushed the little barque out on to the pool. Then she crouched down to watch its passage, her smooth arms folded across her chest. It was a small model of a funerary barque, complete with oarsmen and goddesses, mourners and offerings. It had been made for her by Tahlevi, the King's Court Jeweller, to comfort her when her greatest friend had died. Now she had decked it with flowers and sent it on a voyage, in imitation of Re the Sun God's barque which nightly took its journey on the dark waters of the underworld.

The pool was small because it was indoors, set into an inlaid floor. The room seemed dimly mysterious by contrast with the dazzling day outside. The floor gave off a white glow like moonlight. The pool reflected the silver inlay of the ceiling, the barque with its trailing flowers, and Ta-Thata's intent face.

Now the barque reached the other side, touched it, and turned sideways. There was a slight crunching sound and a cornflower was crushed. Ta-Thata ran round the pool to rescue her barque and send it off again.

'And how long do you play this game, my sister?'

'It's no game – and what is that to you?'

'It is nothing to me – except that it's somewhat dull.'

'Go away, then. Do you think I want you here?'

She and the barque had returned simultaneously. She bent

to readjust the flowers and pushed it off again. 'Six times should be enough, that is a voyage – ' she murmured to herself. 'No, seven – '

Something came whizzing over her head to land with a splintering sound upon the barque. Chips of enamel flew. Offerings and Canopic jars rolled over the side and sank to the bottom of the pool. The barque itself lay with its deck awash and its beautifully arranged garlands all drenched and disarrayed.

Ta-Thata let out a howl, whirled around and sprang at Sinuhe like a young leopard, just as she used to do when they were both much younger.

Sinuhe fought back until: '*Woww* – ' he screamed suddenly, and rolled over on his stomach to protect himself, kicking with an automatic, anguished kick. Ta-Thata slid across the floor and ended up bumping her head hard against an ebony stool. Sinuhe breathed with an awful sobbing sound. She lay and listened, feeling slightly ashamed of herself.

A shadow fell across the floor. A shadow long and broad, commensurate with its owner's size.

'Princess? Disaster, it appears, has struck this Royal Palace.'

She flushed, and lowered her head. The King her father was a great man and a great king, and the Queen her mother a lovely woman who could make Ta-Thata repentant by a single grieving glance. But Hekhti – what was it about Hekhti? He was no one, really: only Chief Royal Architect, and a physician. He had no power; at least, no worldly power.

'Which of you has hurt the other most, Princess?'

'I – I am not hurt.' Ta-Thata scrambled up, ignoring her many painful bruises. 'But I've hurt Sinuhe, I think. He – he spoiled my barque.'

Hekhti crossed to Sinuhe and turned him over. The boy still clutched himself, moaning.

'Take yourself modestly to the terrace, Princess, while I examine him.'

There was a long awful pause, while Ta-Thata stood on the terrace, nervously digging her nails into her palms. At last she heard Hekhti's voice say, suppressed amusement in it: 'I think my lord Sinuhe will survive intact.' And Sinuhe's sulky response, 'I can barely stand.'

There was a scraping sound as Hekhti helped Sinuhe upright. Ta-Thata returned to face her brother across the pool. Responding to something in Hekhti's face, Ta-Thata said impulsively, 'I'm sorry, Sinuhe.'

'That's all very well – I've been hurt.'

'Ah,' said Hekhti thoughtfully. He was looking at the barque. They all looked at it. Then at last Sinuhe went very red and jerked out, 'Oh, all right, then – I'm sorry, too. I didn't mean to harm it, anyway – only to see if it would sink.'

'Unkindness and impiety are to be avoided in a ruler.'

Sinuhe went redder still and stared at his feet. Ta-Thata gave a very faint smirk which instantly disappeared when Hekhti, looking at her, added, 'And the best attributes of a woman, and above all a princess, should improve on those of a wild animal.'

She was relieved to avoid his eyes by glancing towards the doorway where someone was making flustered entrance.

'Prince! I have searched the Palace for you – so has the priest No-Hotep! It is the hour of lessons, as you well know. If my Sovereign, my lord should find –' The tutor's voice trailed away as he noticed the wrecked barque and the young indignant faces.

'There has been a slight – occurrence. The Princess's barque overturned, and both she and my lord Prince in

trying to – er – rearrange matters, have fallen on this hard
floor. My lord Sinuhe would be better for a short rest
instead of lessons. I will send a plaster of figs for him to
– er – apply.'

'But, most noble Hekhti, I would like to understand –'

'We need not trouble our Sovereign, our lord with such
small matters ! Content yourself, my good Khatounh, with
a tutor's duty – "making excellent of the King".'

Khatounh looked undecided but eventually left, half
supporting Sinuhe by the arm.

'And now, Princess, shall we rescue this barque? And in
doing so pay more reverence to the gods?'

Ta-Thata came shyly to stand by Hekhti. She longed to
ask what he really thought of her, but somehow she
couldn't. Was it the sardonic touch to his kindness that
made it impossible? He was looking at her now with his
eyes half shut. Their irises showed dark like rims of coins
between his lids. The lines of his heavily curved mouth
were drawn in as though he clamped his jaw pugnaciously
on something. His stature was comforting, rock-like, but
occasionally she found it a bit too impressive to be easy with
– there was a resemblance to someone she had seen, but she
could never place it . . .

She shook herself suddenly as a little cat might have done
after being in the water. She – she was a Princess ! And
he was only a middle-aged architect, who might be taller
and more broad-shouldered than his compatriots but –

'You are staring, Princess – with those enormous eyes !'

She heard herself say impulsively, 'I do not want to marry
him.'

Hekhti was silent. She could read nothing from his face.
The dark coin-slits still watched her.

Words came tumbling out. 'I – I know it is the Custom,

but do you think my mother would have married with her brother?'

'Your mother the Queen had no brother, Princess: she was an only child.'

'Yes – and she was lucky, lucky! I wish I had no half-brother!'

'Prince Sinuhe is very like the King your father's first Great Royal Wife.'

'And the King my father married with his sister – and look what came of it!'

'Do you then dislike Sinuhe so much?' In dropping the royal title he spoke gently, as though talking to a child. And she was almost a child still, he thought – though not too young to be married soon to Sinuhe, who was two years older.

'I – no; yes! There are things in him I do not like.'

'You will think that some time of all people.'

'Yes – but not perhaps of the same things! Not cruelty – I hate him when he's cruel. When he is Ruler,' her voice dropped to a whisper, 'he will be very cruel. And do you know something, Hekhti? Sinuhe is cruel because he's weak. I found that out.' There was a note of ridiculous complacency in her voice, and Hekhti almost laughed – but it was no laughing matter.

His voice, when he answered, was prosaic, 'You're not yet married to him, Princess, and he's not yet Ruler – nor will he be, while the King your father lives. And if he's cruel because of weakness, then there's hope for you – because a weak man may be ruled by his wife.'

'If he's not first ruled by someone else.' She sounded worldly-wise, almost as though maternally instructing him. 'Sinuhe will be ruled by the priest No-Hotep. And I hate him. I hate him more than anyone I've ever known.' She looked up at Hekhti anxiously under her long dark lashes. 'You think it's bad to speak like this?'

He didn't answer. At the name 'No-Hotep' his lips had tightened again. Presently he said, with a note of compassion in his voice, 'Child, you should discuss these questions with the King your father. See – in the garden are your ladies, looking for you. Is it possible you've been avoiding them? Before they find us, shall we not straighten out your barque of Re?'

'Oh yes!' She beamed at him, putting thoughts of Sinuhe from her mind. 'We'll take off our sandals –'

Together they waded into the silver pool. The barque wasn't badly damaged, as Hekhti discovered when he picked it up. 'Tahlevi will mend it for you easily, Princess. What now?'

'Look – here are the flowers,' she said, bending, 'and here the little jars – ' Her fingers groped beneath the water. Her linen dress was kilted up above her knees in a most unroyal fashion. She straightened again, clutching small figures of the goddesses Isis and Nephthys.

'And then?'

'And then we must complete the voyage: another five times –'

'Ah yes. It is important to complete what one has set out on, in life.'

'I am sure it is.' Child-like, she gripped his hand, and waded from the pool. 'Hekhti – have you completed what you set out on?'

The Chief Royal Architect was placing her little barque back upon the water. He was looking ahead of him, and frowning.

'I, Princess?' he said absently. 'No, not yet. It may be that I only set out on it today.'

Conversation in a Water Garden

While Ta-Thata and Hekhti were gently pushing her barque across the pool, the Lord of the Two Lands, Horus of Gold, King of the South and North, Living for Ever, had escaped with his Great Royal Wife from the splendours of the Palace of White Walls to the simple gaiety and beauty of the Court Chamberlain Ay's water garden. Here they were just Merenkere and Meri-Mekhmet. Here time seemed to roll backward to their first meeting and join the present with the past till it was like one of those scrolls wound into cylinders by the Court Scribes. Only, instead of grave lists and names, this scroll bore witness to happiness and kindness and a touching fidelity.

A kingfisher darted across the water and poised for a moment on a bulrush. His bright eyes shone, and his breast and head were burnished with colour.

'Look at him, displaying his male vanity!' said Merenkere. 'I think he would like you for his mate! But I may say that he won't get you – or not until I'm dead.'

'Don't speak of being dead!' Meri-Mekhmet shuddered. 'I'm certain that our Kas will creep back here, where we've been so happy, and live among these flowers and watch the red fish swim to and fro among my father's lotuses.'

'And then I shall really have to fight the kingfisher for you! Fond though I am of your father Ay, I trust his devotion to you won't make him join us too continually.'

'You forget – he'll have my mother! He loves me so

much because I'm like her. How sad that I hardly remember her – someone who smelt of flowers, and was so very beautiful. Oh!' She went a little red.

'Vanity, vanity!' Merenkere grinned and put his arm around her. 'Each day I should remind you of how plain you grow. You have a golden heart, of course, which is why I married you. One is soon sated with Court beauties – '

She pulled his hair. 'They don't say I married you for your good looks, Merenkere! It was your finer qualities they –'

'They said you had overlooked my plainness for my Throne, and – arkh!' Schloosh.

She had given a wicked laugh and pushed him suddenly so that he fell into the pool. As he surfaced spluttering she jumped in beside him. Fish shot away in all directions. Meri-Mekhmet lay in the shallow warm water, her linen dress fanning out around her like the petals of a lotus, and looked at him with two real ones bobbing beside her ears.

'What were you saying that I married you for, royal husband? Take your august time – a gravely considered judgement in a pool is harder than one in the Throne Room.'

Merenkere gulped up some water and replied, 'Because you're obviously mad – ' and he turned towards her with terrible intent, and ducked her to his satisfaction. Afterwards he kissed her.

'My first sister, how shall we explain this to our waiting courtiers?' He looked at their two soaking forms. 'We ought not to give people like the priest No-Hotep a chance to spread rumours that his Sovereign is a madman.'

'Oh Merenkere!' She was remorseful. 'I'm a worry to you – I never think.' She broke off a lotus bud and stuck it behind her husband's ear. 'But how well a water garden suits you! Better than the Double Crown –'

'That ridiculous object could never suit anyone. It makes me look like a flea in a waterpot – I'm always glad to disguise my shame by my false beard. Do you know, I'm beginning to feel uneasy – what if your Aunt Tut's Ka has taken up residence here, and is watching us?' The King rolled over on his side, and kissed Meri-Mekhmet so that she sank. Then he stood, to pull her up and out.

'Come along, we'll dry ourselves in the sun. How pretty that weed looks in your hair!' They waded out and sat down close together. 'Let us trust that Aunt Tut's brooding as a priestess should over the men who will embalm her, and breathing down their necks to see they do it properly.'

'Oh, poor Aunt Tut!' Meri-Mekhmet's gentle eyes filled with tears. 'She was an old dragon, but I miss her.'

'Yes – it's strange what a gap these old dragons leave behind. They are a part of life, like one's enemies. The priests are in despair about her last instructions – she has demanded a special treatment for her toenails that will take a moon by itself. The priest No-Hotep –'

'That man again!'

'Yes – that man again. He has already made representations against the expense.'

'Merenkere, why don't you send him away?'

'I've often thought of it, but I prefer to have him under my eye.'

'Instead of plotting with others against you elsewhere! That I understand. Though not why he hates you, and all our house.'

'He does not hate us. If he did, it would be easier. I might manage to remove the cause. But he knows I will never give him advancement.'

'Then he does hate you!'

'No – he's too dangerous. A lesser man might waste his

energies in hatred. He is coldly determined, and very, very
shrewd – and he gives me no chance to act against him
that wouldn't be unfair, and perhaps give him allies from
among my enemies. He has friends enough already.'

Meri-Mekhmet gave a small swallow, and said unhappily, 'I was wrong too, when I said he hated *all* our
house. He is gaining Sinuhe's devotion.'

Merenkere's face set hard, and for a moment the Ruler
was apparent. 'I know this. And it's one more reason why
I would remove him from Men-nofer if I could. If I could!
And I am King! I could at least send him on a mission to
the priests at On – but he would be back again within a
moon, having made more mischief while away than he
ever could in three whole moons at Court. My hands are
tied till I can send him on some far-off embassy where he
can do no harm. The worst thing I ever did was to make
him Sinuhe's chief tutor!'

'But you knew little of him, save his reputation for
great learning.'

'Beloved, I *should* have known! But Hekhti, who often
shows a great instinct about people, was away at the time,
and I heard nothing – it was wise of No-Hotep to approach
me then, was it not?'

'You think it was deliberate?'

'Yes – and I was much occupied with matters of the
Two Lands, and that man applied with his sponsors –'

'But both such loyal servants of yours!'

'That was so clever! I wonder how long it took him to
gain their confidence? His butter-smooth smile, and that
infuriating meekness' – Merenkere hit the stone edging
with his hand – '*Ow* – Well, there are other ways
to remove him than by some open slight.' He smiled
grimly. 'Sometimes I wish I were my grandfather – *he*
wouldn't have hesitated: No-Hotep would have had a

nasty pain, and the Court would have mourned the passing of such a promising young man.'

'You would not be you, if you did things like that.'

'Sometimes – *sometimes* – I wonder if my squeamishness is justified, when Kemi lies in my care.'

'Merenkere –'

'No – do not look like that, Meri-Mekhmet! If there is any other way . . .' He sighed heavily, staring at the pool. Even in this private haven the burden of his kingship laid its shadow over him. Meri-Mekhmet couldn't bear him to look so wretched.

'Never mind all this just now! Ta-Thata is having an entertainment for her friends tomorrow. And she has specially asked me to tell you that the Sovereign is not to desert his family on such an occasion. She's peremptory, our daughter! I must speak to her.'

Merenkere smiled, as gently as he did for Meri-Mekhmet. 'Is she sharing it with Sinuhe?'

'She has asked him – naturally.'

'That was her idea – or yours?'

'Of course she would always ask Sinuhe, without my suggesting it!'

Merenkere put his hand under her chin, and turned her face round to him. 'You are a poor liar. Will my Court never corrupt you, I wonder? Tell me one thing, openly. You are against this marriage, are you not?'

'How could I be against Sinuhe? He's your son – ' she said evasively. 'And you say she must marry him.'

'You don't like him, I know that.'

'Sometimes I like him. He can be – very likeable.'

'Can be!' The King sighed. 'He's not just my son – he is the Royal Heir. But his right to the Throne is confirmed only by his marriage to Ta-Thata. You know that, too, Meri-Mekhmet.'

She opened and shut her mouth for a moment, rather as a red fish might have done; then said desperately, 'He could take a Great Royal Wife from elsewhere, Merenkere – people would find it strange that Ta-Thata had given up her rightful inheritance, but she would be happier so. I would rather she were happy – like us. Sinuhe will want many, many princesses in his harem – and he would never consider a woman as you've considered me. He would want to tease Ta-Thata, anyway – even if he loved her. No-Hotep is bringing him up to think about the Custom for this, and the one for that – *he* will not neglect such a way of introducing favourites to Sinuhe, I can assure you! Ta-Thata will be unhappy.' She finished with quivering lips, 'Do you not care?'

Merenkere put his hand over hers in distress. 'Of course I care! And more, to see you so upset. Every word you say is true – but it can make no difference: Kemi's needs come before Ta-Thata's. During my life I can protect her emotions from Sinuhe, at least. She must marry him, and she must learn that there are areas where he will go against her.'

'You make it sound so cold! And it's the most important thing.'

'No – for Ta-Thata it can never be the most important thing. After my death Sinuhe will be Sovereign: the Ruler. And a bad ruler he will be, if he takes a liking for men of No-Hotep's character. Luckily he will share the Throne with my daughter: someone who will not only be there by rightful inheritance but because she is infinitely fitted to rule. If Ta-Thata learns to allow Sinuhe his freedom elsewhere – he will take it, anyway – she will eventually come to rule both him and the Two Lands. She is very much your daughter!' He gave a slight smile. When his meaning sank home, Meri-Mekhmet flushed.

'Merenkere! I have never, not for one –'

'You rule me, anyway.' He turned her hand over, and kissed it.

'But not the Two Lands! When have I even suggested – '

'Now, let me see. Yes – the Festival of Sekhmet: wasn't it you who –'

'I only thought that – You're teasing me!'

'Perhaps. A little. But do you see now why our daughter must marry with my son?'

'But if she left the Throne – and we found Sinuhe a girl of strong character –' she began stubbornly.

'No. She would never be accepted by those around her. And – more important – Sinuhe wouldn't be accepted.'

'When we married, I thought there would be no more problems. Now I see that life is always the solving of one more problem.'

'You are being profound.'

'My Sovereign, my lord knows I am not profound.' She looked at him with great dignity, and Merenkere sensed that she was almost as mutinous as when he first knew her. 'I am just unhappy.'

'And I am sorry for it, with all my heart. I am unhappy for Ta-Thata, too, Meri-Mekhmet my beloved.' She looked at him more hopefully, for she knew what it must have cost him to admit this in connection with his son. But he added in the slightly hard tones which revealed the Ruler, 'Nevertheless, our children must marry, whoever's tears are shed for it, to keep the Two Lands safe. I ask you not to oppose me on this again. Now shall we rejoin our courtiers?'

He Who Becomes the Rising Sun

Ta-Thata was undecided where to entertain her friends: in the Palace, or on one of the royal barges – with harps and pipes to make the evening sweet as they returned at sunset from gliding up the Nile. Now she changed her mind for the fourth time, aided by her two friends and dear companions: Su-Shunut and Keta.

'Yes, Ta-Thata – it would be nicest of all on the river! Shall you bring the Queen your mother's old cats, Ptahsuti and Nutka?'

'But Ta-Thata – the King your father won't have time to stay upon the barge ... it would be lovely, though. I adore the sound of singing on the water.' Su-Shunut sighed longingly. Sinuhe, seated cross-legged just behind her on a carved stool, leaned forward and gently pulled one of her dark curls. She shook her head crossly. 'Don't, Sinuhe. You can never leave my hair alone.'

'*Sinuhe?*' He stretched his fingers to include all the side tresses of her hair, gave a great tug, and forced her head round towards him. She glared, and coloured. 'Let me go!'

'Speak properly, then.'

'Don't be so silly, Sinuhe!' said Ta-Thata. 'We've known Su-Shunut all our lives – and do I make her call me Princess when we're by ourselves? I would be ashamed. Don't always make trouble!'

'But you're only a girl, my sister. Besides, we're all growing up, and Su-Shunut is becoming very pretty.' His grip tightened. 'Su-Shunut?' By tugging heavily he pulled her backward against his knees.

'Oh! Kindly release me, my lord Prince,' she said with biting emphasis.

'Not until you have paid.'

'You *said* when I spoke "properly".'

'Yes – but you were very slow. So now you must kiss me. No, Keta, go away! You're not to help her, or I shall yell, and then Ta-Thata's party may be stopped. Come, Su-Shunut –'

'I will not – ow!' He had dug his knee into her spine.

'Kiss him, Su-Shunut, and be finished with it. He'll go on now until he makes you ... and if I fight him again, he'll have my party stopped.'

'You really want me to, Ta-Thata?' Su-Shunut reluctantly turned her face to Sinuhe.

'Mmmm,' he said, on a note of pleasure. 'Your mouth tastes like sweet fruit –' At last he let her go.

'Have I now your permission to withdraw, Princess?' she asked formally.

'Of course – and you go too, Keta.'

The two girls silently left the room.

'Shall I call them back and make them do obeisance? They have to do it publicly, you know.'

'If you do, after my party I will tell the King.'

'Pretty tale-teller.'

'Telling tales is the only way to stop your teasing – so I'll do it.' Ta-Thata impotently clenched her fists. 'Oh, I wish you weren't Royal Heir!'

'Never mind – you'll have the pleasure of inheriting the Throne for us, dear sister. Very dull this brother-sister thing will be – but at least I shall benefit by your charming companions! Keta may be plain and shy, but she's graceful enough – I love to watch her. You, she, Su-Shunut – I shall begin well with the three of you, shall I not? Our grandfather had a Sumerian princess sent to him, with long green eyes, they say. And a black girl from Punt. Isn't it a shame how the future's limited for you, my sister? No one will send you a tall prince from Shinar to eat you with his white, white teeth.'

'I shall *not* marry you,' swore Ta-Thata between hers. 'Nor will the King our father make me.'

'You think not? But it's for Kemi that we marry. So the King will make you, whatever you believe, though don't think that I particularly desire it – you're prettier even than Su-Shunut, but so strong-willed you can be most tiresome.'

Ta-Thata's stomach grew cold. 'Sinuhe – I'll give you my inheritance! Then you can marry elsewhere.'

'Then someone else would grab you, and cause trouble. No – *our* children will be doubly children of Re, which secures both us and Kemi. Don't scowl so, Ta-Thata, it makes you ugly! Well – No-Hotep says that wives are easier to tame than sisters. He says you should be whipped.'

'How dare you discuss me with that man!'

Sinuhe smiled lazily. 'He's my friend. Don't you discuss me with your friend Su-Shunut – *our* Su-Shunut?'

'Su-Shunut is not *ours*! Her father already negotiates her marriage.'

'Oh indeed? A forward-looking gentleman, the Court Chamberlain Ket.' One corner of Sinuhe's mouth quirked up, and Ta-Thata wished she hadn't spoken. But Sinuhe was only a boy still, and could be nice when he chose, and could have no real power till their father died –

Her long eyes slanted. As her thoughts changed, the colour came and went in her cheeks. Sinuhe, watching her, said suddenly, 'Yes – you're like Meri-Mekhmet!

You'll grace the Throne, as she does. Perhaps I'll be content to marry you, though you're divine only through
the King and not born of his sister. Do you know that,
when he met the Queen your mother, he had ninety-three
princesses living here?'

'Of course I know! All the ones that couldn't be sent
away are still cluttering the women's quarters, poor things
– it must be very dull for them.'

'I might have changed all that – but they would be rather
old for me.'

'I'm so tired of your teasing, Sinuhe.'

'I am not teasing – I shall have more than ninety-three
when the Throne is ours. Ninety-three is nothing.'

'And you're always talking like this. The King would
have to die first.' Her voice trembled. 'Do you not love
the King our father?'

'Yes – I do.' His voice was suddenly uncertain. He lived
often in dreams of himself: the all-powerful Lord of the
Two Lands, rich in pleasure and dominion and women –
visions conjured up by the whisperings of No-Hotep in
his ear. Whisperings of how wise he was already, how
fitted to rule – of how he was born to raise Kemi back to
its ancient ruthless glory which had been lessened by
leniency and a provincial Queen. The day when he would
take the Crook and Flail into his own hands might come
sooner than he thought –

But did he want this? For that day would bring too the
horror of his father's body lying in the hands of his
embalmers who would prepare him for the royal tomb
... A chill of terror went up Sinuhe's spine. Even a king
could die! And so another king could die ... everything
could change, like water flowing. No – surely his own
reality would never change. And reality included his
loving father's vigilance over his children, and Kemi's

peace and plenty. His father was great. There had never been a king, the people said, who so personified Ma'at, or righteousness – that great aspect of the Ruler.

Then he remembered No-Hotep saying thoughtfully that when things reached a peak of perfection they always toppled over into something else – something more interesting and exciting, for it was a Law; and looking at him, Sinuhe –

Ta-Thata was gazing at him now as though she hated him. Why had he wanted to hurt her? It was she who painfully provoked him. He really wanted her to like him, and look up to him. Above all, he wanted his father not to die –

He ran to her suddenly, throwing his arms around her to her amazement, and crying, child-like, 'Ta-Thata! I don't want him to die! I don't! I love him too –'

'Oh Sinuhe! Why should he die? He's still so young.' Her first instinct was to tear herself away, but instead she stayed quietly in his arms, awkwardly patting his head as though he were a little animal. 'Hush! Don't worry. Hathor be implored, he won't die yet.'

Sinuhe said roughly, 'I didn't mean to tease you about Su-Shunut. Do you feel it will be so very bad, to marry me?'

'Well – they won't marry us just yet!' She moved out of his arms, and said, 'Look – let us forget all this at present.' She saw that he was ashamed, and unable to look at her. 'Sinuhe, *you* tell me: shall we have my party in the Palace? Or on the Nile?'

'In the Palace, and then the King will come.' He was already forgetting his distress. Ta-Thata watched the shifting moods reveal themselves on his features, which were stamped with Merenkere's likeness, and were yet – in some subtle way she found disturbing – so unlike.

'That's settled then – and I'll tell my ladies. We will have that strange new dancer from the land of Shinar!'

'Yes – No-Hotep says she has beautiful headdresses of golden leaves and flowers on metal stalks which tremble when she moves. Are you asking the courtiers – or just the King and Queen?' His question sounded casual enough, but Ta-Thata glanced sideways at him.

'I haven't quite decided. The party was for younger people, really.'

'But you'll ask Hekhti, surely. And your ladies will be here?'

'Perhaps – but I don't want all your tutors, Sinuhe! They would spoil things.'

'I must have one or two attendants! Particularly if you have Hekhti –'

'I have not said so.' Again she looked sideways at him. 'I will let you know, royal brother.'

'Don't leave it too late for me to arrange things,' he said sulkily.

'I will not – but the priest No-Hotep may have ritual duties at that time!'

Sinuhe scowled angrily at the floor. *He* would have a better party, later. A fleet of gay barges would progress up the river. The watching, worshipping people would see the son of the Son of the Sun casually seated at the foremost prow, in the place of honour usually kept empty for the Goddess. Song would echo down the river, the waters would reflect flashing oars, the slaves' ornaments of gold, the young courtiers' lapis and carnelian and silver. Lovely girls would sit like a bevy of doves about his feet. Oh, the glory and the brightness and the prostrating –

'And do you know, my brother, that the soles of your feet are very dirty? I saw them when you were sitting on the stool.'

'It doesn't matter – it's a privilege for anyone to see the soles of my feet,' he said loftily, longing to pinch her.

'Then it would be a privilege for No-Hotep to wash them?'

'He is a great man – a priest of Set!' he said angrily. 'It is not his business to –'

'He is too great for you, brother?'

He stared at her, more angry and upset, for with the silky question she had caught him. He, the King's son! Yet very briefly he saw himself as he really was: an inexperienced, lightweight youth, dependent on those around him. And No-Hotep – was he just the smilingly subservient attendant who pandered to his whims? Or an implacably strong and learned man whose aims and intentions were as inscrutable as his smiles? How horribly uncomfortable it would be to marry Ta-Thata, after all! She had a way of looking at him gravely, and –

'I shall leave you now,' he said shortly.

'As the Prince my brother desires.'

Her large brown eyes watched him go. Su-Shunut and Keta were talking with her ladies in the next room, and she knew that her mother would expect her to rejoin them, but instead she slipped from the room and turned left to run lightly down a corridor. Its pillars were so realistically carved that the palm fronds might really have moved above her head, and the painted birds and butterflies have taken to flight. She passed Court officials, who hurriedly made obeisance, and wove her way in and out of labyrinthine passages until she neared a hushed and hallowed region: a sanctuary of Khepri who, in his scarab's carapace which could be shed and yet renewed, represented eternity, and was styled 'He who Becomes the Rising Sun'.

The sanctuary was very still. Lights burned with dim flame in their holders. Khepri himself, vast, black, shiny and carved in beetle form by some forgotten artist, filled the room's centre. He was mounted on a block of alabaster. A small offering table before him held food and a pitcher of wine. There was a faint smell of spicy sandalwood.

Ta-Thata stood and gazed at him. She thought he looked very wise, inscrutable and benign. Some people were scared of Khepri, but she wasn't. She had loved him ever since she'd found him in here when she was a very little girl. Then she had had a good time sliding up and down his enticing back, until a horrified priest had come running in and, not recognizing her till too late, had spanked her soundly while she gave vent to tremendous yells of outraged royal dignity: she had known very well that Khepri, who was so nice and shiny, had enjoyed her visit just as much as she. Later on, her father had explained that many people would have been offended by her action, and since she was a royal princess she must give more thought to her behaviour. So she *did* think – but the more she did so the more her conviction grew that it was all right to visit Khepri now and then, and slide on him, so long as no one found her out.

Once she had grown too old for playing she would come there to sit or lie upon his back, and stroke his beautiful blunt head while she told him all her troubles – things like Sinuhe's teasing, or lost kittens. And nothing bad had ever happened to her for what that priest would have described as sacrilege. Indeed, she'd often gone away refreshed, as though Khepri had absorbed her troubles or folded them beneath his black and sculpted wings.

Now was the time of day when the sanctuary was sure to be deserted. It wasn't necessary to listen hard before climbing up to settle herself comfortably along the scarab back. She stroked Khepri's right wing reverently, and then his nose.

'Beautiful Rising Sun, you haven't shed your carapace since I saw you last?' Of course Khepri never replied, he simply pondered and understood. 'Whenever I come to you

these days, it's about Sinuhe. I'd almost like to die – if I
could renew myself as you can! For – do you know? – I've
only just understood that I shall *really* have to marry him –
I shall be sacrificed to Kemi – I shall be the dark shadow of
Sinuhe's glory as Set's the dark shadow of Osiris! My parents
say they love me, but they'll put me in the cage like some
rare animal – and I shall have to stay there till I die.' Her
tears fell on to his shiny nose. 'You'd think it a happy fate
to be *the* Royal Princess, wouldn't you? But it's terrible!
Will nothing happen to prevent my marriage?'

'What answer are you expecting, Princess?'

She gave a violent start and nearly fell off Khepri's back.
Hekhti stood in the entrance and looked at her with his
remote, clear gaze, the corners of his mouth turned very
faintly upward. As she righted herself, he lowered himself
with dignity to the floor and did obeisance.

'Hekhti! Was that for me? Because you know you
needn't –'

He came upright again, still smiling.

'– or was it for Khepri?' She looked at him doubtfully.
'You do obeisance to Khepri, Hekhti? I've never known
just what you do believe –'

'Perhaps I do obeisance to what he represents, Princess.
And to what you represent.' His smile broadened, and
spread to his eyes. 'So you still visit Khepri – I can remember
when your Royalty was well spanked for it.'

'That was many, many, many moons ago.'

'Very many moons : a whole young lifetime,' he agreed.

'And now I come when I'm sure to be alone – oh!' She
put her hand to her mouth. 'I didn't mean – *You* cannot
think –' She was still perched on Khepri's back, and added
hastily, 'Do you think that I shouldn't be – That I'm treating
Khepri with disrespect?'

'Are you treating him with disrespect? I thought you were treating him as a treasured friend.'

'The priests wouldn't like my sitting on him. Nor, really, would my father, because –'

'If you give offence to other people, then you risk harm to my Sovereign Lord the King, Princess. For that reason alone perhaps you shouldn't be where you are now.'

'No – I see.' She got off Khepri's sleek back regretfully and patted him with a final sort of pat. 'Yet my father the King is all-powerful, Hekhti – so who could harm him? And he's a god too, is he not?'

'I know he is a good Sovereign and a wise man – and that is to be god-like, Princess. As to harm – both men and gods may die, even as Osiris died. And as to power – that flows where it wills, into good men and bad. A man with power is like a crab in its shell – soft flesh, and not so protected as he feels. When he dies someone else may take up residence, or use the shell to purposes he never dreamed of.'

'I think you would warn me, Hekhti.'

'You're little more than a child, Princess – yet you knew I warned you. It's dangerous simply to be good – less dangerous if goodness goes with wisdom. There are men who are both bad and wise – and that's very dangerous indeed, to others and to themselves.'

She was pleased that Hekhti should talk to her as though she were grown up, and yet she shivered suddenly.

'What is it, Princess?'

'Nothing, I – It's what you said then, and I had a feeling of darkness, as black as Khepri here –'

He studied her. 'Yes. Your intuition may well be your safeguard.'

'I wish it would tell me I shan't marry Sinuhe!' She studied him as earnestly as he had studied her. 'Deep inside

you, don't you know how things will be, Hekhti? Somehow, I've often thought you did. Can you not tell me what
will come?'

He shook his head thoughtfully. 'Then it couldn't be
altered, if it was a true seeing. That might not comfort you!
Look into your self, Princess, which told you just now of
darkness. And remember this – which is hard to learn when
you're young: change is the essence of life. You were once
a baby, you may live to be an old, old woman. Today a
girl – tomorrow, if Osiris wills, Kemi's Queen. Foolish men
try to make laws and customs so rigid that things will never
change, but it's impossible, for it is not *the* Law.' He took her
gently by the shoulders, and turned her so that she could
see her reflection in the polished copper panel of the further
wall. 'See yourself! You're not just that young girl, you are
a form for life which flows like the great Nile. And unless
you're conscious of this, other people will use you for good
or evil just as they will: it's for you to try to understand
life's flow, and guide its direction to the right.'

She stared long at herself, as though she had never seen
the sight before. Then she murmured involuntarily, 'The
priest No-Hotep wants to direct good to evil.'

'Yes. And perhaps the girl you see reflected is the only
obstacle that will prevent him.'

'It is a heavy weight, Hekhti,' she said, not child-like at
all, and put her hands up to her hair as though someone
had placed the burden of a crown upon it. Then, in the
polished shield of copper, they both saw above her head
the Double Crown of Kemi: not the elegant Queen's Crown
her mother wore, but the Red and White crowns of North
and South combined into the heavy authoritative shape
that her father – King Merenkere, Living for Ever – wore
when he was enthroned.

'*Oh* –' breathed Ta-Thata, more startled than when

Hekhti had made his silent entrance. She stared and stared into the copper. Behind her, movement was reflected : there stood one of the priests who waited on the Sovereign to care for the God's regalia, and what she had thought a prophetic vision was her father's real and solid crown held high in the hands of its own servant.

'I humbly beg your Highness's pardon! The sound of voices in this sanctuary is unusual at this time, so I thought right to come and see who was within.' He made discreet obeisance as far as he could, for the crown was heavy in his hands, then, with a sidelong glance at Hekhti, he withdrew backwards from the Princess's presence.

She gave a small relieved laugh. 'I am so glad! For a moment I thought Khepri showed me a true seeing.' She looked at Hekhti to see if he were laughing too, but his face wore its habitual gravity.

'There are many ways in which truths are made known to men,' was all he said.

Ta-Thata Entertains

Gay and beautiful was Ta-Thata's party. It began in one exquisite large room which gave directly on to a terrace. Flowering trees had been brought inside to make a sweet-scented semicircle behind musicians who sat cross-legged, or on low stools if they played the harp or lute. And in front of them dancers and jugglers performed, and a charmer piped a dun-coloured cobra out of its basket, and charmed it hurriedly back again when it started to look around as though it might join the guests. A flock of doves had been coaxed indoors with grain, and made a pretty decoration. (A pygmy slave spent the afternoon solemnly clearing up the droppings with a palm leaf brush.) After wine and cakes had been enjoyed the party began to expand, and then to break into groups which wandered out into the gardens.

Sinuhe was late; though he must enter before the King and Queen, as etiquette demanded even on informal occasions. Ta-Thata, wearing a jewelled coronet with a turquoise pendant dangling on her forehead, was very conscious of her obligations both as Princess and hostess. Her usual exuberance was reduced to a regal formality that held a touching quality of slight uncertainty. As time drew on towards the King's and Queen's arrival she began casting anxious looks in the direction of the pillared entrance. Surely Sinuhe was too conscious of his duties as Royal Heir to muddle them? He was to bring four of his companions with him : boys of noble blood reared in his own household

which had its apartments in the Palace. There was no sign
of any of them. Ta-Thata bit her lip –

Notes from a silver trumpet, muted by distance, warned
the scattered guests of a royal approach. There was a hurried
reassembling inside the room, while the entertainers grouped
themselves upon the terrace. Footsteps sounded in the
corridor, the hangings were drawn aside, everyone bowed
themselves to the ground – and Sinuhe, his four companions
at his heels and the priest No-Hotep at his side, made a
perfect entrance. It was so timed that no one had a chance
to rise before the trumpet sounded again, closer at hand.
The group of late arrivals turned and prostrated themselves
like corn before a rising wind. When Merenkere and Meri-
Mekhmet entered, Sinuhe and his tutor occupied the place
of honour that should, on this occasion, have been Ta-
Thata's.

Chairs had been placed for the Sovereign and his Great
Royal Wife. Marshals and fanbearers took up their stance
behind. The King regarded the small forms dispersed about
the room, and gave a slight smile.

'Rise, my children.'

There was a sound as though many half-grown puppies
had suddenly been released. No-Hotep stood head and
shoulders above even the tallest boy. The King eyed him
stonily, and Meri-Mekhmet glanced at her husband and
then away.

'My daughter,' said Merenkere, 'we wish for no great
formality during this day's pleasures. But how is it that your
brother is attended by his Chief Tutor, while your ladies
are conspicuously absent?'

'O Sovereign, my lord –' began Ta-Thata hesitantly.

' "My father".'

'Then, my father, my ladies are absent because – Because
I decided the party was to be just for ourselves. I mean, for

people of our age – Sinuhe's and mine. And for my Sov –
I mean, my parents and whoever your Maj – my father
wished to bring.'

'It is well understood.' The King continued to regard
the priest, who bowed his head and gave a deprecating
smile. 'All the same, my Marshals and fanbearers are here.
Your brother has brought one of his servants –' A cold
wind seemed to have blown across No-Hotep's face – 'and it
would be suitable for a lady of your household to be
present.'

'With my father's permission, I will send for one. And
– and may I ask that my – my parents will also allow me
to send for one more guest. The Chief Royal Architect. I
wanted to invite him, but then I didn't, because –' She
floundered, not looking at No-Hotep.

'We shall be delighted to see my good Hekhti! Perhaps
you, No-Hotep, will prove your excessive eagerness for this
party's improvement by acting as messenger?'

Had the priest stiffened much more he would have been
unable to prostrate himself. Beneath that overwhelmingly
royal stare he bowed himself to the ground, and backed
from the room. His lips twitched at the corners, and his eyes
were dark with something that was better unexpressed.
Briefly his glance crossed with Ta-Thata's, and she very
hurriedly turned hers toward her father's face. She
wondered why he was looking at her so sadly, yet with an
air of resolution that alarmed her. She saw too that her
mother was unsmiling, and wouldn't meet her eye. Meri-
Mekhmet bent her head as though to examine the pattern
of gold threads upon her lap, or her jewelled rings.

'Today is a day for feasting.' Merenkere emphasized the
last word as if it had some special meaning which, so far,
he alone understood. He looked around the room, and then
his exceptional eyes dwelt on his daughter's face, as though

he were mapping each feature separately in his mind. 'Come here to me, Ta-Thata; and you, my royal son.'

She moved forward hesitantly, and Sinuhe followed her. They stood side by side before their parents.

'Kneel down.'

They kneeled. Ta-Thata was rigid with dismay. She guessed now what was coming. There was to be no private discussion of their future. The King would make it plain for all to see.

Merenkere motioned to the Marshal who stood nearest him. 'Where are the silver bracelets, Kouthi?'

'O Sovereign, my lord, they are here. Your Majesty's jeweller, Tahlevi, delivered them to the Palace this afternoon.'

'It is well,' said the King, with a small sigh. 'Give them to Prince Sinuhe.'

Meri-Mekhmet didn't raise her eyes. Nor did Ta-Thata raise hers. Both listened to the Marshal's heavy tread as he crossed to Sinuhe, and the faint chinking as the bracelets changed hands.

'Clasp them on your sister's arms.'

Ta-Thata lifted her arms so that Sinuhe could fix the bracelets into place. As the fastenings clicked home she felt like a manacled prisoner condemned for life.

'Have you the gold necklet, Marshal?'

'O Sovereign, my lord, it is here.'

'Give it to the Princess. Ta-Thata, place the necklet around your brother's neck –' She obeyed, with trembling fingers. Merenkere stood up to place Sinuhe's right hand in Ta-Thata's, and his left in her left.

'Bring me wine,' said the King, returning to his chair. 'And to the Queen, and to my royal son and daughter who will succeed my Majesty on the Throne of the Two Lands : the Doublegrant.'

Wine was brought. The King and Queen drank from crystal goblets, but the one Ta-Thata and Sinuhe drank from was blood red, and held to their lips in turn by the Marshal. Ta-Thata could barely drink, and gave a gulp which she felt must echo around the room, where their friends stood gaping at the simple, unexpected ceremony.

'You are bound to each other by blood, and to the Throne of Kemi,' murmured the King. 'By the exchange of gifts and the drinking of wine I pledge you to each other. May the great Sun Re, Isis and Osiris bless you and watch over you.' He raised his right hand wearily, and summoned them to receive his kiss and the Queen's. Meri-Mekhmet's cold lips touched her daughter's cheek, which was colder still. Sinuhe and Ta-Thata kissed their parents' hands.

'O my father,' said Sinuhe, with a slight squeak in his voice from nervous excitement, 'may I choose this time at which you honour us with your decision, to ask one favour for the two of us ?'

'Today you have only to ask, Sinuhe,' replied Merenkere, smiling.

'When we are married, Ta-Thata's household will join with mine ?'

'It is the Custom.'

'My father, Ta-Thata's present companions may have marriages arranged for them, and so leave her. But she's greatly attached to Su-Shunut and Keta, and so am I, and we both grieve at the thought of losing them. You know, my father, that *their* fathers will be greatly honoured if the Sovereign agrees that they may enter my women's quarters instead, when Ta-Thata becomes my wife.'

'My son, this is no time and place to discuss such matters,' replied the King, most displeased. At his side Meri-Mekhmet had given a small outraged movement. Merenkere fixed his gaze sadly on the boy who had known too well how and when to make the request so that it was impossible for it to go ungranted. Traditionally it was an honour to be singled out by the Royal Heir. Now it was unavoidable that the Court Chamberlain Ket should hear of it, and be upset if his daughter were rejected by the Sovereign as though unworthy of his son.

'Forgive me, my father,' replied Sinuhe meekly. 'All the same, I beg your Majesty will consider it, later, both for Ta-Thata's sake and for my own.'

The King gave him a very searching look. The boy had been frail at birth, and spoiled for a long while before he strengthened. He might anyway have developed deviousness, as weak people often do. But behind Sinuhe's words Merenkere fancied he heard a different voice and a serpentine opportunism which spoke through him as a mouthpiece. There was a cold feel around Merenkere's heart.

No-Hotep must go, he thought in agitation – just as the priest re-entered the room. A bland smile was back upon his lips, as though the insult he had swallowed had proved digestible after all. Beside him walked one of Ta-Thata's ladies, and with him too was Hekhti, who bore in his hand a scroll inscribed with a message for the King.

The Dancer from Shinar

'"To my King, my Sun, my God,"' read Hekhti from the scroll, '"may it please your Majesty to know that Thamar, Princess of Canaan, with two of her young sons, has reached the Palace of White Walls, and humbly requests audience with my Sovereign, the Lord of Diadems. By the hand of Rhama, Chief of the King's Scribes".'

'Thamar!' exclaimed Meri-Mekhmet happily, smiling for the first time since her entrance. 'Here already!'

'Let us see her at once!' said Merenkere, glad to change his thoughts from a distasteful and melancholy subject. 'Tell them to admit the Princess, with her children, Hekhti. They time their arrival well!'

Thamar felt slightly shy after her many years away from the great Palace, and kept her eyes downcast as she was ushered into the Presence. Phut clung to her skirts, and Casper and Cefalu trotted like black shadows at their heels.

Through his whiskers Cefalu issued instructions to his offspring: 'Do not treat a king's Court as though it were your home – manners should be easy, not familiar: a gentle licking of the shirt front is the farthest you may go. Courtly love is expressed by a mere showing of the pink tongue tip, effusiveness is common. Now – these are the Sovereign's feet before us. Follow my example.' And he bowed himself on his stomach in a single graceful curve, with a slight rise in the arrogant tip of his tail which said plainly: 'Gracious

I may be, but inferior I am not.' Casper's imitation, though sincere, lacked true expression.

Thamar's obeisance was unsteady, cluttered as she was by Phut, but she was warmly greeted by both Merenkere and Meri-Mekhmet, who at once had a chair placed for her between them. Thamar sat down, still somewhat over-awed – she had almost forgotten Merenkere's gentleness and his royal simplicity.

'Why – it is Cefalu!' said the King. 'And which child is this – Phut? If that is obeisance he's attempting, he need not : it looks uncomfortable. They told me you had brought two sons?'

Thamar flushed. 'O Sovereign, my lord, yes. But Sadhi is very tired after the journey, and – and – I have left him in the apartments that your Majesty's Chamberlain has allotted me.' Above her head Meri-Mekhmet and the King exchanged a glance.

'Very sensible,' said Merenkere tactfully. 'And how is my good friend, Reuben? We're both sad not to see him here, and particularly on such an informal and happy occasion – my son and daughter are soon to wed, and are entertaining some young friends, as you see. It's not often the Court can throw off its cares in this simple fashion.'

'W-wed, your Majesty?' stammered Thamar, thinking how very fiercely Joshu would object to marrying his sister Miriam. 'How – how delightful.' She saw the shadow on Meri-Mekhmet's face, and added quickly, 'My husband is well, and sends your Majesties many humble greetings. I – I had to come alone this time, because there's so much for him to do in Canaan. He will follow me as soon as possible, but there was haste for Sadhi, and –' She faltered and bit her lip.

The King said kindly, 'Later you shall tell us everything. Now, my daughter's friends await us – they've found some wonderful new dancer from Shinar, and we're not meant to know that she is dancing here today. Let us go out on the terrace, as a sign that we're ready to be thoroughly surprised!'

Couches had been arranged for the King and Queen and those privileged to sit with them. After Thamar had been presented to Ta-Thata and Sinuhe a group of musicians began their tinkling, fluting and harping. Timbrels jingled with a violent jingling as small girls shook them with all their might. A gigantic hairless Nubian clashed his cymbals – Clinggg! – and again and again until his audience could scarcely bear it. Then, just as they were almost stunned by the vibrations, the dancer from Shinar was suddenly among them, twirling as though someone had set her in motion with a whip: round and about the couches, in and out of the groups of guests, touching no one, spinning lightly here, there, everywhere. Thamar had never seen such dancing in her life. The air seemed to crackle with displaced energy.

Now a Clinggg! from the cymbals sent the performer off again as though driven by the sound. Clanggg! and she twirled to Thamar's feet. Clinggg! and she circled the Queen. Clanggg! and a pattern of flying arms and legs lost the King to view. Each clash gave fresh impetus, till it appeared she was the spirit of the cymbals, expelled from them violently by their meeting and flung from one point of the terrace to another by their vibrations. Sometimes her peacock and gold skirt swished within an inch of a nose and then, as she did something unusual with her muscles, her stomach flew round and round before Phut's astonished gaze. It was tremendous, it was fiery, it was too much to be borne. Cefalu retreated underneath the Queen's skirt, and told a hiding lizard, 'Not at all what we're accustomed to in Canaan.'

The cymbals ceased their clashing. The dancer sank down at the King's feet : had she died? The petals of her skirt lay about her, so still, it was incredible to think they had been part of that wild motion : did she breathe? — so gently, it was hard to believe anything had happened. But her long dark hair was drenched with sweat, and the jewelled flowers of her headdress, nodding on their stalks, were still agitated as though a wind blew through them.

The music began again : this time with a slow, insinuating air, strange harmonies, sudden calls and flutings like the sound of mating birds. Immediately the dancer was on her feet, standing very still. She held the painted palms of her hands outward and gazed upward at the sky. The metal flowers fell back behind her head to frame it in a peacock tail of blue and gold. She was brown and strong, a magnetic woman, lithe as a leopard. Her face was painted to a mask : white eyelids, an almost orange mouth, eyes outlined in green and black and blue. She was singing now. The voice was low and surprisingly sweet, emerging from the lips of that exotic face to strike the hearers with the strangeness of a contrast.

> '*Sweet to love is the Heiress of the Sun!*
> *The light of her glance draws the longing of the men.*
> *Sweet to love is the Heiress of the King!*
> *The heart of his son is netted with desire*
> *As with her companions before his eyes she stands . . .*'

Before Ta-Thata the dancer from Shinar, Beltethazar, stood and sang as though honouring the girl who had asked for the performance. But now and then her eyes moved to Sinuhe's face and then on to Su-Shunut's. Thamar, watching the Princess, saw colour come and go in her face, and how she drew herself up with a regal dignity the image of her father's. What gossip there must have been . . . She saw the

King turn and say something to his Marshal, who stepped forward and brought the singing to an end. The dancer most humbly prostrated herself.

'The song does not please my Majesty! It is unfitted to its audience,' said the King.

'O Sovereign, my lord,' said Beltethazar, and her speaking voice was husky with foreign intonation, 'if your servant has sung badly before your Majesty's royal son and daughter, may she be counted as one dead.'

'My Majesty did not speak of death. Go. You shall be paid.'

'O Sovereign, my lord, treat not your servant as one who would deliberately err! It is your servant's ruin. No fee will I take for a performance that has displeased so gracious a Sovereign. I ask only to be allowed to sing again so my work may not be cursed before all hearers and my living lost.' The words were humble, but there was nothing humble about their speaker. She was extended like a victim, yet haughtiness was in every line of her. 'Listen, my King: I ask only to sing one little song so old that even some people in my land have forgotten it; so short, it can scarcely disturb the royal ears for –'

'Sing!' said the King peremptorily. 'And then go. My Majesty would not spoil an artist's living, but your performance does not please me.'

The dancer leaped to her feet, ran lightly to the little girls, bereft them of their timbrels, and returned to the central position. She clashed the timbrels angrily, as though she would shake them to pieces. When the sound died she sang without musical accompaniment, and in her foreign tongue. The song was brief, exultant, and ended suddenly on a strange cry: shrill, like the call to sacrifice. It was an odd ending to a performance for the young Ta-Thata's party. There was no clapping, only a sense of unease.

Then Thamar saw that the tall, broad-shouldered man who stood behind the King's couch had understood the woman's tongue – there was dark indignation in his face.

Hekhti leaned forward to whisper in Merenkere's ear, 'Your Majesty! Will my Sovereign, my lord allow that woman to sing praises to her goddess Ishtar-Inana before your Majesty's very face? She is impious.'

'My Majesty thinks you speak truly, Hekhti!' said the King. And added harshly to the woman, 'Go!'

'She was a strange one,' said Phut wonderingly. 'Wasn't she? She did things with her belly, it went round and round. The King didn't like her, nor did that big man.'

'They were sensible. Now, Phut – you know it's time for bed. Come along –'

'I *am* along –' Phut looked around him appreciatively at the apartment he was sharing with his mother. He had been royally appointed his own quarters, with maidservants, but he preferred to be with Thamar because – he said – she was really afraid of the dark. 'Is that a weasel painted on the wall? Can I have Casper in my bed?'

'Yes, it's a weasel, and no, because Casper and Cefalu are asleep.'

Phut submitted to have his short robe removed. He stared down at his stomach and made earnest efforts to revolve it. 'Won't,' he said sadly, and climbed naked into bed.

'Have you prayed?'

'I have – I mean, I'm praying now.' He closed his eyes and his lips moved. 'I'm praying that my belly –'

'Be quiet about it, and go to sleep.'

There was a lengthy pause while Phut breathed heavily, and patient Thamar sat with her hands folded while she waited for him to fall into the concentrated slumber that would keep him unaware of hated darkness. She was

sorrowful without Reuben, and imagined that the Palace
felt different to when she last was there. Kemi had always
its cruel, rapacious side, but this time she was conscious of
a general sense of threat, as though the evening brought
with it thicker darkness than used to gather by the Nile.
Perhaps she was nervous, so far away from home. But
– there *was* something odd, she was sure. It seeped into the
Palace, a challenge from the realms of Set – yet that
challenge, in Kemi's worship, had always been there : and
the King's Ma'at, with his enlightenment, had held the
balance on the side of light. There was some legend, she had
heard, of Men-nofer – it was called the Balance of the Two
Lands because here, in the Temple of Ptah, Horus and Set
had been reconciled, and the duality of creation was –

'She came from Shinar, that belly one . . .'

'*Yes* . . .' Once Phut began to talk, he seldom went to
sleep.

'Like all those people . . . 'n caravan th't joined us –
coming.'

'They came from Syria,' said Thamar in a soothing voice.

'Didn't – came from Shinar,' said Phut's voice, positively
and less sleepily than before. 'They was talking when they
didn't know I was hearing – they wasn't going to tell anyone about Shinar because . . . I don't know why. C'n I have
Casper in my bed ?'

'If you really go to sleep you can have Casper. But if
you don't, I shall take him away again.' Thamar sighed and
rose. She disentangled Casper from the sleeping Cefalu and
deposited him on Phut's chest, where he settled down
comfortably with a fortunate and soporific effect. Soon
the room was filled with noisy breathing.

Thamar quietly went away, leaving a torch burning in
a bracket. Shinar ? she wondered. There was a little niggling
sense at the back of her mind that it was something she

should tell the King. But this idea was soon driven from her memory once she entered the room where Caltah sat watching beside her heavy responsibility – her sick and hating son.

A Question of Sadhi

'It is a problem,' said Merenkere, next morning. There was a shining brightness about him, or so Thamar thought. Each day began for the King with ritual purification before, in his role of Kemi's Great High Priest, he made the sacrificial offerings to Re the Sun.

'O Sovereign, my lord, it is.' There was a quiver in her voice.

Meri-Mekhmet patted her hand. 'Let us ask Hekhti, my lord?'

'Hekhti?' asked Thamar doubtfully. 'His Majesty's Chief Royal Architect? Forgive me, but is an architect the right person to help my afflicted son?'

'Hekhti is no mere architect,' said Merenkere, pacing to and fro. 'He's a strange creature. His knowledge seems to embrace everything. Astrology, mathematics – medicine, My more jealous priests dislike him thoroughly! Yes – I think we will consult Hekhti about your son.' He clapped his hands, and his bodyservant entered and prostrated himself.

'What is the King's will, O Sovereign, my lord?'

'Find my honoured architect for me, Hemi. And tell the Princess of Canaan's servant to bring her son, Sadhi, to his mother.'

'O Sovereign, my lord, it is done.' Hemi withdrew.

Merenkere noticed Thamar's apprehensive expression. 'There's no need for anyone to fear Hekhti,' he reassured her. 'Sadhi will not be faced with strange rites and practices that might upset him!'

'O Sovereign, my lord, it is not that –' Thamar's lips quivered still more violently. 'But I cannot tell how *Sadhi* will behave! You see, we – we failed with – He's sometimes like a wild animal. He may bite!' She looked nervously at the King who was believed to be a god. Should one's son bite him? 'And by now he is so – so odd, and ill.'

'Poor child! Reuben's herd dog tried to savage me in the past, and failed. Benoni has bigger teeth, my Majesty is sure, than has your son.'

Thamar gave the ghost of a sigh. 'O Sovereign, my lord, that is true.' Her eyes filled with tears. 'If only Reuben were here, now,' she added, with a sob.

Hekhti came quickly in answer to the King's summons. 'We have a patient for you, my friend. No – not the Princess of Canaan! Her son. He has been deaf and dumb since illness struck him many, many moons ago. He pines from sheer misery, and can be ruled by no one. My orthodox physicians would say that evil spirits inhabit him, and prevent his hearing and his speech. See him for my Majesty's sake, and tell us your opinion. Ah – here is the Princess's servant, with the child.'

Hekhti frowned when he saw Sadhi's emaciated condition, but he answered readily, 'My Sovereign, my lord is as always obeyed. May Your Majesty forgive me, but examination will be easier in his mother's presence alone.'

'We are duly dismissed,' said Merenkere, laughing. 'Send for your assistant, Hekhti. There is a couch in the next room where you may examine the boy, while the Queen and I wait in here. Go with Hekhti, Thamar – and don't worry if Sadhi tries to bite him, for he is very strong.'

There was no doubt of that. Hekhti lifted Sadhi as though his frantic efforts to free himself and violent kickings were nothing, and bore him to the next room, where he placed him on the couch. Sadhi immediately rolled off and tried to crawl beneath it. With a sound of distress Thamar started forward, but Hekhti waved her aside and gently recovered his escaping patient.

'Princess – please sit right away from him, upon that stool ... Ah! Here is Amrat –' For Hemi was ushering in the young assistant – 'Just when he's needed! Prepare a pastille for me, Amrat, and quickly ... That is right.' A little dish was placed near Sadhi's head, and the pastille set alight. Hekhti stood back and allowed Amrat to hold down the child. Sadhi stared as though hynotized, while fumes drifted up his nostrils. Then his eyelids began to droop. Amrat looked towards Hekhti for further instructions, and Thamar was comforted by the obvious confidence that the young man had in his master.

'It's enough! He is young, and easily affected – a little more, and he will be asleep!' Hekhti gently lifted Sadhi's chin in his hand. 'That is just right –' His examination was very quick, thorough and assured. He completed it as Sadhi, making his one gobbling sound, began to fight again. Hekhti patted him on the head, and avoided a vicious attempt to scratch his hand.

'Now I advise you, Princess, to take the child back to his own apartments, and try to comfort him. I will speak later with the Sovereign, who will discuss the matter with you as soon as he is able.'

Thamar gave Hekhti a beseeching look and opened her mouth to question him. Then she shut it again, for she saw it was useless. Apart from Merenkere she had never known a man of such quiet authority before. Caltah picked up the struggling Sadhi, and she followed them obediently from the room.

*

It was late when the King sent for her. She found him alone, looking anxious and abstracted. His mind was less upon Thamar and Sadhi than on his heavy duties and the subtle yet increasing influence of No-Hotep upon his son. He spoke abruptly to Thamar in a way unlike himself, and wounded her. 'Hekhti tells me he thinks your child may be incurable, Thamar – but he cannot even put it to the test until the boy co-operates. For this reason he wants me to send you away from him.'

She turned very pale and sat down, forgetting she was in the Sovereign's presence. Such unprecedented behaviour made Merenkere look at her in surprise, then realize how harshly he had spoken. He went to her, and put a hand upon her shoulder. 'Thamar, if there's anything Hekhti *can* do, he will do it.'

'But – to send me away, O Sovereign, my lord!' stammered poor Thamar. 'And if Hekhti thinks him incurable, anyway? How could I have Sadhi feel that his mother had deserted him – when perhaps he's dying?'

The King said gently, 'Tell me : do you think you can improve his condition ?'

Thamar stared at her toes. 'No, your Majesty, but –'

'My Majesty was far too outspoken. It's true that Hekhti cannot pronounce upon a *cure*, but he believes that he might bring the child to accept what has happened – perhaps even find some way of communication. From what you say, Thamar, it seems that Sadhi's will is set against you, and himself. He wills to die. It may be that he desires to torment you, that you, his mother, may share his desperation. Hekhti insists upon a brutal truth – there is no hope, while you're with Sadhi.'

Thamar twisted her hands together. 'O Sovereign, my lord, Your Majesty makes me feel a failure !'

'Thamar, that's beside the point and unworthy of you.

For there's small time left, as you must know. If my Majesty can advise on such a subject, take Hekhti's advice and let him try!'

Almost inaudibly Thamar said, 'And if Sadhi dies? If he dies sooner, because I leave him?'

'That would be a terrible thing. Hekhti tells me that the child will suffer, anyway. So it is a terrible choice you have to make – as a mother.'

'O Sovereign, my lord – you can prevail on Hekhti! He is your Majesty's subject! Please tell him that I'll let him try, but I *cannot* leave the Palace.'

Slowly the King shook his head. 'It would be wrong for my Majesty to command Hekhti in this way. He knows already what a risk you and he take with the boy – but he dares take it, on his condition : Sadhi must be handed over to him so completely that there's no chance of his seeing you at all, or running off to you.' Watching the struggle in her face, Merenkere added, 'If Sadhi were my own child, Hekhti should take the chance – but I'm only a father, not a mother! Will you talk with the Queen about it all?'

'O Sovereign, my lord, I will be glad to do so,' replied Thamar faintly, seeing she was dismissed. She made her obeisance, and the King called Hemi to conduct her to the Queen.

Early next day Thamar and Phut left the Palace of White Walls, to lodge with the aged Court Chamberlain Ay. Cefalu elected to remain with Casper in the Palace. He had always thought its luxury almost adequate for any cat, although there were a few things he would have liked to alter. 'It is peculiar, for instance,' he said, 'that the King and courtiers don't eat fish. One would think that what a cat enjoyed would be considered a universal delicacy.'

'Age makes you exacting, Cefalu,' replied Thamar absent-mindedly. Her thoughts, just then, were all with Sadhi.

'I express an opinion. I shall stay on here, however, out of kindness. The Queen may have promised to send you frequent reports, but we all know that there's no one like a cat for subtle inner knowledge of a situation. You shall have word from me twice daily.'

'Thank you, Cefalu,' responded Thamar meekly. She was well aware of his great liking for the Palace cooks' ways of roasting waterfowl.

'Think nothing of it. Now today I am taking Casper to the tomb of Meluseth. He is the right age for an exalting experience – I am confident it will leave its mark for life.'

Thamar had already left the Palace when Cefalu and Casper made their way out of the city to the Necropolis, and entered the shaft leading downward to Meluseth's funeral chamber. The tomb was very still. There was a smell of fragrant spices. Meluseth's sarcophagus stood in the inner chamber, which was as yet unsealed since its wall paintings were unfinished. The sarcophagus was most elegantly made, as befitted the resting place of one who had been the greatest cat beauty in the Two Lands. The inscriptions on the wall were very clear, the hieroglyphs sensitively drawn.

Cefalu recited a text aloud from memory. '"The Eternal House of Meluseth, She Who Loves the Moon. I was the honour of my sister Sekhmet, a fragrant guardian of the Two Lands –" '

'How was she a fragrant guardian of the Two Lands?' asked Casper, as his father finished and wiped away a tear with one deft paw. 'Will *I* have a little house like this, one day?' He sat down and began to gouge out his left ear.

'She just was,' said Cefalu shortly. 'And no – not if you

behave like that. Come outside at once.' And he took Casper away and spanked him, not only for his vulgar behaviour but also to impress the gracious memory of the occasion upon his mind.

An Opponent for Hekhti

The Chief Royal Architect had his own apartments in the immense rambling warren of the Palace. Caltah carried Sadhi into Hekhti's presence, and left him there. At first he made no attempt to escape, but seemed overawed, and sat where he had been placed on a pile of cushions in the centre of the floor, and looked around him. Like a small animal he was sensing the atmosphere of his surroundings.

Hekhti's main room was large, high and rectangular, its ceiling supported by the conventional columns topped with lotus buds. The floor was black and white inlay of some stone which felt warm to the soles of Sadhi's feet. The room's three entrances – to right and left and at one end – were covered by hangings of plain white linen. Decoration was confined to the ceiling, where bee and plant, vulture and serpent, all symbols of the Two Lands, were repeated in gold and turquoise and lapis again and again.

Sadhi lowered his gaze to where Hekhti himself sat cross-legged upon the floor. At his side was a low table, covered with plans. He was writing on a length of papyrus, but looked up occasionally at his small patient, smiled, and returned to work.

The silence, the austerity, Hekhti's presence : Sadhi summed them up and didn't like them. Pining and frail he might be, but he could still summon up the nervous energy that some sick people show. He was suddenly on his feet, darting for the nearest entrance. He grabbed at the linen hangings and pulled them apart. Outside stood one of the King's Bodyguard, who smiled pleasantly but raised his spear to a horizontal position and barred Sadhi's path.

The child stared, backed away. He wheeled and charged across the room, only to fall into the arms of another guard outside the second entrance. Sadhi made an inarticulate sound of rage and charged the third entrance even faster – with the same result. All the time Hekhti paid him no attention, and continued to work.

So it went on: Sadhi didn't give up easily. He feinted towards one entrance and made for another. He almost succeeded in twisting out between one soldier's feet. Yet each time he was caught, and gently prodded back into the room again. His rage mounted. It was impossible to show quite what he felt – his thin chest heaved, he gasped, he pummelled, he fought. At last he expressed his sense of outrage by kicking and kicking at one of the eternally smiling soldiers, and then retreated to the cushions, lay on his face, and thrashed with all his limbs as though hoping to break the floor.

Presently his physical condition told on him. His frenzy gave way to stillness, except for an occasional heaving sob. Then even that ceased. After some while he sat up again, his hands pressed over his eyes. He looked a pathetic, beaten object, but there was something about the way he sat – Hekhti, eyeing him thoughtfully, rose, put down his papyrus, and picked up a jug of fruit juice from the table by him. He filled a carved cup, bore it to Sadhi's side, placed one hand on the child's shoulder and, when the guarded position relaxed very slightly, offered him the cup.

Sadhi's thin brows slanted downwards and then together in a frown. Sadhi's eyes peered upward like a nervous and suspicious oryx's. He drew back an arm and struck the cup away from him so forcibly that it fell from Hekhti's hand

and shattered to pieces on the floor. A stream of golden liquid spread across the patterned black and white.

Hekhti showed no reaction – but waited quietly, his hand still on Sadhi's shoulder. After a second's scowling into that impassive face Sadhi shrugged out from under the architect's hand and struck wildly in the direction of his mouth. Hekhti was too quick for him, and moved aside. Impetus carried the child forward on to his face. Before he had time to start flailing at the floor he was picked up and returned firmly to the cushions. While he was still sitting there, dazed with surprise, Hekhti returned to the room's far end, re-seated himself, and clapped his hands for Amrat, who came running to clear up the spilled juice and remove the shattered cup. When the room was silent once more, Hekhti resumed his work.

Sadhi stayed where he was, and did nothing for some while, but his tension grew and grew till it was unbearable along with his hatred and frustration . . .

Hekhti was carefully inscribing on his papyrus when Sadhi charged at the table like a small bull. He banged into it heavily, hurt himself, and leaned sobbing against the top; then, with one sweep of both arms, he sent everything – plans, writing materials, fruit juice – cascading to destruction on the floor. Hekhti paid no attention whatever, but continued writing until something like a miniature cyclone hurled itself upon him from behind. He let fall his scroll, turned, and caught Sadhi by the wrists to lift him effortlessly and carry him back towards the cushions. Violent attempts to escape from them were restrained without violence of any sort. Meanwhile Amrat, who had heard the crash, re-entered to deal with the resultant chaos. Once Sadhi's hysterical fighting had quietened down, Hekhti returned to his writing, ignoring an occasional exaggerated sob.

The pattern of rising tension, attack, and sobbing continued throughout the day. At one time Amrat came to serve Hekhti with food and wine, and then carried a plateful of wild duckling with green shoots to the scowling boy. Immediately a trail of broken pottery and duckling spattered across the floor. Hekhti, paying no attention, ate and drank. It wasn't long before the cup was dashed from his hand, yet he couldn't be moved either to fury, outer anxiety, or placation; nor did he try to soothe the raging child as Thamar, Reuben or Caltah would have done. He simply warded him off and returned him to the cushions. Food and mess were cleared away, and the room left exactly as before.

Still Sadhi wouldn't give in, though there was no Mother to be bullied, no Caltah to hold him, just this dreadful stranger whose strength and impassivity seemed endless. If only that patience could be broken! Throughout the day Sadhi did his best. Furies, thrown food, heel-drummings, attacks. His own nervous endurance seemed similar to that of madness. But as the day waned toward sunset there were longer intervals between his outbursts. Sometimes he would sit quite silent, with drooping head. Hekhti thoughtfully observed the difference.

Now he himself sat silent, and Amrat removed the finished scroll. Slaves brought torches and stuck them into holders on the walls high above Sadhi's reach. Just before the sun began his nightly journey through the underworld the torches were lit, and Hekhti made his evening ritual. Sadhi sat watching, motionless except that his thin chest rose and fell with the uneven flutter of a bird's. The corners of his mouth drooled slightly. His hair was black with sweat. He gave a sudden desperate sob that wasn't one of fury, and keeled over upon his face.

It was what Hekhti had been waiting for: in an instant

he was kneeling on the floor at Sadhi's side, his hand on the child's wrist. A faint pulse beat there, fast and erratic. He gently touched the sweat-drenched head, then stroked it. Sadhi made a brave, compulsive effort : he tried to bite. But when Hekhti picked him up and nursed him in his arms like a sick baby he lay there still and panting. Hekhti walked slowly round and round the room, holding the child comfortingly close, and aware how tensely the thin body lay; Sadhi might have been forced to a standstill but was still unbeaten. He carried him through into the next room.

This was where he himself slept. In one corner a small bed had been prepared for Sadhi. Hekhti sat down with the child in his arms, and called for Amrat, who brought a special draught of strongly fortified fruit juice cunningly mixed with herbs that had a sedative effect. By now Sadhi's thirst was tremendous, and in spite of the remnants of his fighting desires he couldn't resist the enticing draught. Before succumbing to sleep he forced his weary lids open, and gave his opponent a last, long, hating glare which said plainly, 'Don't think I'm beaten – tomorrow we will fight again.' Hekhti gave a deep sigh; he was tired, as well, and he had still to prepare a report that could be sent to Thamar without dismaying her.

Once Sadhi was in bed, Cefalu emerged from the shadows underneath it with his tail indignantly erect. He might dislike Sadhi, but he was disturbed that a Prince of Canaan's son should be treated by such unorthodox methods. The man is a fraud and dupes the Sovereign, he told himself. How things have gone to pieces in this Palace since I left it ! But he was too goodhearted to alarm Thamar, and his own message, carried by one of the younger Palace cats, merely said that Sadhi was now asleep.

The next day Hekhti found the child so tired that he refused to let him up; kept in bed, Sadhi still refused his food, but no one spent a long while tempting him to eat as Thamar had. Once food was angrily pushed away it was removed altogether, and nothing else was brought until Hekhti himself ate again. Sadhi couldn't restrain his thirst, though, and eventually gave in to the extent of swallowing more fruit juice, which was this time laced with something to make him thirstier. He was even thirsty for the soup that Hekhti offered him, and drank that, too, while eyeing his captor with a sullen stare.

Later in the day, since he seemed stronger and more rebellious, he was allowed up to sit on cushions in the next room. Here his determination reasserted itself, as he looked round at the scene of yesterday's humiliation, and ruminated on it. The battle was resumed.

Sadhi's will was even stronger than Hekhti had suspected, and by the fourth day he had grown increasingly worried although he wouldn't show it. This keeping the boy from his mother was distasteful to him, and Thamar's anguished daily messages made him wince. Each time he looked at Sadhi's drawn features, the huge circles beneath his eyes, his hair darkened with sweat, he winced again. It was a brutal business, and if it went on much longer Sadhi wouldn't only have defeated Hekhti, but have defeated himself in that inner place where defeat can, alarmingly, be misread as victory.

Then, quite suddenly, half-way through the fourth day, Sadhi's determination crumbled. He had been raging round the room all morning, showing reserves of nervous energy which seemed incredible. He had hurled cushions, sobbed, attacked just as before. But around midday when the sun stood at full strength high above the Palace, and the heat was infernal, and the shadows of columns black upon the floor, Sadhi gave a great sigh of exhaustion. He raised his eyes, which now looked enormous, and gazed at his impassive tormentor. His glance travelled over Hekhti's face as though seeking some sign of a crack in that relentless impassivity. There was none. No evidence of strain, of fright, of possible giving up. He knew at last that no one would bring Thamar here with Caltah, nor let him free.

Of course, he could punish them all by starving himself until he died. One part of him – no, more, a *great* part – wanted to do just that, and watch them wring their hands and be unhappy around his bed. But where *were* his mother and father – and where was the terrifying pleasure of reject-ing life if he couldn't see their alarm and enjoy inflicting pain on them? There would only be this stranger to sit by him, kindly compassionate but not sorry enough – no, not *nearly* sorry enough ! – to make it all worth while. He glowered across the room at the man who couldn't be beaten, who wouldn't raise a finger to stop him going alone into the darkness of which, when he really thought about it, he was so very much afraid ... Amrat was just bringing in the midday meal, and looked at Sadhi, beckoning to him. The child took a few wavering steps forward, and received the full warmth of Hekhti's encouraging smile. Just to eat once meant nothing, Sadhi thought. He could refuse again any time he chose. In a very dignified manner he approached. Hekhti made a simple, downward gesture. Sadhi sat. Then he put out a hesitant hand toward the food.

But, to his utter amazement, Hekhti prevented him by taking hold of his hand in a firm grip and tapping twice on it. Sadhi looked at him, very puzzled. Hekhti released his hand and gave him the bowl; as he started to eat, removed it from him, took his hand, tapped on it as before, and again handed him the bowl. Sadhi's ferocious scowl began to form. He was almost ready to start throwing things, but he was so hungry by now and the food smelled too enticing !

In spite of himself he ate, casting suspicious sidelong glances at his companion.

When Amrat approached to serve them with a light wine, Sadhi snatched greedily at the cup, but again Hekhti intercepted him. He doubled Sadhi's hand into a fist, closing the child's fingers inward and holding them there. It was done twice and then he was allowed the cup. Quite suddenly Sadhi got the message. That gesture meant 'drink' just as the first had meant 'food' or 'eat'. Someone had managed to break through his lack of communication and the awful silence of the outer world! He was so surprised by the blinding revelation that you could actually speak *without* speaking that he gave Hekhti a wondering smile.

Something of Reuben's charm appeared on his pinched features. Hekhti was more moved by that pathetic smile than he had been by anything in the preceding days. He put his arm round the child to draw him to his side, and kissed him on the forehead as Reuben would have done. Sadhi stiffened. Then, lulled by a strange sense of confidence in this man he couldn't make afraid, and by the pleasure of a full stomach, he leaned heavily against Hekhti and went straight to sleep. For a long while Hekhti sat there holding the child's fragile body in his arms. He sat as still as he always did, and there was very little expression on his features except one of faint surprise.

Matters for the King

As Hekhti had foreseen, the fruits of that first capitulation weren't brought to maturity without further trouble. Sadhi had been wild and destructive for too long, and re-education was a slow affair. When he failed to understand what Hekhti meant – or failed to make himself understood – he would revert to tantrums more suited to a child like Phut. At times it was Hekhti's great patience that he fought against. He would refuse to puzzle over what his teacher tried to show him, curl himself into a ball with his hands over his eyes, and cut himself off into his world of silent stubbornness.

So there were setbacks; and yet to balance them came days when his understanding was suddenly enlarged by his grasp of some new sign-series – such as those that dealt with colour. He had just displayed a bad bout of temper one morning, and kicked Hekhti viciously on the shins. Hekhti had responded by complete calm, and by picking him up to seat him on a nearby table. Then, while Sadhi stared sullenly into space, the Chief Royal Architect began to lay out a row of objects, all coloured turquoise, beside the boy. Sadhi still sat determinedly withdrawn. Hekhti placed another row of objects nearer him. This time they were green. A third and final row contained only yellow ones.

Sadhi peered reluctantly sideways at this fascinating sight: what could it mean? Seeing his attention caught, Hekhti picked up three amulets – turquoise, green, yellow –

and tapped on Sadhi's hand the sign for 'amulet' that he already knew. He replaced them in their separate rows, indicated each row in turn with a pointing finger, and accompanied each gesture with another sign. Sadhi frowned, and frowned harder. It was touch and go whether he would fall into another tantrum. First an amulet was an amulet, and then it was ... All at once fresh understanding came to him. He leaped from the table, ran to touch a green cushion, rushed back and grabbed up the green amulet to tap it rather painfully and triumphantly on Hekhti's hand in the correct colour sign. Then his head drooped, and an unaccustomed sense of shame affected him. How hard and often he had kicked his patient deliverer! Very shyly he put his arms around Hekhti, and hugged him. It was the first sign of affection he had shown another human being for many years.

That evening Hekhti went to see the King. On his way he heard swift footsteps behind him, and the priest No-Hotep caught him up. Hekhti made a polite inclination of his head, and slightly increased his pace. No-Hotep increased his too, walking with his curious smooth gait which flowed along in almost inhuman fashion and had led his detractors to compare him to an eel.

'And how is your little patient, the Princess of Canaan's son? We hear tales that a magical cure is soon expected.'

Hekhti raised his eyebrows. 'A wise man like No-Hotep does not listen to such chatter, surely?'

'It would be impious not to believe that invocations to the gods may produce great results.'

'Ah,' responded Hekhti, 'you must forgive me – I thought we spoke of magic.'

'It's the common word for it,' replied the priest. 'I do not wish to offend you – or the gods!'

'I'm not easily offended. As to the gods, a true priest never offends them, for his conversation is discreet and concerned only with the truth. As for the child –' Hekhti hesitated. He had been going to speak of his new method, but some instinct warned him to say no more. There seemed no reason against such an innocent revelation, but he had learned to trust his intuitions. 'Sadhi is probably incurable,' he finished evenly, 'but makes some physical progress under my care. I am on my way to our Sovereign Lord the King to tell his Majesty.'

'Then it is not for a mere humble priest to detain one who has dealings with the God ! I ask only how long you will be there, for the Royal Heir has desired me to deliver personally a message to his father.'

'The length of audience his Majesty graciously allots is decided by his Majesty.'

'Very true, most noble Hekhti ! A wise man waits patiently until the Sun rises, for it surely will not rise at his own bidding.'

'It's edifying to hear that you keep such thoughts constantly in mind, O No-Hotep, for in no circumstances should it ever be forgotten. Now his Majesty awaits me.'

'Wisdom must always wait upon greater wisdom.' The priest smiled. 'I'm sorry to hear that your considerable skill has failed with this poor child.' He allowed Hekhti to escape him.

The Sovereign was playing draughts with his Great Royal Wife. It was a rare occasion when he could relax, and he frowned as Hekhti reported that No-Hotep sought admission. 'My Majesty will not see that priest tonight! He is always pestering, with the excuse of a message from the Prince. Hekhti – we have heard it was No-Hotep who brought that woman from Shinar to the attention of my children.' The King's hand moved impatiently, and swept an ivory piece from the board.

Hekhti retrieved it. 'O Sovereign, my lord, may your servant have permission to speak on the subject of Shinar?'

'And what of Shinar?'

Meri-Mekhmet rose gracefully. 'You are beating me, my lord! And as I see that Hekhti is here to speak of grave matters, I shall leave you both together.'

'I am troubled, O Sovereign, my lord,' said Hekhti when the Queen had smiled at him and left, 'for I have a strong impression that No-Hotep is engaged in something of no value to the Throne. Is your Majesty aware that when the recent Embassy from Shinar was at Court, the minor officials were often closeted with that priest of Set?'

'Are minor officials of importance?' asked the King, surprised.

'No, your Majesty – unless they act as messengers; or – unless the most unnoticed, the most discreet of them is in fact the King of Shinar's younger son under a false name.'

'Hekhti!' exclaimed the King. 'Can this be true? And why have you waited so long to speak of it? The Embassy left nearly a moon ago.'

'Forgive my correcting your Majesty – three men did not leave: this young "official" and two attendants. He had been most unwell, and left only after I called to see him late last night. While I waited for him in a side room his attendants came out, quarrelling. They had been drinking, and their tongues were loosened – this is how I learned the truth about whom they served. It was impossible to see your Majesty earlier today, and I cared not to send the information by someone else.'

'You were quite right!' Merenkere rose, and paced the room. 'Now, what means this? There's always plotting in Men-nofer, as you know, my Hekhti, and most of it can be dismissed. But No-Hotep, if my Majesty's instinct is not at fault, is a man who moves only to his own advantage. A sharp rebuke shall be sent to Shinar for discourtesy – if for nothing worse ! And, Hekhti – your information decides me about something I've been brooding on all day : my Vizier has to hand the right opportunity to rid me of this priest – one which cannot sound offensive and so make others pity him or seek to espouse in him a cause. It's time to send an Embassy to Syria, where loyal friendship to my Throne and Kemi has never been in question. Upon this journey, so regrettably beset with dangers as it often is, the priest No-Hotep shall soon be sent. What do you say, my architect ? Pretend you're my Majesty's Vizier, and advise me !'

'Why, your Majesty, that it's indeed not for the King's architect to voice an opinion – but since your Majesty *has* asked me, I would say that if trouble befalls this priest through a dangerous journey, then it befalls a man who has only brought it on himself.'

The King remained silent for a space, then said, 'Soon my son shall be appointed a new Chief Royal Tutor and better counsellor. My Majesty has it in mind to give you this task.'

'I'm ready to serve your Majesty in any way my Sovereign pleases.' There was resignation in Hekhti's voice and, in spite of himself, dismay.

The King laughed ruefully. 'Are you so, my friend ? Well, there's no hurry – Sinuhe has many tutors already, crowd-ing each other for position. My Majesty would in any case be patient – so no one could hint you had managed skilfully to oust No-Hotep. The sooner my worthy priest of Set has his new appointment, the better. It shall shortly be announced. Now : what of Canaan's son ?'

Hekhti laughed. 'O Sovereign, my lord, I came here

intending – no, hoping – to steal from your Majesty on his behalf.'

'My Majesty thought it only the good jeweller Tahlevi who stole – and that in the past! What is it you need, Hekhti? You may have anything except the Queen and the Crown. And at least you wouldn't want the Crown, it is a heavy weight.' His face grew sombre.

'O Sovereign, my lord, that is very true; and yet it's what No-Hotep wants.'

'The *Crown*?' asked the King incredulously.

'The power behind the Crown, at least. But your Majesty, who wishes to remove him from the Royal Heir's household, is aware of that already. With regard to Canaan's son, and with my Sovereign's gracious permission, may I borrow the Princess Ta-Thata and her two companions?'

'By great Osiris, my friend, are you thinking to set up a harem? I don't believe the Queen would quite approve!'

Hekhti smiled broadly. 'O Sovereign, my lord, it is not so delicate a matter! Your Majesty has been much occupied, so I thought it unfit to trouble my Sovereign with too many details about Sadhi. Even the Princess of Canaan only knows at present that her son's physical state has generally improved under my care, that he now trusts me and is less inclined to violence. Your Majesty, I'm trying a new treatment on the child, one I'm in the process of inventing! It's a method of communication by signs. Since he has mastered its rudiments his general condition has improved out of all knowledge.'

'But that is wonderful, Hekhti! You'll bring new hope to countless people. Your fame will be great in the Two Lands, if you accomplish this thing.'

'If your Majesty pleases, I would still keep silent about it. I – I cannot quite tell why. It is some – intuition.'

'As you will.' Merenkere understood the desire to keep

quiet about a discovery till it was complete. 'But Sadhi's mother? Should she not be told? Shouldn't she come to see the child, if he's better?'

'Not just yet, your Majesty,' replied Hekhti quickly. 'Sadhi could still set his face against recovery, and firmness is yet required. But he should have young companions – and there's little sense in teaching him a language he cannot share. The Princess, Su-Shunut, and Keta would be very good for him – and could be sworn to secrecy!'

'You would teach them this new language too?'

'O Sovereign, my lord, that is my idea.'

'Wouldn't a boy be a more suitable friend? My son could visit him.'

Hekhti looked downward at his Sovereign's sandalled feet. 'If that is your desire, O Sovereign, my lord,' he said without expression.

The King turned his back on him, and walked to the window. It was a sudden action, and Hekhti glanced at him anxiously, but it wasn't annoyance that caused Merenkere to turn away. It was a sickness of heart that, because it must go for ever unacknowledged, was almost greater than Thamar's. 'I told you, Hekhti, you might have whatever you needed,' he said over his shoulder. 'As to secrecy, surely some time his mother must be told?'

'Your Majesty is most kind. And yes – the Princess must soon know of this new teaching, although if she came here it could be bad for my hard-won authority! Sadhi might visit her – in a short while; perhaps every other day, at first. If the Princess Ta-Thata and her companions would go with him, they could show her the rudiments of this new language.'

'Do as you please, Hekhti.' The King turned his head and smiled, but he sounded remote and sad. 'It's your treatment and I confidently leave it in your hands. But don't forget –

no, my Majesty knows you will not – that my daughter must soon face the rigorous Court training of a woman who will also be a Queen and one who, it's hoped, will strengthen her husband. There will be little time for Sadhi – though she will give you what she can.'

'O Sovereign, my lord, that is all I ask,' replied the Chief Royal Architect.

In fact Thamar already knew of Hekhti's experiments. Cefalu had brought the news himself.

'I have revised my opinion of this fellow,' he had told her, sniffing delicately and thoughtfully at a bulrush, 'and have discussed him with my son Ptahsuti, who has grown to be as noble and discerning a cat as you could wish. We are in agreement.'

'But why hasn't Hekhti himself explained to me?' Thamar sounded perplexed. 'It's most odd of him.'

Cefalu pushed the bulrush with his whiskers and then let it rebound against his face in a pleasant manner. 'He wants' – push whiskers – 'success to be' – push – 'assured, before he tells you. He has even sworn young Amrat to secrecy, so I beg you'll let no one know I've told you of this invention.'

'I must send news to Canaan!' insisted Thamar in an agitated way. 'It's not fair to keep this to myself, and if my poor –'

'My poor Master will be much happier with a larger, later surprise than a smaller, earlier one,' said Cefalu firmly, tiring of the bulrush, and rolling over to rub his spine against a cushion of springy green plants. 'Women will act too quickly. Even that Pearl of Wisdom, Meluseth, would act too quickly now and then.'

'Cefalu, do you *really* think Meluseth was – ' began Thamar incredulously. But her voice trailed off, for Cefalu had shut his eyes tight till they were no more than two black lines in his triangular face, and, looking determinedly deaf, was rubbing his spine yet harder along the ground.

Sinuhe laughed in amazement when he heard that Ta-Thata was to visit Sadhi every day.

'What is the King our father thinking of? And what are you to do for Sadhi – feed him?'

'Just be with him a little, I think,' said Ta-Thata evasively.

'And that pleases you? Dear sister, you're as mad as he is!'

'He isn't mad – he's sad. He is the underside of life.'

'All the more reason to stay with the topside of it, then!' Sinuhe twirled about the room on his toes, admiring himself in a sheet of polished copper on the wall. 'You'll take Keta with you, but you may leave Su-Shunut here.'

'Alas, my brother,' said Ta-Thata demurely but with pleasure, 'that Hekhti has asked for all three of us to go, and the King has granted his request.'

Royal Architect, Royal Tutor

Companionship was just what Sadhi needed, as Hekhti had foreseen, and he was soon paying visits to the delighted Thamar at Ay's house, accompanied by Ta-Thata, Su-Shunut and Keta. This freed Hekhti – whose duties as Chief Royal Architect had been temporarily disrupted – to pay a visit of inspection to the desert site where the Royal Tomb he had designed for Merenkere was almost complete. At one time the King had set his face against his priests' demands for the raising of a Great Eternal House; he was willing to tax the people for a temple, he had said, but not for his own tomb. Later he had come wearily to see that the people themselves would feel their security shaken if their King were not to rest in unrivalled majesty, and that the Throne itself would lack power if any symbol of his royal divinity were withheld.

'Sometimes,' he had told Meri-Mekhmet, 'I'm appalled by the blindness of my countrymen! They would sooner have the body of a cruel, exacting king in a vast stone monument, than the bones of a compassionate king in a plain mastaba. Still, let them be reassured by the sight of grandeur, if they must – ' Then he had sent for Hekhti to give him his commands, and had finished by saying, 'If worth had anything to do with it, the Queen's Tomb should be larger. But Custom decrees, Meri-Mekhmet my beloved, that yours shall be smaller altogether. Shall you mind?'

'Yes – if you really mean to put me there! But I've

secretly determined to lie in a hidden chamber next to yours, so we shall still be near each other. Hekhti, you must arrange it! Then they must promote some other woman, who dies when I do, to lie buried under the name of Queen in the second Royal Tomb.'

Hekhti had obeyed; and had chosen the site for Meren-kere's Great Eternal House with care, close to the Nile which now carried him by King's Royal Barge to the landing stage. He was pleased to see how much progress had been made during his absence. All was as he had imagined it. The King's Tomb was outwardly complete, although within it was still undecorated. The sealing devices were ready in their places. The stone mortuary way where the illustrious dead would pass was almost finished, so too was some of the temple complex to the East, and the priests' apartments. The Queen's Tomb alone was as yet nothing but a marked-out site.

As Hekhti looked around him he could see that his overall plan had marvellously succeeded, every separate part of it combining to make an imposing whole. If this were cause for rejoicing, he rejoiced; but he couldn't see this place without entertaining sombre thoughts, since its purpose could only be fulfilled once the King were dead and the priests made here their offerings to him as Osiris. Even the roughly constructed labour barracks were more encouraging to look at, for they at least teemed with human life, ignorant and miserable though it might be.

He spent a long while at the site with his overseers and his Chief Assistant, Phenue. Afterwards, as he was walking back towards the landing stage, he looked about him, sighed, and said, 'What strenuous efforts we make in this life, and it all comes to stone and silence in the end!'

'The noble Hekhti sounds melancholy today!' said his assistant, smiling. 'But all men praise what you have done.'

'All men! The world is very wide – wider than this narrow valley. And death is very deep, and – in spite of what we pretend – we know nothing of it.'

Phenue misunderstood the reason for Hekhti's melancholy, and said encouragingly, 'Great fame may spread slowly, but it is sure, and comes, as certainly as death, to him who deserves it. Now men make offerings to Imhotep your great forerunner – nightly the poor and mendicant and sick lie by his tomb, hoping for a cure, and many are announced. Was he not also physician and architect combined?'

'He was great,' said Hekhti. 'Phenue, I don't aspire to what you think I do! Let them visit Imhotep and make their offerings and prayers, he's more likely to cure them than am I. Always he has been my patron, and I am grateful to him – I do not grudge him fame!'

'Still, you should build your own tomb close to his!' said Phenue half-jestingly. 'Then there will be two of you!'

'For my part, they may dig a pit and put my body in the sand,' said Hekhti curtly.

The conformist Phenue was deeply shocked. 'And lose your eternal life, like any poor foreigner who knows no better!' He peered closer at Hekhti. 'Don't you believe that embalmment ensures eternal life?'

Hekhti shrugged. 'Who am I to disbelieve it? Surely it would be better if it weren't so – considering the number of tomb robbers who exist.'

'The devices you have invented for this tomb will keep them out.'

'No device keeps a tomb robber out. What one man may invent, another may discover.'

'True, O Hekhti.' Phenue stared around him, seeking for something to raise the Chief Royal Architect's spirits. 'All looks almost ready to be occupied!'

'*Yes,*' said Hekhti. Unsmiling, he went on board the barge, and stood silently on deck as the slaves bent to their oars. 'Men don't want wisdom or knowledge,' he said sadly to himself, 'they want show.' On the way back to Men-nofer he turned his eyes toward a grove of date palms on the western bank, a little way inland. A few squat white buildings stood among them, but no life could be seen.

'A lovely place!' The new young bargemaster stood at his elbow and indicated the date palms with a sweep of his arm. 'Would that I could afford to build my tomb in such a place, most honoured Hekhti. Surely the gods favour it, and those who lie there. Haven't I heard that it shelters the tomb of a great nobleman – Tak-te? And some story of his daughter, a beauty who died sad and young?'

'Yes, her story was indeed tragic, but it made the gossips happy for a season,' replied Hekhti bitterly on an almost savage note; and he turned brusquely away, wiping his forehead with a gold-braceleted arm.

When she heard him entering his appartments, Ta-Thata ran to greet him – she and Sadhi had been hard at work on their fascinating new game. Hekhti made ceremonial obeisance, but she stamped her foot just in front of him.

'Oh Hekhti, not when we're alone!'

'Your Highness must grow accustomed to it.'

'Must I?' She looked at him uncertainly. 'You seem very sombre today, Hekhti – something is the matter?'

'Nothing, Princess.' He regarded her unsmilingly. Isis, but she is young and beautiful, as well, he thought un-willingly, and life will be cruelly heavy to her, too.

'Don't stare at me like that as though – as though I were the Ka of someone dead!' She laughed gaily, but sobered when she saw him wince. 'Hekhti? Something *is* the matter?'

He continued to stare at her. What he had just thought, and what he had felt in the precincts of the new Great Eternal House, seemed to herald some miasma of evil ready to approach. He brushed his hand across his eyes. It couldn't wipe out the picture of Ta-Thata's face – her eager red lips parted in a smile, the eyes that were Meri-Mekhmet's, the gaiety of her expression. All this he saw superimposed on another lovely face, long dead.

'Hekhti?'

'How is Sadhi?' he asked mechanically.

'Oh, he grows more clever with each day – and so do I! We've been adding to your new language – you aren't cross? Come, and I will show you.' She held out an eager hand to him, and was a little hurt when he drew back and said formally, 'I am not cross, but honoured. Lead the way, Princess, to your discoveries –'

Sinuhe *was* cross. He hurled a priceless vase across the room and broke it.

'What *is* happening in here?' asked Ta-Thata, entering the apartment with Keta in her train.

'Your precious Hekhti has been at work behind my back.'

'What nonsense! And he's not my precious Hekhti, he is Chief Royal Architect.'

'What that rising draughtsman is after is to be my tutor! *Chief* Royal Tutor, just as he's Chief Royal Architect. The King hasn't said so – but I can guess, because I'm not a fool. Well, the King our father *is* a fool.'

'Sinuhe, don't speak so of the King! You make me angry.'

'But No-Hotep's to be sent away from Court!'

'Oh, splendid . . .' cried Ta-Thata, throwing her arms in the air and beginning a most unroyal dance. Sinuhe flung his arms round her from behind, and shook her.

'*Will* you listen! Go to the King and beg him not to send No-Hotep away – it's all your fault.'

'You told me it was Hekhti's – ow! Don't pinch like that, Sinuhe, or I'll pinch you back. Now listen, Hekhti doesn't want to be your tutor, you know it's nonsense. Why, I shouldn't even think he likes you,' she added frankly. 'As for saying it's my fault – No, in my opinion our father the King dislikes that upstart priest No-Hotep, and I won't beg for you to keep him here, not if you pinch me till I'm black and blue. I'm glad, glad, glad he's going – and I hope he stays away for ever.'

Sinuhe was glowering at her when a familiar voice spoke behind them. 'Why – how sorry any man must be who, having basked in the Princess Ta-Thata's presence, is now unkindly spoken of! Who is this unfortunate, may I be allowed to learn?'

Ta-Thata jumped, blushed, forgot her courtly training, and responded in confusion, 'You!'

'I am miserable indeed to find disfavour.' But No-Hotep merely sounded faintly amused. Ta-Thata recovered her dignity and replied, 'You overheard what I was saying, which I'm sorry for – yet I don't think we need to pretend that you and I have ever liked each other.'

'Pretend!' The priest threw up his hands in mock amazement. 'I hope that I'm ever loyal to all the Royal House.'

'You know very well you've told me often that she should be punished,' said Sinuhe sullenly. 'And that when she was my wife you would advise me how to do it.'

No-Hotep's heavy lidded eyes gave him a look which caused him to hang his head. 'My Prince, your memory is much at fault, perhaps your mind is overstrained by –'

Ta-Thata was laughing openly: peal upon peal.

'It's no use, Chief Royal Tutor! We both stand discovered! And as you won't be here when I'm married, I'll forgive you. Believe me, I hope you have a pleasant journey – if a long one.'

The priest bowed to her, but said nothing. She found herself staring at the crown of his head, and wondered what went on within it.

'Were you looking for me, No-Hotep?' asked Sinuhe, somewhat ill at ease.

'Our time together, Prince, will be curtailed in these next days – but we still have lessons, *intensive* lessons, awaiting us. So, by your leave, Princess – ' He did not make her the ceremonial obeisance, but drew aside so that Sinuhe might walk out ahead of him, then followed his pupil from the room. Ta-Thata and Keta, like two rude small girls, stuck out their pink tongues at his retreating back.

'And then Apep will arise from the depths, where he lies curled at the bottom of the Nile, and he will swallow up the sun! The priests are ready to make many offerings – and – and work is at a standstill, while people crowd into the temples. You see, Princess, when the power of Re is broken in the daytime and all is dark, then Set's powers are freed against his royal brother Osiris! At such times even the King my father is deeply threatened, and the ritual purifications are increased. That's why people say my brother chooses wrongly, to hold his party the day before Apep rises – the gods may be enraged. But the King my father hasn't stopped him – and as the High Priest Nmem and his priests of Set go with us perhaps it is all right. What do you think?'

They were in Ay's water garden. Su-Shunut, Sadhi and Keta could be heard playing with Phut farther off. Ta-Thata knelt beside Thamar and dabbled her fingers restlessly in the water.

'You don't answer me?'

'Because I cannot! You see, I and my husband Reuben worship differently in Canaan – we worship only the one true God. Here you have many gods, Princess, and – as Reuben says – perhaps they each represent an aspect of one truth. Reuben always believed that the King your father thought much as we did, but here in Kemi –' She stopped, in perplexity, and shook her head. 'As for this talk of serpents swallowing the sun,' she murmured sceptically, 'it's hard –'

Ta-Thata was looking nervously over her shoulder. 'You don't believe it?' she almost whispered. 'Certainly the sun's so large – may Re be praised ! – and a serpent so small; and then, however big Apep grew, how could he get into the sky?' Her brows knit together. 'No-Hotep of course says that Apep does, but how could anyone believe No-Hotep? Yet all Set's priests are very venerated, and must be honoured now. That's why my father won't send No-Hotep away till Apep has given up the sun again, or he would have the priests against him.'

'It must be very difficult ruling the Two Lands, with all this going on,' said Thamar roundly.

'Oh, it is! It is almost impossible! If it isn't Apep it's Sekhmet, or Wepwawet or even Thoth! Still,' added Ta-Thata more cheerfully, 'the King my father and the Queen my mother are coming with us on the river, which has greatly pleased the old High Priest, who is going about telling everyone how the Horus honours Set – in other words, himself! It was Sinuhe who thought of this good idea that we should go by barge to see Hekhti's royal tombs : that will be partly religious, you see, and will offend no one for we'll go very simply, eat on board, and perhaps hear the Temple singers at the site. Usually Sinuhe wants everything very grand with all the courtiers, yet this time he seems content with the King my father's presence, and all these priests of Set – and Hekhti.'

'Then Sadhi must stay here, if Hekhti is in attendance on the King.'

'Oh, Princess, you won't mind?'

'Mind? Sadhi is my *son*,' said Thamar hotly. 'Of course I'm delighted whenever Hekhti lets him come! All this banishment from him has been intolerable, but I've endured it for Sadhi's sake.'

Ta-Thata coloured. 'Oh please, Princess! I really meant that the King and Queen would have wanted you and Sadhi, as well as Hekhti, but it's partly a religious occasion and you would feel –' she floundered.

Thamar patted her hand. 'Yes, I would feel out of place!'

'They must not take Casper with them,' put in Cefalu, who was present. 'It might shake his nerve.' He touched Thamar's knee with an urgent paw. 'Please make that scatterbrained Ta-Thata realize this.'

'Your cat seems upset! Why is he mewing like that? Do you think he wants some fish?'

'*Really*,' said Cefalu, getting up and stalking away, '"mew", "fish"! No wonder she thinks that serpents swallow up the sun! It would make one laugh, if it were not so sad –' and his tail went stiff with anger and quivered violently towards the tip.

Part Two

No–Hotep

In the Great Eternal House

The river had fallen, leaving behind it the rich, black alluvial deposit that would be sown for Kemi's harvest. Many people working for Government and King on building sites and other places were allowed home for the planting, while in the labour barracks only slaves or prisoners remained, which almost brought work to a standstill. The river's fall was so unusually rapid that the priests frowned. They said that Apep, threshing in the depths, had drawn the water off or swallowed it as he prepared to leave the river-bed for his attack upon the sun. It was thought a bad augury that a sowing of the usually fertile land should coincide with the death of Re, however temporary his enclosure in the serpent's maw might be. Some people said openly that their labour would be wasted, the harvests doomed long in advance. In Men-nofer it was rumoured that the King would allow his son to hold a riotous party on the Nile, with music and dancing girls. His subjects raised their hands in horror. It would bring sorrow on the poor and on the Two Lands! The rumour was soon contradicted by a public proclamation of the truth which, however, seemed to reach fewer ears – and on the day Sinuhe's party slipped down the Nile on two of the royal barges the river banks were almost void of worshippers.

On the first barge Ta-Thata looked about her and thought this could hardly be called a party, it was like a Court occasion, only duller. There were the same fanbearers standing behind the Royal Family, as though royalty couldn't breathe unless the air about them were agitated by gigantic ostrich plumes. Court Chamberlains, Marshals, and Officers of State were replaced today by Set's High Priest Nmem, and other priests of Set – grim-visaged men whose function in Kemi was to serve and placate the darkest of the gods and killer of his brother Osiris. Ta-Thata felt their presence about her as she would have felt a chilly wind. Goose pimples rose upon her arms and she shivered. She would sooner have travelled in the second barge – the Chief Royal Architect's – which had now fallen behind, but her request had been refused.

'What is this, my daughter?' Merenkere had asked her with the ghost of a teasing smile. 'Is it to be nearer Hekhti?'

Ta-Thata had blushed vividly.

'But of course she loves Hekhti!' Meri-Mekhmet had told her husband when they were alone together. 'She is just the age for it.'

'Great Hathor, *he* is years older than I am!'

'What has that to do with it? I believe that I love Hekhti too.'

'But this is a disaster! Perhaps Hekhti would like to leave Court with No--Hotep? A rival for his Sovereign *and* for Sinuhe? And wasn't his father my present Vizier's head gardener? It's most unsuitable!'

'My great-grandfather was a gardener!' said Meri-Mekhmet.

'Which explains why roses grow so well in your family –' Merenkere took her hand and kissed it.

'Try to look on Hekhti as another rose!' Meri-Mekhmet giggled irresistibly. 'All women love him – it's partly his solitariness and because he's kept them at a distance since Tak-te's daughter died.'

'You know that story? I haven't heard it spoken of at Court for many years.'

'Oh – I heard it when I was a little girl, everyone knew it, it was so sad. The gardener's son and the nobleman's daughter, and how her marriage was hurriedly arranged elsewhere, and then on the eve of it – There were all sorts of rumours : that she threw herself in the Nile, took poison –'

'Poor Hekhti – what a tragedy! He didn't deserve such a misfortune,' Merenkere sighed.

Meri–Mekhmet held out her hand to him comfortingly. 'As the gods will it, so life goes : we know that.'

'At least what the gods will has brought me you ...' He bent and kissed his wife.

'Our destination's in sight; look ahead instead of trying to see behind you, my child,' said the King's voice with a faint note of reproof in it.

'It – it all looks very fine, O my father,' replied Ta-Thata, although her first sight of the royal tombs had given her a horrible feeling – as though time had ceased to exist, and she and Sinuhe were journeying downstream together in solemn procession as they would one day when – after – She glanced at Sinuhe, but he was staring at the empty banks and wishing there were many people on them come to see the great ones make passage on the Nile.

The priests were silent, too. It was impossible to imagine them laughing or dancing as the priestesses of Hathor did. Ta-Thata looked downward at the water. The huge paddles were painted with a formal green design, a pattern of papyrus buds, and drove in and out propelling the barge on its course. In and out, pushing the water backward. What would happen if one of them touched the head of Apep?

'It stands beautifully,' said Meri-Mekhmet's voice, 'and Hekhti has chosen well. I see no one about.'

'There are few people left near the site, O my Queen,' murmured No-Hotep, 'for they are gone already to the planting, as my sovereign lady knows.'

The barge glided onward as though in a dream; the only sounds were the driving thrust of paddles against water, the creak of timber, the low-toned commands of the King's bargemaster. Other boats, warned in advance that the Horus of Gold, Kemi's great High Priest, would make passage that day upon the Nile, were pulled in to the river-side where they fluttered with slack sails, butterflies seeking a border, or rode at anchor with oarsmen motionless. The King sat in silence as the royal barge sought the landing mark and the shadow of his own tomb fell inescapably ahead.

The party disembarked in a leisurely manner, while the other barge was still some distance away. Preceded by his fanbearers and the High Priest Nmem, the King strolled beside the Queen's litter up the causeway. Sinuhe approached Ta-Thata and took her hand. 'Come, my sister! It's good practice for us to walk together in procession. And bad manners – do not turn your head! – for a Princess to concern herself with the late arrival of an architect.' Ta-Thata let her hand remain limply in his, and contented herself with giving him her fiercest glare. She could hear the other priests' discreet, sandalled shuffling behind her. The vast stone slope up which they all toiled seemed as though it would never end. They passed empty plinths where statues would be set and, on the right, the site for the Queen's Tomb. At last they reached the open shaft leading into the heart of the great stone edifice that now towered above them into an empty sky.

Torches were lit, and the High Priest Nmem with

No-Hotep and half the priests of Set filed into the building. Ta-Thata looked back. People from the second barge were toiling up to them. Her father paused as he was about to enter the shaft, and she heard him say, 'But where is my architect?' And then Hekhti's assistant, Phenue, had arrived and was prostrating himself, and explaining in some distress, 'O Sovereign, my lord, there must be some great error – for the Chief Royal Architect was not with us in time to sail after your Majesty's barge at the appointed time and distance! I sent back a message to his apartments before we left the quay at Men-nofer, but I greatly fear, O Sovereign, my lord –'

'We shall not wait.' The King cut him short. 'Whatever has become of Hekhti, this heat is fierce and we proceed without him!'

'At your Majesty's pleasure,' murmured Phenue, still distracted, 'but without the Chief Royal Architect –'

'– his assistants are doubtless capable of explaining a design,' completed the King, a slight snap in his voice. 'Lead the way, my good Phenue, before the Queen and I entirely melt.'

The stone passages were cold, after the heat outside. As the royal party entered, Ta-Thata once more looked back. The land was white with sun. Even the river was almost white, reflecting that majestic brilliance. Down by the labour barracks she could see some activity.

'I thought the peasants were on the land now –' she said to Sinuhe, who shrugged.

'Some slaves and prisoners remain, but what is that to us, my sister?' As he led her through the torch-lit passages he gripped her hand more tightly and she could feel his slight nervous trembling. How dwarfed was humanity by this great stone labyrinth where her father would lie after his death! Just then she was glad to hold Sinuhe's hand –

she squeezed it, and he squeezed hers. She thought : at least we can sometimes share our terrors. The second phalanx of priests walked behind the young couple, and their sandalled shuffling sounded intensified by echoes. It was too easy to imagine that the priests shuffled beneath the weight of a royal bier.

'Well,' said the King's voice ahead, 'my good Hekhti shows himself a most admirable designer ! Ah – here we reach the first chamber, it's a roundabout approach we have come.'

'O Sovereign, my lord,' said No-Hotep, 'since the inner chambers are still – empty, I have arranged for chairs to be provided for your Majesties and their Highnesses, and for two of the royal cupbearers to await your Majesties with refreshing wine.'

'Should my Majesty drink in my own tomb?'

'Isn't my Sovereign, my lord the water of life to this thirsty land? Can it be wrong to refresh the living water ?'

'Your reasoning may or may not be ritually correct, No-Hotep – but my Majesty is willing to accept it after that tremendous heat, and now this coldness.' He shivered.

They were in the outer of the two inner chambers. The King looked thoughtfully upward at the stones above him, so irrevocably shutting out the light, and gave a small, sad sigh. Meri-Mekhmet gently touched his arm. She was engulfed by a sense of unfathomable terror. Here is what will part us, she was thinking. Stone and silence, and the dark. How is it possible for so slight a thing as a human's Ka to survive this horror? Although they were not alone together she took Merenkere's hand and pressed his fingers fiercely as though she would melt their bones together.

The chairs were now brought forward for the King and Queen, Ta-Thata and Sinuhe to seat themselves. Ta-Thata was absently staring at No-Hotep's sandalled feet, and then noted that one of his toes had developed a twitch. She was fascinated. If I look up, will his face be twitching too? she asked herself. I wouldn't have thought him a twitching sort of man. She did look up, and under her innocent gaze a muscle in his right cheek began to jerk and quiver.

The young cupbearers advanced from the inner chamber where they had waited, and stood before their Sovereign and his Queen. They kneeled to offer wine.

'Ah –' said Merenkere as he drank, 'this is very good – it brings life into this place –'

Meri-Mekhmet received her cup from the second cup-bearer, and drank. Then it was brought to Ta-Thata who was glad to wet her dry lips with the sweet white wine.

'I'm thirsty too!' complained Sinuhe. 'Am I not to drink with my sister?' The King's cupbearer rose hurriedly and crossed to him, but was intercepted by No-Hotep who took the cup into his own hands. Meanwhile the High Priest Nmem, old and frail, bent before the King, and in a quaver-ing voice besought his Majesty to view the inner chamber.

Sinuhe said imperiously, 'No-Hotep! I am *thirsty*!' But No-Hotep paid him no attention, he was watching the King, who rose and walked to the inner entrance. Merenkere put his right hand on the lintel. When he was one step over the threshold his left hand went to his head. He muttered, 'But I feel –' crumpled suddenly, and fell.

Meri-Mekhmet gave a little cry and sprang to her feet. The High Priest Nmem tottered forward towards his master. The glistening cup fell from No-Hotep's hand and spilled its contents on the ground.

There was sudden chaotic movement with the King's body the centre of it. Over all, the priest No-Hotep's voice rose gratingly – the ring of granite in it was appropriate to the place. 'Stand back from the Sovereign! The cup was not poisoned. His Majesty merely sleeps.'

Meri-Mekhmet and Ta-Thata paid little attention to his words, for in their terror they were barely conscious he had spoken. They were kneeling by Merenkere, who breathed shallowly and whose hands, palm upward on the icy floor, were very cold. Meri-Mekhmet was cradling the King's head in her arms, while Ta-Thata wept soundlessly from fright. Sinuhe stood upright and hesitant, his head now turned toward his father, now toward the Chief Royal Tutor, whose words had sunk into other ears. The High Priest Nmem gave a tremulous and horrified gasp. The cup-bearer who had given the King to drink looked at his own hands in dreadful disbelief. One of the fanbearers cried, 'Treason!' in a shaking voice and, staring at the entrance, saw the priests of Set standing there each armed with a long and cruel knife.

At the word 'treason' a general, terrible silence fell. Even Meri-Mekhmet looked up, and understood, and was glad if she could die with Merenkere, whom she held closer still. Ta-Thata leaned against her mother as though exhausted. Sinuhe nervously licked his lips and stood rigid as though he were a painted statue by a funeral bier. Over all, the torchlight flickered. Ta-Thata felt that she was in some evil dream when eyelids try to open but stay shut.

'But this – this is outrageous!' gobbled the High Priest Nmem quakingly.

'Ah, Sanctity, you're old for your high office – neverthe-less, you'll not endanger our Sovereign, our lord by some senile misunderstanding,' replied No-Hotep blandly. 'His Majesty will not die – if all obey me.' He kneeled by Meri-Mekhmet, who drew away from him, feeling as though she had encountered Set in all his living dreadfulness here in this tomb. 'Madam! I repeat: the King will live while no resistance is made by *anyone*. So – take the Princess by the hand and sit with her on those chairs.'

Meri-Mekhmet looked downward sorrowfully at the King's face. She hesitated, but a knife glittered menacingly in the torchlight as its bearer raised it. Very slowly she stood up, drawing Ta-Thata with her.

'Royal Heir, will your Highness have the goodness to stand upon one side? For the King your father must be moved from his uncomfortable position on the ground.' Sinuhe shakily obeyed. 'Help me lift the King,' said No-Hotep to the cupbearers, 'and place him on the litter in the inner chamber, where you waited.'

It was done. Meri-Mekhmet, scarcely able to breathe, held her trembling daughter's hand, stared at the ranks of knives so near their heads, and decided if the King should die to throw herself on one. When No-Hotep emerged from the inner chamber he looked at her penetratingly as though he read her thoughts.

'Be reassured, my Queen. His Majesty's sleep is harmless, although its nature could be – changed.' He glanced around him. To Ta-Thata's appalled gaze he seemed to have grown in size since he cast off his role of the obsequious tutor.

The poor old High Priest Nmem opened his quavering mouth to protest.

'Old man,' said No-Hotep warningly, 'don't meddle if you wish to live and be High Priest. It would be a pity if you had to be – retired, for you've done the Two Lands and the great lord Set much service, the people trust you and know the tender love you bear his Majesty. All this is very useful!' He looked at his ranks of armed priests. Behind them now showed strange and foreign faces. 'In the land of Shinar slaves and courtiers are killed when their King dies, and are buried with him to be of service in the next world. Here is a King who only sleeps – but a greater King than he of Shinar. The servants of the Lord of the Two

Lands shall go before him, though their Kas wait long before great Osiris joins them.' His glance lingered on the cup- and fan-bearers, and the shrinking Phenue.

He made a sign. The ranks of priests parted as foreign soldiers threaded a way between them. Meri-Mekhmet, fearing massacre, threw herself before her daughter, but she was ignored. The King's servants, limp with terror, were bound and carried out. Then there was no sound except Ta-Thata's gasping breath. No sound for what seemed a long, long time. At last there was one faint cry which might have been a desperate child's wail a long way off. A child forced to something it cannot bear. Meri-Mekhmet shuddered uncontrollably. The two boys were little older than her daughter, and she had known them all their lives . . .

'The cup of Shinar,' said No-Hotep's voice soothingly, 'is potent and painless. No – calm yourself, my Queen, the King doesn't owe his sleep to it!'

For the first time Meri-Mekhmet answered him. 'How can I believe you! Obviously you plan to kill us all – For myself, I care only to live or die with the King. I might beg for our children's lives, but into whose hands would they fall? Yours? Even in their youth they would do better to fall into the Judgement! But take care, No-Hotep – deaths are already on your conscience, and, though you've gained possession of this Eternal House, outside is Kemi, and the army, and the Court! Do you really think to hold *Kemi* in your hand? A man with enemies – like you?' She clenched her fists as though she would hit him.

No-Hotep looked at them and smiled, and answered obliquely with a good temper that was thoroughly alarming. 'At present, anyway, you won't be parted from the King. Kiss your daughter, if you wish – and the Royal Heir! They are leaving with me, now. I'm sorry to keep you and my

Sovereign in this cold and dismal place, but the outer world must see you have decided to separate yourselves from it, and stay in contemplation here in this Eternal House until the Sun God Re makes his escape from Apep and floods the world with light.' He glanced toward the inner chamber. 'Apep –' he repeated softly. 'Symbolic, is it not?'

'I won't go with you!' said Ta-Thata in a fierce though shaking voice. 'I'll stay with my father and mother, even if you poison me, or entomb us all!'

'You're a silly child, Princess. Do you want to watch your mother knifed before your eyes? No? Then see that you obey me.'

Ta-Thata looked hopelessly at the priest, and then at Sinuhe, as though she couldn't believe what she was hearing. All this time her half-brother had stood quite silent. He stared at No-Hotep with something unreadable in his eyes – was it horror? – and muttered between lips which seemed to move stiffly as the jointed lips of a wooden toy, 'You – you've done much wrong, No-Hotep! You swore that if I brought the King my father here today you wouldn't have to leave the Court. You said you'd help me to great glory, soon! You didn't say you meant anything like this –' His words ended on a childish whimper. He saw Meri-Mekhmet's face, and added quickly, 'Madam, don't – don't look at me like that! I wouldn't harm the King!'

'What could you have thought he meant?' asked Meri-Mekhmet faintly.

'Say? Was it necessary to *say*?' No-Hotep's lips smiled warmly at his pupil, but his eyes were cold. 'And do not speak of *wrong*. What are servants' lives, my Prince, when Kemi's glory is at stake? Has the goodness men praise in the King your father strengthened the Two Lands? Has he given Set his rightful place? Now is the time to right these matters and, believe me, all I do is only for your future greatness. Take the Princess's hand, it's time to go. And remember – no harm need come to anyone.'

Ta-Thata shrank away, but one glance at No-Hotep's face and she accepted Sinuhe's outstretched hand with repugnance – it was sweating like damp stone – and bent to kiss Meri-Mekhmet on either cheek, while their tears mingled on their faces. When Ta-Thata turned longingly toward the inner chamber No-Hotep made a furiously impatient gesture which caused Sinuhe to tug firmly on her hand. She thought contemptuously that he was afraid to look upon the King's face.

As they left the outer chamber she strained back still to catch a last glimpse of Meri-Mekhmet. Then she was stumbling toward daylight, preceded by a torchbearer and priests of Set, her hand fast in Sinuhe's, No-Hotep in the rear. Behind them remained six other priests of Set. Six fierce, silent men, with drawn knives, who were now her parents' only guards.

The Court Jeweller's Son

Outside the Great Eternal House were grouped the Temple singers, humbly waiting in the heat for the royal party to emerge.

'Smile, Princess,' said No-Hotep's voice softly in Ta-Thata's ear. 'You're happy to be honoured by the singers, and *untroubled* by the King your father's decision to remain secluded until Apep's rising is accomplished.'

'I will not smile.'

'Ah – but remember the Queen your mother!'

So Ta-Thata smiled at the singers, who promptly sang praises to Isis very lengthily till No-Hotep stopped them with a gesture.

'Now we proceed at leisure to the completed Temple. Prince, I beg you to talk and smile with your sister as though nothing strange had taken place. Keep hold of her hand, and look at her lovingly. Think of your coming marriage . . .'

Smiling and talking, Ta-Thata and Sinuhe moved between the singers' ranks. When Sinuhe accidentally looked into her eyes he saw there a shadow of scorn darker than any he had known, and a hatred which almost chilled his spine. Why should she look at me like that? he wondered in self-pity. Could I tell what would happen? She's unfair . . . No-Hotep *cannot* mean harm to our parents, he would be afraid. But there his thoughts finished in confusion and a doubt he didn't dare to face.

They reached the Temple's shade, where No-Hotep dismissed the singers, thanking them courteously in the King's name and requesting them to wait upon the second barge. The priests of Set, who had put away their knives but looked even grimmer than before, escorted Ta-Thata and Sinuhe through the Temple entrance. Inside, they found soldiers waiting in concealment: men who had come disguised in those caravans that had joined Thamar's escort to Kemi. The King's children were jostled hurriedly past them toward an inner chamber almost cut off from the light outside. Ta-Thata looked around her wildly and felt her knees begin to tremble. She sank into a chair. No-Hotep's face was turned away from her, he was speaking low to someone who had caught him up outside the entrance. She couldn't hear what was being said, except the last word '... Hekhti'. On a note of grief she cried, 'Hekhti didn't come! Where is he?' and heard the revealing sound of terror in her voice. She couldn't see the expression of mingled doubt and consternation on No-Hotep's face, but recognized the menace in his tones as he replied, 'That, Princess, isn't your concern.' There was a scuffling sound, a silence, and then No-Hotep gave a peremptory order that she couldn't overhear.

Luckily for Hekhti, a minor misfortune had overtaken him in the shape of sudden sickness with fever, sweating and vomiting: common symptoms among those who dwelt near the Nile. Yet it was rare for the Chief Royal Architect to fall ill, and as he lay exhausted on his bed he thought bitterly that this seemed a bad omen for the day when the King and Queen were to visit the Great Eternal House. Very early, he had dispatched a slave to the King's bargemaster, to convey most humble apologies to the Sovereign; yet by mischance the boy was already succumbing to the same sickness that had laid his master low – he had staggered on gamely in the hot sun but, having a weaker physique than Hekhti, had been quickly overcome, and collapsed before reaching the waterfront. He had gasped out a few disjointed sentences to the people who gathered round him, but they were much occupied in stealing his amulet and ring, and had then rolled him into the shade, and left him to delirium. At last two women carried him to their hut, and nursed him unenthusiastically but with hopes of later recompense.

So Hekhti's message to the King went undelivered; and when later in the day Phenue's messenger arrived hot-foot the Chief Royal Architect was much disturbed, and sent him back hurriedly, telling him to hire a boat and hasten to the King. Other messengers were sent to search for the missing slave, while Hekhti lay and fretted with vexation. He was a bad invalid, anyway, being one so seldom, and irritation rose faster than his fever. Far worse than irritation would have affected him had he known that, by the time Phenue's man neared the pyramid, Phenue himself was already dead of the cold poison of Shinar.

The messenger climbed the steep stone way just as the King's children were standing with No-Hotep and the priests in the hot sunlight to hear Isis' praises sung. He hesitated : should he try to find Phenue, perhaps deep within the giant monument? Or deliver the message to No-Hotep, whom he knew by sight? In the end he discreetly followed the priest of Set toward the Temple. No-Hotep had been feeling most uneasy about Hekhti's absence, which he had only dis-covered while inside the Great Eternal House. He was relieved to learn that there was nothing premeditated about his proposed victim's escape. As a reward for bringing such good news, Phenue's man met his death there in the little Temple. Sinuhe and Ta-Thata heard nothing of it, for he gave only one outraged gasp as the long shining knife slid into his side. Then two of No-Hotep's men left hurriedly to take the dead man's boat back to Men-nofer, and catch the Chief Royal Architect unawares.

A number of important people had already been quietly silenced that morning in Men-nofer, or overpowered and imprisoned. Two army commanders fell unexpectedly ill of a sickness more final than was Hekhti's. The Vizier, who had unwisely visited Set's sanctuary to meditate on Apep's rising, found himself unable to leave again. Some Marshals and Chamberlains who were antagonistic to No-Hotep received strangers in the King's absence and unexpectedly received their knives as well. Some of No-Hotep's adherents died, too, but no one loyal to the Sovereign managed to raise an alarm, although the Court Chamberlain Ket struggled to the outer entrance of his home before he died. Men of the Royal Bodyguard who had come off duty marched as usual to their barracks, and found themselves surrounded. Those who had relieved them in the Palace fought a short battle with silent intruders from Shinar, retreated down a corridor, and managed to barricade themselves inside a storeroom. While all this was taking place the gay populace of Men-nofer went busily about their humdrum duties, quite unaware of what had happened.

Towards noon it was rumoured in the city that many nobles had secluded themselves to appease the gods during Apep's rising and attract favour for the King, who himself, with his Queen, would remain in ritual isolation at his Great Eternal House. This rumour arose simultaneously in different parts of Men-nofer, no one quite knew how.

Hekhti didn't hear it. He lay cross and feverish in his bed, wondering why illness always made the mind so gloomy, although thankful at least that Sadhi had been sent to Thamar the day before, accompanied by Keta and

Su-Shunut. He would have been less relieved had he known that the Court Chamberlain Ay, watched over by two young servants who had only lately joined his household, was suffering from an obscure and violent indisposition; and that Thamar herself had been advised not to leave the house, in case she spread this new, strange sickness elsewhere.

The Chief Royal Architect turned over on his side with a groan, raised himself on one elbow, and put out a hand for water. Over by the entrance there was movement like a flowing in of small shadows. Hekhti blinked to clear his sight.

'Treason!' shrilled Cefalu on a piercing note.

'Fly!' urged the noble though shaken voice of Ptahsuti beside him. Ptahsuti's fur, which was even longer than Meluseth's – but black, so that he was more like a thundercloud set with green eyes than a cumulus cloud set with blue ones – stood on end with his vibrant physical terror. 'Death is everywhere!'

Beside them Nutka's legs failed her from fright as she skidded into the room on her behind. Her one green eye and one blue expressed her feelings, but her small mouth opened and shut soundlessly. As for Casper – *he* had fitted himself under Cefalu's stomach for comfort, so that it looked as though the latter had eight legs.

But for all his wisdom and knowledge Hekhti didn't speak Cat. He stared, frowned, wondered if he were delirious, and drank more water. Then he looked closer – surely these animals were terrified? What could have frightened them so? And why had they fled in here? Come to think of it, why hadn't his messenger reached the King, and –

Feet stumbled in the next room. Cefalu darted to Hekhti's bed and scraped at him with an urgent paw.

Hekhti stiffened and called out, 'Who's there?'

No reply. And then a timid voice, breathless from running, whispered, 'My lord – my lord Hekhti –'

'What – who *is* it?' Hekhti pulled himself clear of his coverings, and cursed to find himself so weak.

The linen hangings at the entrance were dragged aside. A very frightened boy stood there.

'Oh, it's you, Henmut!' Hekhti relaxed again, having recognized Tahlevi's son. 'I really thought –'

'My lord, you must go, quickly! I came to warn you – they'll kill us – there's no time to lose –' The boy looked over his shoulder as though assassins were already there. 'Treason,' he panted, 'it's – it's everywhere! I think they've even killed the King – please come and hide – oh, *quickly* –' There was no doubting the note of terror in his voice. Hekhti's heart thumped even faster than it had with fever. The words 'they've even killed the King' struck him with a dreadful sense of recognition. The miasma of evil he had lately sensed had realized itself as one black overwhelming disaster. He dragged himself out of bed and sat on its side looking up at Henmut.

'When did who kill the King? What of the Queen and – Princess Ta-Thata?'

Henmut caught at his arm. 'Come now, my lord, or you are dead! No-Hotep . . . it's he who – The Queen and Princess are both prisoners and I don't think he means to harm them – yet.' Again he glanced over his shoulder, but there was no sound from the direction of the outer room. Hekhti, who had only wanted to be left alone, had sent Amrat off duty. So the silence was in one way right, and yet it held an edge of threat.

'Who else is dead?'

'I don't know – they who love the King – *Please*, my lord – Is there no back way? You *cannot* serve the Queen by staying here. They'll kill us!' Hekhti's lingering put

Henmut in greater terror. 'They come soon . . . with knives. I came a shorter way – My *lord* –' He tugged.

Hekhti made up his mind. If such a calamity had befallen Kemi, then it *was* pointless to stay where he could be cut down, useless to anyone.

'There is a back way to these apartments – but they may come by it.'

'Either way they may come!' gasped Henmut. 'Yet it's our only chance! No-Hotep's men are in the Palace.'

'Wait!' Hekhti shook him off. He crossed to his box of implements and extracted two sharp operating knives. 'We'll fight for it, if we must,' he said between his teeth as he gave Henmut the longer knife.

'Are you coming naked, my lord?' asked Henmut with the ghost of a grin. He was a brave boy and felt braver with that sharp blade in his hand.

'Better naked than dead,' responded Hekhti grimly; but he picked up his linen kilt from a chair and thrust his feet into sandals. 'Now, through here –'

There was a curtained alcove in one corner, and when he pulled back the hangings a small square-cut entrance was revealed, leading to a passage. He listened. Henmut listened. There was no sound ahead of them and still none from the outer room.

'We'll try – Come, child. Keep to the left-hand wall, your knife ready, and – What are you doing?' For Henmut had darted back into the room. He snatched a cloak from the foot of Hekhti's bed and held it up.

'Outside you must hide your face, my lord.'

'It was well thought of. Come –'

The cats jostled through at their heels as the hangings fell into place behind them. While No-Hotep's two assassins entered the Palace front, Hekhti and Henmut reached the sunlit gardens at the back and fled through them in the savage heat. Hekhti was panting and his head reeled.

'My lord, can you manage?'

'Yes. But we're turning too far left for the back way.'

'We mustn't use it. He will have his men there too.'

'Fever makes me stupid.' Hekhti stopped. His chest rose and fell in great gasps. 'How, then?'

'Over the double wall. I know a way.'

'Of course you would know one! Are you not Tahlevi's son?' Hekhti's lips gave a faint upward twitch. Since he was in the King's confidence he knew of Tahlevi's past.

They went through the royal gardens, crouching behind bushes, doubling up paths, pausing in the shadow of a tree to scan the way ahead. They saw no one, not even a gardener. The tinkle of fountains was an accompaniment to apparently unbroken peace. The running of the cats' paws behind them was like the pattering of rain.

At last they reached the inner of the two great walls surrounding the Palace. A tamarisk grew near the place where Cefalu had fought his epic battle with the bandit cat Khnum-Put and routed him. Henmut bent to search in a small hollow at the tree's roots, while the cats crawled up the tamarisk and stretched themselves out on a slender branch overhanging the wall, Casper dangling from Nutka's mouth. When Henmut straightened up again he held out a number of sharpened copper pegs. 'See, my lord Hekhti,' he whispered, 'this is how we'll climb the walls – it's how I came. But you're heavier than me –' He looked up anxiously. 'At least the tree and bushes shield us.'

'They'll shield an enemy's approach as easily! The wall looks too smooth for climbing, Henmut.'

'It's not so smooth as it looks. Watch –' The boy confidently examined the wall's surface. His fingers had the sure touch of a blind man's. Hekhti saw that he almost lived through his hands, it was uncanny. Henmut forced in a peg and tested it; put a bare foot on it, and then forced in another support higher up. 'If only they'll take your weight, my lord . . .'

Hekhti now had time to ponder the extent of the Palace calamity, and to wonder why he'd so quickly, implicitly believed young Henmut's story: how could the boy know all this? And yet something within Hekhti told him it was true. He was seized with terrible sorrow for the King, and fear for Ta-Thata and the Queen. Henmut hadn't mentioned Sinuhe: probably the Royal Heir was indispensable to No-Hotep's plans; the man couldn't be fool enough to think that he could actually mount the Throne himself? While Hekhti waited he found himself making inner supplications to Isis and Osiris . . .

At last he heard a whisper in his ear, 'Come! I've managed enough on this side. Both inner sides are done already, for I left them prepared when I came in. On the outer, street side, we must choose our moment, and let ourselves drop!'

Panting, Hekhti began his ascent, and was soon standing between the walls in comparative safety. They saw Cefalu's flattened form above on the first wall, and heard a peremptory mewing which told the other cats, 'Hold back on the tamarisk till this business is well advanced, or we may give ourselves away.' Cefalu examined the double wall with a most sentimental expression. 'Look – here are the very marks where I fought Khnum-Put.' He leaped stiffly on to the other wall, crouching low. Henmut and Hekhti were just lowering themselves for the second time. Once Cefalu had seen Hekhti drop he called back over his shoulder, 'Quickly! It's time – for I see men with spears emerging from those bushes.'

As he spoke, Ptahsuti landed gracefully on all four muffed

fur paws beside him, conspicuous on the skyline – a black, fluffy cloud with another cloud behind it for a tail. There was a shout, and a spearhead clanged against the walltop before clattering into the ditch.

'They've seen the cats!' cried Henmut. Hekhti looked up as Cefalu hurtled downwards, braking with spread paws. Ptahsuti seemed to blow gently like a cloud to earth, but Nutka gave Casper a final vigorous shake and jumped with him into a bush. They were safe.

'Are *you* all right, my lord Hekhti?' asked Henmut anxiously; for Hekhti breathed fast, was running with sweat, and held one hand to his side as though in pain. Hekhti nodded briefly. 'Well enough,' he gasped. 'Where now?'

'To my father's house.'

Hekhti shook his head. 'Ah, no, Henmut – I should endanger him! As yet there's no reason for No-Hotep . . .'

'To bother with a mere Court Jeweller?' Henmut put his firm brown hand on Hekhti's arm and urged him forward. 'My father's as loyal as you are.' He sounded affronted.

'No-Hotep will stamp out loyalty wherever he finds it,' said Hekhti soothingly, 'but his activities are likely to spread *outward* from the Palace. I could bring Tahlevi death quicker than he may find it on his own.'

'Then where else will you go?'

Hekhti tried to think. Fever made thought harder to catch than the glittering fish that swam in Meri-Mekhmet's water garden –

'To the Court Chamberlain Ay!' he said, inspired.

'The Queen's father?' Henmut was as shrewd a boy as any fathered in Men-nofer. 'My lord Hekhti, if he's still alive it is Re's own miracle!'

Hekhti groaned. How widespread were the tentacles

of evil? What of Sadhi and his mother, Su-Shunut and Keta, if Henmut were right? He was almost overcome by grief; and the sky and white walls began to whirl around him. With an effort he steadied himself, to hear Henmut saying, 'See – my father will keep you safe hidden near his work-shops, and no one will guess your whereabouts – providing, my lord Hekhti, that we hurry! Those men who saw the cats may be suspecting that they followed someone, and rush to the nearest Palace entrance. *Quickly* – don't you want to live and serve the Queen?' With these words he overcame Hekhti's feeble resistance, threw the cloak around his head and shoulders to disguise him, and urged him on their way.

'Separate, separate!' said Cefalu testily to the other cats. 'Are we to be the undoing of this excellent stripling's plan? If anyone should see four honoured Palace cats out-side Tahlevi's the whole neighbourhood will talk! Nutka, guide Casper to Meluseth's tomb and lie up with him behind the sarcophagus; you may take him to Tahlevi's after sunset. Ptahsuti, try the Temple of Sekhmet – fish offerings and fresh milk. As for myself, it's a duty to find Sadhi and my Mistress. By the way, how does this boy *know* the King is dead? I've not heard Hekhti ask him. And we only know of the struggle in the Palace.'

'Hekhti is too feverish,' replied Ptahsuti wisely, 'to think of more than one peculiar thing at once. But whoever goes to Tahlevi's will learn soon enough. There is a man who sees straight through to his son's heart.'

Cefalu looked thoughtful. 'Together we'll go there, though not at Hekhti's heels. We may slip in unnoticed by ourselves. Afterwards, noble offspring, we'll go our separate ways to Ay's house, and Sekhmet's Temple.' He sighed through his whiskers, remembering his trysts with Meluseth at the goddess's granite feet.

Tahlevi and Reuben

When the assassins found that Hekhti had escaped them, they considered how the priest No-Hotep might react to failure, wisely lost themselves in the darkest part of Mennofer, and were not seen again. Henmut and Hekhti reached Tahlevi's combined workshop-dwelling in safety, although the Chief Royal Architect was in physical distress as he was guided through a side door in a wall and the miniature garden that was Tahlevi's chief delight. Flowers and sky seemed to come very close and then retreat far off as Hekhti blinked at them. Henmut's small warm hand half led, half dragged him up the path. Inside a dark entrance he pushed Hekhti down on to a stool and said, 'You wait here, my lord – '

Hekhti put his reeling head in his hands and watched the lights go round behind his eyelids. 'Treason' they flashed, and 'the King is dead', and 'Ta-Thata'. Soon he heard ringing steps which to his distorted hearing sounded like great hollow hammers hitting stone. Tahlevi peered down at him anxiously.

'Royal Architect! You're very ill – '

'Treason,' mumbled Hekhti automatically.

'Help me get him to a couch – quietly !' said the enormous bearded Tahlevi to Henmut. 'Then call your mother, but no one else must hear.'

Hekhti later remembered little of being half carried to a side room except his sense of outrage at being treated as he himself would have treated Sadhi. Tahlevi's wife came to cluck over him, and provided a warm and soporific drink. Then, dreadfully aware in a far corner of his fevered mind that he was needed somewhere else, he sank into troubled sleep.

Henmut was led to Tahlevi's own room and asked for a fuller story than the few bald facts he had already blurted out.

'And is the Sovereign really dead?'

'Yes, I think so, Father.'

Tahlevi sat down heavily upon a chair. 'Treason!' he exclaimed sorrowfully. 'Who would have believed that a man like No-Hotep could destroy our great King Meren-kere?' Suddenly he peered closely at his son, who began to shuffle. 'Why were you in the Palace, Henmut? How was the King killed? How did *you* come to see this? Was the God in audience? I've often thought it would be easy for some assassin – But there's the Royal Bodyguard. Stay! I remember now: the King went today with the Royal Heir to –' He paused. Henmut looked bashfully down-ward. Something pushed his calves consolingly from behind with a furry, heartening push. It was Cefalu, who with Ptahsuti had insinuated himself into the house through a small window.

'Just where have you been?' thundered Tahlevi at his wriggling son.

'You'll be angry, Father –'

'I will – I will be very angry. You've been creeping about inside other people's tombs! And the *King's* tomb! The priests would burn you for trespassing on holy ground! There'll be no more of this – in future you shall learn your trade with my enamellers. My son shall not grow up to be a dirty thief – I was one myself, and know all the horrors of it.'

'But I've stolen nothing, Father.'

'Hhhuh! That's the next step.' In spite of himself a look of quickly suppressed longing and excitement appeared above Tahlevi's beard. 'I would whip you till you lay upon your face for a whole moon, if it weren't for the importance of this disastrous news you bring. Come here!' He drew back his right arm and biff! boxed his son heartily on both ears. Cefalu watched approvingly. This was how he had always dealt with kittens and it had had excellent results, producing tireless toms and fine mousers.

'*Now* – tell me everything, and leave nothing out.'

'Well, Father,' said Henmut, gulping and wiping his eyes, 'there were some friends of mine – down by the waterfront –'

'Faugh!' put in Tahlevi, darkly.

' – boys who – whose fathers are – sort of interested in tombs and that sort of thing, and sort of – '

'Sort of rob them? Enamelling for you, my son!'

'They said one of them had – had *managed* to see a plan of the noble Hekhti's, half torn up –'

Tahlevi groaned; yet there was a kind of envy in the groan.

' – and there was a secret way into King Merenkere's Great Eternal House. So we – we thought it would be exciting if we could find a way in – and – and perhaps watch the King himself come for a ritual Seeing.'

'It's impious!' said Tahlevi roundly. 'Not to say pointless, for there would have been no jewels.' His eyes glittered strangely.

'But we're not *thieves*, Father.' Henmut modestly lowered his eyes as Tahlevi's hand flexed again. 'We – we thought two of us could search for this second entrance by night, and we'd draw lots who was to enter alone if we found the tiny secret Queen's Chamber which Muto's father thought was there. So we went, and the stars looked extra large that night – almost as though they wanted to guide us! We found the second way in quite easily, but we couldn't shift the outer stone. So next night *four* of us went back and moved it, and oiled the edges, and it swung easily when it was pushed.'

'Very prudent,' said Tahlevi, 'that's just the way – ' and then coughed harshly. 'Go *on*.'

'Next day we drew lots, Father. Muto won, but he was sick, and the others chose me instead. They honoured me, you see, because you'd been the most famous tomb robber in Men-nofer.' He looked innocently at his father.

'What! They know me, in spite of my great beard!' Tahlevi looked aghast.

'But of course! Only stupid people like the noble Vizier think you're just a jeweller! Why, Muto's father says the way you stripped the tomb of Tak-te's aunt has been a model for –'

'Enough! Tell me of the King.'

'*Yes*, Father. Last night I took some food, and borrowed Muto's papyrus boat, and sculled downstream. I hid the boat in the reeds, and crept up behind all the new stone-work. There were people in the labour barracks – I thought they were slaves. I peered in, and they were drinking and swearing, and some were talking a strange tongue – *they* looked like soldiers. Anyway, I reached the Queen's Chamber before dawn. Ugh, it was creepy, I can tell you! The air was bad, and made me sleepy. I'd lit a torch, but when the King came I knew I'd have to put it out or the flame would show – you see, there were concealed spyholes, as well as a hidden way into the inner chamber. The spy-holes were set at an angle – I could see into both inner and outer chambers if I turned a bit. I had to be very, very careful when the procession came! It was wonderful, Father – the Queen was so beautiful, and the Princess prettier than you can imagine. I was happy, just looking at her. And – and then it *happened*.'

He gulped, and put a hand across his eyes. 'I was so scared, I almost screamed. It was horrible.'

'Tell me,' said Tahlevi gently. 'And come here.' He put an arm around the boy's quivering shoulders. 'They killed the King? Who did?'

Henmut repeated all that he had seen, and added, 'The trouble is that you can *see* into those chambers, but you can't always *hear*, if someone turns away as they're speaking. What puzzled me was that No-Hotep threatened harm to the King if the Princess and Royal Heir weren't obedient. But the King was put into the inner chamber, and looked dead. And – and – ' he swallowed, and went on – 'the cup-bearers and the noble Hekhti's assistant and the fanbearers were killed. Then I was terrified, Father – I knew what would happen if I was caught.'

Tahlevi held his son closer. 'They were knifed? Before the very eyes of the Queen and Princess ?'

'No – they were taken out and poisoned. I heard that priest say it was the poison of Shinar. That's why I really think the King *is* dead, for he drank a cup of wine. No-Hotep wouldn't let the Royal Heir drink, and then the King fell.'

Tahlevi made a great growling sound. 'So Hekhti's illness was most merciful – he too would have died if he had gone ! Tell me, my son, could the Royal Heir have plotted this? They say No-Hotep is his greatest friend.'

'It sounded as though he planned to get everyone there. But he scolded No-Hotep, and I think he hadn't guessed what was to happen.'

'He's a fool! And fools get used. How did this arrogant priest take a scolding?'

'He – he sort of put the Royal Heir in his place, as though he was a little boy, and – and I *think*, scared him.'

'He might well be scared – of his great friend! Fool, fool, *fool!* I've always said that boy dreamed of nothing but his own glory. No doubt he was careful *not* to guess –' Tahlevi's hand clenched as though he would like to box Sinuhe's ears as he had Henmut's, earlier. 'And then – ?'

'The Queen was left guarded in the outer chamber, and the King left lying on a litter in the inner chamber. Once I thought he moved, so perhaps he *is* alive. No-Hotep took the Princess and Royal Heir back outside. I was shaking all over, Father, but I had to learn what would happen next. So I got out, and crept from shadow to shadow of the other buildings, until I could hide behind the little Temple where No-Hotep took the Princess and Royal Heir to imprison them. There was a tiny chink far up in the wall of one room –'

'They've trained you well on the waterfront!' murmured Tahlevi.

'– and I saw a messenger arrive from Men-nofer to say that Hekhti was sick and couldn't attend the King. No-Hotep had *that* man killed, too.' Henmut shuddered, 'and I heard him order Hekhti's death. So I ran and pushed Muto's boat out of the reeds and paddled away very fast – it's so light and small that I could land at an easy place Muto talked of, a narrow canal very near the Palace. I was just able to reach Hekhti – I slipped on blood, getting there.' And suddenly he leaned against his father's enormous strength and began to whimper like a very little child.

Cefalu and Ptahsuti, who had heard enough, slipped from the room to go their separate ways. Cefalu left a sign at the back entrance to tell Nutka, when she arrived with Casper, that he would be at Ay's house if there were special news to be passed on to him.

The cunning of No-Hotep's plan – so carefully synchronized in all its aspects, so quietly and ruthlessly achieved – appalled Tahlevi. How wholeheartedly he wished for Hekhti's quick recovery! In his vulnerable state it would be necessary to hide him well. A Court jeweller keeps many valuable things upon his premises, and long ago Tahlevi had secretly caused a strongroom to be constructed within the thick sun-dried mud walls of his dwelling. Its whereabouts was known only to himself, his wife and son, and its ventilation hole was outwardly hidden by a thick green vine. So, in this narrow place and among gems and gold and silver, his wife prepared a makeshift bed, and the sleeping Hekhti was safely bestowed – not without effort, for he was a large man. All the time Tahlevi despairingly wondered how, single-handed, he could take advantage of Henmut's discoveries and No-Hotep's ignorance that they had taken place. Always his mind returned to: If only Hekhti – If there were only someone he could trust like Hekhti!

He sighed heavily and went back to his own room, Henmut trotting silently at his heels. Someone awaited them. An unexpected arrival today might have jolted anyone. Tahlevi's hand went speedily to his copper dagger. Then he stared, smiled in relief, gave a great shout of welcome, '*Reuben!*'

'Tahlevi, my friend – my dear, dear friend –'

Once they had embraced each other, the smile faded from Tahlevi's face. He gazed earnestly at Reuben. 'So – my Prince of Canaan! What good fortune brought you *here*? You've not been to the Palace?'

Reuben looked downward, very thoughtfully, as though weighing something in his mind. 'No,' he said, 'no. I came straight here. I've not yet seen Thamar who – as perhaps you know – is lodged with the Queen's father.' He raised his head and gazed sombrely at his friend. 'There's something wrong in Kemi, is there not? I – I heard this, before entering the city.'

'It was *already* spoken of?' asked Tahlevi incredulously.

Reuben seemed reluctant to reply. 'It was not – not rumour that I heard. Yet it was made clear to me . . .' He stopped. It wasn't necessary to explain much to Tahlevi – that natural artist – who could recognize the look of a visionary when he saw it.

'So – it was made clear.' Tahlevi nodded to himself, remembering the still small voice that had guided Reuben in the past. 'Then what of Thamar?' he asked briskly. 'You – heard she is all right?'

'Nothing of Thamar, Phut nor Sadhi.' Reuben gave a weary sigh. 'But if they weren't – protected, I do not think I should have been sent here.'

Tahlevi nodded again, satisfied. 'Things seemed as usual in the city? No one tried to stop your retinue entering it? As Prince of Canaan you surely did not come alone?'

'Men-nofer was unchanged except . . .' Reuben frowned, seeking for words. 'There was a – a sense of dark excitement. Milling crowds here and there which I partly put down to this expected hiding of the sun, and the dread it causes in such a – forgive me, friend! – superstitious people. As for my small retinue, I left it, with my other children, at one of the King's outer forts; and then came on alone, riding Anak, and muffled like a bedouin! Tahlevi, outside the city – some way off toward the wadis – there was a curiously large company of men encamped. I would have thought them soldiers, though not the King's, and I avoided them. *What* is happening here in Kemi?'

'So! In one way it was made clear, but not –'

'Not in so many words.'

'Henmut!' Tahlevi dropped his enormous hand on his son's shoulder. 'Fetch beer for the Prince of Canaan and myself. Now, Reuben – I will tell you all I know.'

When Henmut returned carrying the beer, Reuben was prowling up and down the room like an angry cheetah. He was struggling with several feelings: sorrow, fury, and determination on swift action to assuage his grief.

Tahlevi took the beer from his son. 'Go to your mother and ask her for a basket of our best figs and grapes. Then take them to the Court Chamberlain Ay's house, and say you come from the priestesses of Hathor with offerings for the Princess of Canaan. If you can see her, tell her that her husband's here, and warn her secretly of what has happened; but only enter the house if all seems outwardly at peace. Wait, child – take this headcloth, and wrap it so that no one sees your face too clearly. And use well your instinct and your wits!'

'Father, I'm so well known to all the noble Ay's household that if someone suspects me of – of spying or – They will guess you sent me! You won't want that, will you? But if Muto's better today, *he* will go.' Henmut looked up at his father earnestly.

'It's well thought of!' Tahlevi patted his son's shoulder. 'But wait: can we trust Muto? He must tell no one but the Princess, nor speak of these things afterwards.'

'Trust Muto? Why, Father, his family are famed as the most honest tomb robbers in the whole country! Trust Muto – I should say we could!' And Henmut ran out, laughing. The horrors of that morning were already fading before the excitement and importance of the present.

'A delightful boy, and full of enterprise,' said Reuben; but absently, for his mind was already sifting weightier matters. 'My thoughts turn constantly to this secret inner chamber that your Hekhti built. If, by the Lord's grace, the King does live – and we must act always, I think, as though he does – then *there* is the path to rescue. But this cunning priest has had the skill to divide his hostages, and can threaten us both South and North, so to speak.'

Tahlevi brooded, then said suddenly, 'I've just remembered something! Yesterday I was with the King. His Vizier was present, and there was talk between them of how the Army Commander in the Western desert had asked permission to bring his men nearer Men-nofer when the sun's darkening by Apep's rising comes to pass – for the soldiers suffer when they're kept far from their wives at such a time. The King agreed to grant the request. Now – we know the priest No-Hotep has laid his plans too well here for us to manage a quick counterstroke within the city. But there *is* a chance he took no steps against a possible reaction from that desert section of the army, if he'd no cause to think the danger imminent.'

'A *chance*, yes,' said Reuben grimly. 'But he seems to me a careful, thorough schemer.'

'That Army Commander, Akhtat'nat, is most loyal to the King. If he's still in command, then it's all right. If he is "sick" – or dead! – then No-Hotep's triumph will be wide indeed. One of us – you, my friend, because my absence from the workshop will seem odd if too prolonged – should go and see.'

'Yes, and if he's there, get him to turn his men aside and wait until some plan of action can be formed.' Reuben nodded, mulling it over.

'He's a good, strong fighter, and his troops seasoned men. I'll guide you on your way, overland, and we'll make our cast wide toward the Sovereign's Great Eternal House, and see from some distance off all that we can see.' Tahlevi clapped Reuben on the shoulder, and said comfortingly, 'But we'll wait first for news of Thamar. Meanwhile my wife shall prepare you supplies of food, and wine, and water. You may be in the desert for some while.'

Apep Rising —

The next day the Nile, which had retreated even farther during the night, developed a strange appearance that was, in fact, illusion and the reflection of a curiously overcast, greenish sky. It was as though everything were a little swollen or had wavy outlines, and distance itself became another illusion. Men-nofer's buildings looked weightless and seemed to swim in air, rows of dusky pearls. Trees were black shadows with silver leaves. Land and sky appeared to merge into one another, and all was pale green, white and sepia, and very hot and still.

Towards midday it was realized that Apep had risen from the Nile, and soon afterward his jaws could be seen darkening the sun as he began to swallow it. The people of Kemi stood groaning in the streets as they watched their Sun God disappear, or they sought refuge in the Temples to make offerings. By King Merenkere's Great Eternal House the Royal Heir and Princess Ta-Thata issued from the priests' Temple, and prostrated themselves at the water's edge. They were accompanied by the High Priest Nmem and the priest No-Hotep, who hovered humbly in the background. When the royal pair had made their offerings they were escorted back again and the doors closed on them once more.

It was a full sunswallowing; and, to its many watchers, it seemed long before Apep slowly disgorged the God again. As the eerie darkening faded, leaving the former greenish light triumphant, messengers took ship for Men-nofer bearing scrolls marked with the King's cartouche and the High Priest's name. The contents were read aloud in the Throne Room of the Palace to No-Hotep's followers assembled there with courtiers and minor officials, and the less powerful Hereditary Officers of State who, surprisingly, seemed to be the only great ones present on that day, together with two or three High Priests of various cults who were exceedingly mystified by the pronouncements.

'From the Lord of Diadems, Horus of Gold, the Sovereign Merenkere, your Sun, your God, your King, Living for Ever –

'My Majesty makes known to those who serve my Majesty and all my Majesty's people that during the swallowing of Re, which brought heavy sorrow to the Two Lands as being the loss of all we live by, it was made known to my Majesty, Son of the Sun, that the gods' displeasure has fallen upon Kemi, wherefore the Sun God almost abandoned us to rest for ever in the jaws of Apep. This punishment was only averted by the offerings made by my Majesty and the Great Royal Wife in my Eternal House, and those made to Set and Apep by the Royal Heir and Princess Ta-Thata. Ma'at itself and Men-nofer the Balance of the Two Lands have been endangered by the lack of honour paid to Set, who determines that his reconciliation with Osiris in the House of Ptah can only be maintained in this manner :

'For the space of two moons the High Priest of Set, Nmem, with all his priests and particularly his brother priest No-Hotep, shall be honoured and hold precedence above every High Priest in the Two Lands, even those of Ptah and Sekhmet.

'The Royal Heir and Princess Ta-Thata, whose offerings have won them favour, shall immediately be married in the

Temple near my Majesty's Eternal House before the High Priest Nmem and all his priesthood, at which ceremony you are in loyalty bound to appear this day.

'My Majesty and the Great Royal Wife, remaining in seclusion here or in the Palace of White Walls, shall submit ourselves to rigorous ritual and purification while the Royal Heir Sinuhe and his wife Princess Ta-Thata govern for the space of two moons wholly and entirely as Regents in our stead.'

When the messenger lowered the scroll with a flourish there was complete silence. People looked over their shoulders as though a sudden draught had surprised them. They glanced sideways and around them and noted for the first time the lack of many familiar faces. The High Priests of Ptah and Sekhmet exchanged glances, moved toward each other, and were intercepted as though accidentally by two strong priests of Set. Everyone guessed that something extraordinary had happened, though no one quite knew what. The messenger stepped smoothly down from the Throne steps where he had spoken, and passed through the crowd with the sublime indifference of a god. People began obediently to follow him, subdued because bewildered. If the King had truly commanded –

And it seemed that he had. For, when the barges carrying the diminished Court arrived at the landing stage near the Great Eternal House, there were the Temple singers chanting and shaking sistra in ecstatic praise of Hathor, Goddess of Love; and there, entering the Temple, were the Royal Heir and Princess Ta-Thata on their way to marriage; and afterward, accompanied by the High Priest Nmem and other priests, the Royal Heir and his wife emerged hand in hand, garlanded with myrtle, and smiling upon everyone as corn was scattered on the ground, and harpists played, and the jokes about fertility, that were a time-honoured custom associated with these great rites of Hathor were enjoyably repeated.

Then Prince Sinuhe made a short speech. 'Our offerings to Set and Apep at that moment of greatest danger have caused the King our father to shower approval on us his Majesty's children, by raising us now to greatness in his stead.' Only once while her husband was speaking did the Princess Ta-Thata glance toward that dark shaft entrance which showed forbiddingly behind the serried ranks of priests. But the Prince shook his head at her, and she smiled at him, smiled continually; and if anyone noted the trembling of their joined hands, or their pallor, it was no more than what might be expected at such a solemn moment. The priest No-Hotep brooded smilingly upon the scene.

The rows of courtiers prostrated themselves. Sinuhe and Ta-Thata trod delicately between them to board the great Royal Barge and seat themselves gravely on Merenkere's and Meri-Mekhmet's chairs. The priests of Set ranged themselves about them, and no one mentioned the absence of the fanbearers. Huge paddles dipped, and thrust backward; the green lotus patterns rose and fell into the water, as the blades propelled the barge toward the capital of Kemi. Hekhti's receding building gleamed with a silver whiteness under the gaze of Re. At its base was a small dark scar, entrance to the secrets of another world and those of No-Hotep.

Ta-Thata's distracted glance strayed towards Men-nofer and lighted on the Temple of Sekhmet. If it could have pierced into the dim sanctuary of the lion-headed goddess she would have seen Ptahsuti in all the regality of his black fur coat posed at Sekhmet's feet where his mother Meluseth used to sit. His black cloudy tail was curled around his front paws as he sought to be inspired in meditation. Then he drank the offering milk and chewed a piece of offering fish, wiped his mouth on his paw, and left the sanctuary. While he gazed hopefully at the goddess some intuition had told him that in this hour of danger his place was in the Palace. His ageing heart beat faster, but on soft and cloudy paws he padded home.

When Ta-Thata reached her own apartments she found him there, curled up on a couch. No-Hotep had solicitously advised Sinuhe to withdraw to his own rooms, and had more solicitously sent two priests there with him. Then he hastened to rejoin Ta-Thata, who was now nursing her mother's cat for comfort. He sat down beside her. It was an unheard-of insult. Ta-Thata was terrified but retained her dignity, and rose and walked away.

No-Hotep chuckled. 'So : we're very proud, aren't we, my Princess? A little pride is a good thing, and admirable, but too much invites — breakage.'

Ta-Thata's fingers dug into Ptahsuti's fur. She said nothing.

'Well, you're now a happy wife. And your husband instructs you that he has appointed me your tutor too, and desires you to obey me in everything.'

'The King my father has not told me so.'

'Your Highness wishes me to bring the Prince's written command with the King's cartouche?'

'It would be false. It would change nothing.'

'Princess — I have to remind you yet *again* that your parents' health depends on you?'

Ta-Thata raised her hands and let Ptahsuti bound lightly to the floor. 'You'll kill us all, I'm certain ! Now I wonder for the first time : does it matter when?'

'I thought you a silly child, Princess, but I find myself appreciating your courage.' His admiration chilled her, as well as his alarming gentleness of manner as he said, 'It may matter *how* someone dies.'

There was silence as they stared at each other. Then No-Hotep turned his head and looked toward the entrance where footsteps sounded. The hangings were drawn aside, and a woman stood there. Ta-Thata started forward and then gave a gasp and halted. It wasn't one of her ladies who had entered, but Beltethazar, the dancer from Shinar.

No-Hotep rose. Beltethazar tapped her foot upon the ground. 'You are late!' she said. 'I thought something had gone wrong.' She looked from him to Ta-Thata, angrily.

'Nothing is wrong. I instruct her Highness in her duties, that is all.' He took Ta-Thata's unwilling hand and led her forward. 'Now, here, my child, is your new companion – no mere dancer, but a priestess of Ishtar-Inana and the Prince of Shinar's sister! You will look upon her as your guide and friend.'

'No warm greeting from her gracious Highness?' mocked Beltethazar.

Ta-Thata remained silent and mutinous, staring downward at the floor.

'She'll learn,' said No-Hotep brusquely, dropping her hand. 'Now that her mother isn't here to spoil her she will learn very quickly; or she will be whipped. You hear me, Ta-Thata? It would hurt the Priestess most grievously to inflict pain on you, but she will stifle her feelings for the good of everyone.'

The Priestess laughed as though she enjoyed the prospect very much. Ta-Thata still made no reply, but raised her eyes to No-Hotep's face. For the first time since he had embarked on his bid for power something in him quailed. If he had known her great-grandfather, who had been given to the use of crocodiles, he would have trembled at a sudden likeness. It was his turn to lower his eyes. He thought uneasily of Hekhti. What had become of those two accursed assassins? No one could tell him, except that they had disappeared, and the Chief Royal Architect couldn't be found. They must surely have accomplished their task, or had they never reached the Palace? In which case, where *was* Hekhti? If he had walked out, someone must have seen him. And yet, and yet — There was no blood in his apartments; that had been checked.

The insolent woman and frightened girl were summing each other up as No-Hotep ruminated, frowning at the floor. It was unfortunate, this niggling doubt ... He said suddenly, 'The Chief Royal Architect has vanished. So your first act, my child, will be to issue a proclamation recalling him to his duties. You will say that by order of the Horus of Gold the boy Sadhi has been reclaimed from Thamar, his mother, and will badly need the services of his physician, if they're long withheld. It's just possible the noble Hekhti has guessed at — er — changes in the Palace, and fled to save his skin. If devotion to the Royal House will not bring him back, it may be that the needs of a — perhaps dying? — patient, will. You will phrase the proclamation in your own words, so that he knows it comes from *you*.'

This was horrible. Ta-Thata thought achingly of Hekhti and then of her father and mother in No-Hotep's hands. She knew already that she had no choice, but she still had spirit left to say, 'If Hekhti *did* escape you, I hope he'll be wise enough to stay away!'

And Hekhti was both sick enough and wise enough. Fear wouldn't have kept him back, but a dead man couldn't help Ta-Thata and the Queen — nor the King, if he were still alive. Hekhti's violent fever was soon over, but even his physique was temporarily weakened. He sat up on a couch in Tahlevi's room, and thought desperately of what might still be done.

'Are there no rumours of the truth in Men-nofer?'

Tahlevi shook his head gloomily. 'None that I hear, although many fantasies arise about the King's strange actions. Men remember that he once was nearly mad. This priest has worked too cleverly. All is confused, but seems to stem from the Lord of the Two Lands himself. By the time great nobles in the farthest Nomes begin to doubt, they will find themselves confined to their estates, or worse.'

'He has killed or confined too many who are loyal, already!' said Hekhti passionately. 'Otherwise – But to go with the news of this to some uncertain person would itself be madness! If only your friend Reuben would return.'

'Yes – and I want to know who are these men he saw encamped near Men-nofer?' Tahlevi pottered up and down the room; his whole bulk seemed to brood. 'There have been many caravans to Kemi lately. They may be soldiers, but perhaps they came disguised? This is something that one of Henmut's older and skilful companions could dis-cover for us. Speaking of children, my heart bleeds for Thamar – that that man should take Sadhi back into the Palace! At least we know she and the little one are safe.'

Hekhti's face twisted with sorrow. His anger too was deep and terrible as he thought of No-Hotep's using of Sadhi as a bait, and his possible ill-treatment of the child. It made Hekhti feel like returning openly to the Palace –

He said violently, 'Tahlevi, I *must* keep hidden! If No-Hotep can be induced to think that I'm dead and he is safe from me, he may grow careless. We can only hope that Sadhi's with the Princess Ta-Thata, and that this man won't fulfil his threats –'

'We will hope so, indeed,' said Tahlevi, very gravely.

No-Hotep brought Meri-Mekhmet back to Men-nofer later that day. He had meant to bring the King as well, and keep them both close prisoners at the centre of the tight knot he was drawing round the Palace; but then he changed his mind, for he was a very careful man, and those of the Royal Bodyguard, who had fought so bravely and then barricaded themselves inside a store room, were still a possible threat, although a minor one. Once he had brought them to obedience – and at least tried to learn the truth about Hekhti's disappearance – he might let the King return, and then ... The priest No-Hotep smiled approvingly to himself when he thought how many people were in for different surprises one way and another.

Meri-Mekhmet forsook all regal behaviour and wept uncontrollably when they parted her from her husband. He took her hands in his and tried to comfort her, but it wasn't easy in the presence of Set's priests and under the gaze of their cold eyes. He guessed himself already doomed, and had come to terms with it – as much as any man may. But his fears for Meri-Mekhmet, Ta-Thata, and his son : *those* were a different matter. He was pale and drawn, anyway, from the after effects of the strong sleeping draught he had been given, and he was paler still from unhappiness. Tears marked his face as well when he kissed his wife good-bye. The last he saw of her was the pale linen of her dress as they dragged her away along the dark passage to the outer world. Then, hiding his cold and desperate rage, he said stonily, 'How shall you entertain my Majesty in this enforced solitude we now enjoy?'

Imprisoned and helpless though he was, his whole aspect was so regal that the priests of Set peered at each other with uneasy eyes, and then about them, and then back at the King. They couldn't answer him. They were suddenly frightened by the insults they had offered to the God, the Son of Re.

– and No–Hotep Expanding

The Prince Sinuhe and his Princess, Ta-Thata, were seated on their parents' thrones. Jewels and gold and coronets lent them the appearance of two exquisite dolls. They were stiff, too, like dolls, though with terror. Only their eyes seemed alive in their blanched faces. No-Hotep stood before them, looking them up and down.

'Now, Royal Heir, I'm sure you understand my devotion to your interests! I have raised you to sit upon your father's throne and *lent* you his power. But understand, my little Ruler, that although I prostrate myself' – and he did – 'and the Princess Beltethazar also postrates herself' – which she did – 'your Highness will utter no word, take no action, make no move without our consent.' He rose again, followed by Beltethazar. 'When the hangings are pulled aside, and the petitioners and courtiers enter, you will remember this. You will remember for the King's sake and the Queen's, and for your own safety which I have much at heart.'

Beltethazar was carefully arranging herself on the throne steps at Sinuhe's feet. No-Hotep leaned forward and placed one finger under Ta-Thata's chin to tilt her head a fraction upward, as though settling her doll-like pose to perfection. He nodded, and went to stand in an attitude of priestly humility behind her as soldiers threw back the hangings and a sound of silver trumpets ushered in the waiting people.

Ta-Thata had thought that even Sinuhe's presence beside her in this evil dream would be some support; now she found it wasn't so: she was truly alone. He might still play on her feelings, occasionally, by acting like a frightened child, and then she could be sorry for him, with a faint sense of kinship in disaster. Otherwise it was like being with a stranger, and to think they shared the same father was almost unbelievable. She sat now just as No-Hotep had arranged her, and wondered if her parents were really still alive. However impossible it might seem – she swore fiercely and courageously to herself – she would one day have No-Hotep fed to crocodiles. She thought only passingly of Hekhti; or her bravery might have been undermined by the bitter knowledge that he had failed her, leaving her to the dreadful powers of No-Hotep which seemed to reach out and grasp at her with the black, compelling forces of the dread god, Set. No-Hotep was a vast spider who was binding her securely into his gigantic web. Each of her false smiles, each of her obedient playacting gestures before the Court, was another thread to hold her more irrevocably there. Now came the rising panic . . .

With an effort she lowered her gaze and forced a rigid smile. A tall man, muffled in a bedouin's robe, was prostrating himself before Sinuhe. She didn't hear what was said, for her distraught mind made nonsense of the words, and of Sinuhe's high-pitched and nervous reply. No-Hotep had bent to whisper in the Prince's ear. Sinuhe spoke again – *why* couldn't she hear? She tried to relax, and at last the words made sense as the tall man ended, with a foreign intonation, '. . . and thank your most gracious Highness, and beg your Highness to convey to our Sovereign, our lord my humble thanks. Life, prosperity, health !'

Sinuhe inclined his head. The petitioner's eyes met Ta-Thata's. She saw a great kindness in them, and anxiety.

She leaned a little forward, her lips parted. Now he was backing from the Presences, still looking at her. She had seen him before, several times, when she was a little girl. His eyes were like Sadhi's. She heard No-Hotep move behind her, and felt a touch upon her arm. Hurriedly she leaned back again, a model of decorum, but her heart was beating faster. Sadhi's father. Here in Kemi. The Prince of Canaan was her father's friend . . .

Once the audience was over and Sinuhe and Ta-Thata had withdrawn to their separate apartments, the priest No-Hotep, together with the Princess Beltethazar, himself gave audience to the young Prince Kalda of Shinar who had been waiting in an anteroom.

'Soon!' Kalda said passionately, striding up and down before them both. 'It must be soon! I'm tired of waiting out there in the desert! I — my father and I — have lent you force enough to put you where you are, No-Hotep. The Palace is in your hands, Kemi sleeps, you are Vizier in all but name. We've done our part for you — but now on your side there is hanging back. I'm horrified to learn the King is not yet dead.'

'Be not so anxious, little brother,' soothed Beltethazar. 'All goes in order. When our dear friend No-Hotep thinks it should be done, done it will be. When he's your Vizier you will learn to trust his judgement! When Set's priests stand higher in the Two Lands than they have ever done, when the Goddess Ishtar-Inana receives her rightful place in Kemi — in short, when No-Hotep stands at *your* right hand or behind your throne, you will learn the width and penetration of his understanding.'

Kalda gave his sister the look of one who had known her always and disliked her. 'This may be true,' he said sulkily, 'but I want action.'

'Action !' The priestess raised her fine eyes to heaven, as though she saw action there and regretted it. 'Why are the sons of kings always raised as soldiers? It addles their wits.'

'My Prince, soon to be my King,' put in No-Hotep, 'your impatience does you some credit. All the same, you do not know this people. They are stubborn, conservative, religious. It takes time to get some new thought into their minds, yet when it's there, it stays. A fresh Dynasty upon the Throne, this is a great upheaval. *But* – so long as it's seen to be both legal and in favour with the gods it will be accepted. Therefore : all things in the right order. Once our grip on Men-nofer is complete, the King shall return to his apartments. Unfortunately, the sacrifice our gods will exact for Apep's regurgitation of the Sun will be the turning of Merenkere to Osiris. In other words' – he spoke now as to a barbarian – 'his death. Whatever the final stage, it will be tactful. Your Highness knows that Sinuhe must survive him a short time, to accustom the people to Ta-Thata as their Queen. Whoever marries the King's widow, if she have also legal right to the Throne, *is* King.'

'Why shouldn't I marry that great beauty Meri-Mekhmet?'

No-Hotep sighed patiently. 'Prince, I have thought this matter out! Meri-Mekhmet did *not* inherit the Throne, she has *no* divine right, she is of lowly stock although the people have forgotten it, at present. But the little Ta-Thata – there they will see the true Daughter of Re, alone and young and forlorn. The Heiress. What more natural than she should take as consort a Prince of Shinar ?'

'And if she will not ?'

'Until you have children for Kemi we will keep Meri-Mekhmet alive. Her health shall be the stake for Ta-Thata's compliance.'

'You've thought it all out,' said the Prince, chewing his lip. 'I will be patient. At least the Princess, although not beautiful, is very pretty and she pleases me.'

'*You* will certainly please her better than Sinuhe!' said Beltethazar, laughing. 'For no one could please her less.'

'And your Highness is wrong,' said No-Hotep to Kalda in a low, thoughtful voice, 'for she's not merely pretty. A year or so and she will be even lovelier than Meri-Mekhmet. Your Highness is a very lucky man.'

Once the Prince had taken his departure, Beltethazar threw back her head and laughed again. She raised her arms and beat the air and made a crowing sound of triumph. Then she came to No-Hotep, who stood grinning blandly at her, and put her arms upon his shoulders.

'What a fool! What a fool he is!'

'Do not mock him, Princess! Value him. Fools have an intense value in this world, they make all things possible for the rest of us.'

She grew serious. 'You're right, dear friend. Your Sovereign was something of a fool to send you once on that Embassy to my father's court, was he not?'

'It was not the King, it was his Vizier, who knew me very little.'

'I see he did!' She pondered. 'I wish we could have done without Kalda altogether. He's rash, and could make mistakes.'

'Yes: rashness – kills.' He looked at her more blandly still. 'But we're agreed – are we not? – that his rashness will kill *him*, at the right time! And we had to use him. His soldiers are better trained than my limited adherents!'

'Do you know, my friend, I'm quite frightened of you myself?'

'I am relieved! For I'm singularly afraid of your beauty, Beltethazar.' He sat down beside her, and put his arm

around her narrow, muscular waist. 'Mutual fear is good
– better even than mutual love, which can vanish.'

'Yours had better not,' she said warningly.

'Have no fear – it's your dangerousness that makes you
so attractive to me.'

'And yet you plan to marry with Ta-Thata, when the
path is clear!' Her eyes glinted at him stormily.

'It's essential. She must have heirs for Kemi.'

'She may have Sinuhe's heir.'

'No, indeed! I'm keeping them apart, except on public
occasions. If he wants girls, before he joins his august father
in a tomb, they shall be provided. There's Su-Shunut, there
is Keta.'

'You're attracted to Ta-Thata! And you think I'm not
jealous?'

He didn't look at her, for he was thinking of Ta-Thata
and afraid Beltethazar might read his thoughts. He said
evenly and sensibly, and there was nothing in his voice that
she could fault, 'You've no cause for jealousy. The Kings
of Kemi have always many women, but there will be only
one High Priestess of Ishtar-Inana, whose worship shall be
great! Only one Beltethazar, to stand beside the Throne.'

'The Queen sits beside it,' she said unsmilingly. 'So who
will be the greater?'

'How can you ask? You – the only woman for me. Are
we not alike? As for Ta-Thata, you've nothing to fear.'
He bent his head to kiss her hands, and she couldn't see
his eyes. 'I promise you, even when she's Great Royal Wife
she shall be most polite. I've already taught her to smile as
she is told, and how she hates me for it! You shall help me
with her education.'

'It will be my pleasure,' she said between her teeth.
She was still staring at his bent head, and wished she could
see inside it, in case there was a picture of Ta-Thata there.

'Good! She shall spend much time studying obedience. Once I have completed Ta-Thata's training I shall command even her thoughts. She doesn't know it yet, but she will end by worshipping a Sun King who combines the dark power of Set with —'

'You will enjoy this,' she said suspiciously.

'Of course I shall! She has called me an upstart priest — and for that I shall daily humble her colossal pride, enjoying it all the more because she's a true Daughter of the Sun. Yet even these little Court entertainments still to come will never take my mind off you.'

Friends in Council

'She is well,' said Reuben sombrely, 'and brave. But she is terrified, poor child – I read it in her eyes.'

Hekhti paced the room. He was already stronger but his rage, deep and black and smouldering with Set's own violence, made him shake. 'He is the Prince's friend, and yet he stands behind her throne. Sinuhe is married to her, his right to Kemi now assured, but No-Hotep . . .' Hekhti's voice trailed away, as Tahlevi entered the room.

'Henmut's comrades have been invaluable!' said Reuben, smiling at him.

Tahlevi looked proud of his son. 'Yes, they are good boys. And now we know for certain that those men you saw encamped are Shinar's, Reuben.'

'Shinar!' exclaimed Hekhti. 'Of course! The young Prince Kalda will be with them, then. Which is why the Princess Ta-Thata is still more important than the Royal Heir.' He stood in thought.

'Why?' asked Reuben, staring.

'Why has young Kalda provided help for No-Hotep? Out of loving friendship? No: he expects reward – the Princess, and the Throne.'

'But No-Hotep has married her to Sinuhe!'

'That is a stage in this deep game he plays – he *is* very deep.' Again Hekhti began to pace the room. Mentally he was groping for something which was still unclear to him.

'Has he killed the King – or does he keep him alive?' Reuben's brow wrinkled. 'All Henmut heard and saw seemed so contradictory.'

Hekhti shook his head, and sighed. 'We will try to believe that our Sovereign, our lord is still alive. And our Queen ... No-Hotep is a tortuous, methodical man, and an upstart. People must be convinced by what he does – so there will be a show of legality and, above all, the guidance of the gods! What will he do? I think he'll bring his Majesty back to the Palace. But the King isn't strong, perhaps his purifications and sacrifices for Kemi will have "weakened" him. After all, he has been ill before now.'

'So the King will die – quickly. And the Queen too?' Reuben sounded incredulous. 'The people would be convinced by *that*?'

'The Queen could still be kept alive,' said Hekhti in a controlled voice, 'to put pressure on the Princess, who is by nature both brave and rebellious! As for the Royal Heir –'

'A moral weakling!' Tahlevi's voice came fiercely from behind his beard. 'And a physique no stronger than the King's.' He nodded to himself. 'Yes, he could quickly deteriorate under the strain of his father's sudden death! All will go in due order, Reuben – King Merenkere's murder; Queen Meri-Mekhmet's "seclusion"; the Prince's death – the marriage with Shinar's son.'

Hekhti struck one hand into the palm of the other. 'And that priest has been so fiendishly clever! One would say he had Set's very ear! He keeps his royal captives apart. Rescue will be trebly difficult.' His hands clenched as though he would strangle No-Hotep there and then.

'Yes,' muttered Tahlevi, 'in spite of Akhtat'nat's men –'

'That was well thought of, my friend.' Hekhti paused in his restless pacing to put a hand on the jeweller's shoulder.

'At least you've saved a few loyal men for the King! They are making for Imhotep's tomb, Reuben?'

'Disguised as suppliants.' Reuben looked amused, recalling the smart, well-disciplined troops he had encountered in the desert. But his smile faded quickly. Sadhi ... Thamar, he thought; and continued speaking with an effort, 'Well, we know where Akhtat'nat is, if we can use him. Hekhti, what surprised me was to find this priest No-Hotep so young. He has carried out his plans with the assurance, efficiency and speed of an experienced older man. Last time I was in Kemi he was never spoken of at Court – or if he was, I don't remember it.'

'He was many moons with an Embassy to Shinar.'

'We know now how he spent them! He takes much trouble to make Kalda of Shinar the Lord of the Two Lands.'

For the second time Hekhti struck one hand into the other. He stared at Reuben as though light had broken. '*That* is it! That's what is wrong with this whole edifice of thought we have been building! For it's out of character that anyone but No-Hotep should benefit from all this effort and bloodshed.'

'He will be the new King's Vizier, I imagine.'

'Vizier? A Vizier who knows much to the new King's discredit – and might soon smell better dead? No, Kalda is Force, he is the Soldier: he who does the dirty work and is then pushed aside, or worse. When a fresh Dynasty is proclaimed it will be No-Hotep himself who takes the Royal titles: Lord of the Two Lands, Horus of Gold! To marry with the Heiress will be worth a sea of blood.'

'No, but Hekhti! He is priest of Set! Can he marry her?'

Hekhti said impatiently, 'The King himself is Kemi's Great High Priest. No-Hotep will just step upward.'

'Ah yes –' Reuben slowly nodded. 'You're right. There was his proprietory attitude toward her, his indifference to the Prince. I forgot to tell you that there was a woman who sat upon the Throne steps, at the Prince's feet. A handsome creature – ' Hekhti looked up sharply as Reuben described Beltethazar.

'Ah yes – the dancer from Shinar, she who sang a hymn to the goddess Ishtar-Inana before the King, and enraged him. It was No-Hotep who introduced her to the Court. Doubtless her presence has a darkness to match the rest.'

(Here Nutka, who was lying with Casper curled up beside her tail, cuffed him awake. 'How will you acquire the Wisdom of Meluseth if you're for ever dozing? What I've just learned of people would be a warning to any cat, while all you do is blow my fur in and out each time you breathe.' Casper sat up hurriedly and paid attention.)

'Well, if you judge right, the King is doomed –' Reuben began to pace the room like Hekhti – 'unless he's rescued before No-Hotep brings him to the Palace.' (Was Thamar safe at Ay's house, with No-Hotep's servants there? Was Sadhi safe? If they weren't, why had the still small voice sent him *here*?)

'. . . Reuben!'

He started. 'You were saying?'

'That they must all be rescued simultaneously. It's easy, is it not?'

'No-Hotep has men discreetly placed around the Great Eternal House,' put in Tahlevi. 'As Reuben and I saw when –' He broke off, interrupted by Henmut's impetuous entry. 'And where have you been, my son! You look a strange colour.'

'Muto painted me, Father! For a joke. We've been beggars all this afternoon – I had one eye closed, and a bandage, and Muto limped. We've been chased from the *Palace kitchens*! And Muto is all bruised, but no one asked us how we got in past the guards!' He proudly opened his hand, to reveal his climber's pegs. 'We've discovered something for you – the Queen is closeted in her own apartments, we heard the slaves whispering about it.'

'That is good to know,' said Hekhti thoughtfully. 'But with the Palace as it is, you're lucky someone didn't knife you.'

'One tried, most noble Hekhti –' Tahlevi moaned – 'but Muto tripped him, and we ran. He didn't bother to chase beggar brats very far! We've learned something else for you, too: where the King's Bodyguard are – those who fought and got cornered. They've got food and wine in a storeroom. We spoke to them, and told them what had happened.' He looked around him, and his small chest expanded with self-approbation.

Reuben gave a great laugh. 'What it is to be a tomb robber's son!'

But Hekhti frowned. 'I hope you roused no suspicions that outsiders are too interested in the Palace? It could be disastrous. Where are these men?'

Henmut looked crestfallen. 'We didn't rouse *anyone's* suspicions. We're much too cunning, I can promise you. When we were being chased from the Palace kitchens we passed one end of a corridor that was quite heavily guarded – there were soldiers sort of yelling insults through a door. When they saw us they stopped and began to come for us –' Tahlevi groaned – 'but we escaped. Then we had a war council, Father! We thought we might find out what was up. We crept into the gardens and looked till we found the outside of that storeroom. There was no window, only a very small square hole for air, high up, and too small for anyone to get through. Muto climbed up the wall while I kept watch. Some of the King's Bodyguard were inside. Three were wounded and one dead.'

'But how many are alive?' asked Hekhti intently.

'Twelve. So many of No-Hotep's men got killed trying to get in there that they've simply sealed the passage off. They're waiting for the food to run out.'

Hekhti still looked troubled. 'If you were heard talking –'

'Really we weren't! Muto whispered – and some of the King's men made a noise to cover up.'

'And what did Muto whisper?' asked Hekhti severely.

'Oh –' Henmut looked at him uncertainly, a little scared. 'Just that No-Hotep was in control, but the friends of the Great House – the royal family – worked to free them. Was it too much?'

'Too much? I think you've done magnificently!' said Reuben. 'His future profession is assured, Tahlevi – he will be a spy.'

'A *jeweller*,' said Tahlevi crossly. 'If it weren't for the anguish of these times I would whip him soundly.'

Henmut's expression grew very grave, but he was trying not to laugh. 'Father – my lord Hekhti – I – we heard something else. It seemed such a pity to go without learning all we could, so we crept round the Palace front, and hid in the bushes, where we could hear what anyone said as they came out after the daily audiences were over. People were wondering if the King was mad again, and saying the Royal Heir looked very nervous. Was the *King* ever *mad*?'

'Almost – once – a long time ago,' said Reuben.

'Oh . . . We were just leaving when two or three men strolled past together. One was grumbling – it was old Nuphe, the Assistant Royal Bargemaster, and he was very angry. He said why should it always fall on him, when duties happened at late times? *He* needed sleep as much as anyone else –'

'Ah!' said Hekhti, suddenly even more alert. 'And – ?'

'And how it was one thing to take the King's barge downstream by daylight, with a good chance of getting back to eat with his wife, and another to go downstream at night to the new Great Eternal House.'

Hekhti looked his despair. 'So No-Hotep moves already – tonight! Once the Sovereign's back in Men-nofer it will be harder still for us to rescue him. That priest will keep guards round him till he is dispatched – all the hostages in separate quarters, doubtless, and the Palace to be searched for them!' He sat down suddenly, his face looked drawn.

'Ah no, my lord Hekhti – it's for *tomorrow* night. Nuphe will take the barge downstream very late, and wait until the moon has set. Then the King will embark, and come back to Men-nofer before dawn. Nuphe was very angry about it – he said the King must be involved with some new rites, why couldn't the God stick to the ways of his fathers, it was flying in the face of Re.'

'You're *certain* it is not for tonight?'

'Completely certain,' said Henmut with such confidence that they believed him.

('I hope you take notice of this splendid child,' said Nutka to Casper. 'Could you act so? I doubt it. Now watch – his father will send him off to bed for not telling them first what he would do – when he would have been forbidden to attempt it! There: I said so. *And* he has been cuffed as well, which will teach him fortitude under injustice. An excellent father!' And she tucked her nose approvingly into her tail.)

'So,' said Hekhti most heavily to Reuben and Tahlevi, 'the priest's plan proceeds. Even his temporary parting of the King and Queen within the Palace will be accepted by the people as part of the new ritual purifications that have been proclaimed. He will surround them with his priests of Set, and then –'

'Then we must act first, and recapture the King: in the Great Eternal House or on the barge.'

'And rescue simultaneously the other hostages! An easy matter.' Hekhti put his head in his hands.

'It – seems – to – me –' said Reuben very slowly – 'that we're looking at this the wrong way round. Should we not concentrate on two people: the King and – No-Hotep!'

'No-Hotep himself?' Hekhti considered for a while, then shook his head. 'Perhaps even harder. He may be anywhere in the Palace, well protected. And if he got a chance to order the Queen and Princess harmed –'

'He won't have them harmed unless all is obviously lost – they are his pathway to the Throne. And he may be well protected, yet will he expect personal attack without a general one? Therefore, one quick stroke –'

'Mmmm. He must act as though he expects general attack, even if he doesn't. He may be less careful if he believes me dead than if he doesn't. How are we to know?'

So Reuben and Hekhti argued the matter back and forth, with Tahlevi an almost silent third; and when at last they went to bed nothing had been decided. Hekhti's brain reeled with tiredness. He lay awake, seeing Ta-Thata's face against the dark; the King's face, dead; Sadhi sick and woe-begone without his physician. The after effects of fever only increased the Chief Royal Architect's despair. In the next room Reuben firmly prepared himself for sleep. Haunted though he was by fears for Thamar and Phut and, above all, Sadhi, he was still capable of calling up reserves of trust in the Lord God of his fathers; and – unlike Hekhti – he was fully well. Just as his eyelids drooped the window darkened slightly, and something slipped through it and landed with a heavy plop upon his legs.

'Nutka sent word that you were back,' said Cefalu. 'Dear Master, I am glad to find you, but it is tiring to run round Men-nofer at night, and I feel my age.' He stretched himself contentedly on Reuben's chest and extended one paw beneath his chin.

'Dear Cefalu! Where have you come from?'

'The house of Ay. Where else?'

'Thamar is all right? And Phut?' asked Reuben anxiously.

'Well enough, though almost prisoners. They send you every loving greeting. They may not leave while the noble Ay is ill, in case they carry sickness – so they are told. Phut has bitten one of No-Hotep's men, who is now festering.' Cefalu licked his shirt front, and added, 'I have a message from Ptahsuti. He makes it his business to move constantly about the Palace and know all that happens.'

'Hah! Could he find out where No-Hotep will be, at a given time?'

'He could try. That priest is secretive, and doesn't always speak his thoughts aloud. When he does, it's usually to that stomach-whirler – the dancer from Shinar.'

'Ah yes, Hekhti spoke of her. No-Hotep favours her?'

'He loves her. Even crocodiles can love, they tell me, so why not No-Hotep? Master, she is no simple dancer, but a priestess, and the young Kalda's sister. Ptahsuti was wide-eyed beneath the couch when that crocodile kissed her – faugh! It put him off his fish! They plan Prince Kalda's death – after Prince Sinuhe's. Then No-Hotep will mount the Throne with Ta-Thata as his Queen – and the priestess at his side.'

'More or less as we expected,' said Reuben thoughtfully. 'Except this dancer. Could their proposed trickery be used to divide No-Hotep and Kalda?'

Cefalu yawned, showing a pink throat and tongue. 'It would be hard to divide bandit cats, one is on top and the others beneath, that's all there is to it. But you know your own species, Master.' He pumped with his paws to show that he was settling, and added, 'One thing else: our little

Sadhi is with Princess Ta-Thata, and some comfort to her. No-Hotep doesn't know they "speak" together in the hand language that our noble Hekhti taught them. Sadhi may be sometimes ill-treated –' Reuben made a sound of pain – 'Yes, I am sorry, but it's so : No-Hotep is a natural oppressor of the weak – but Sadhi's free to roam the Palace, since the priest looks on him as little better than a cat.' Cefalu stretched out his claws and examined them reflectively. 'A man with such attitudes may not last long. Now – shall we sleep?'

Ta-Thata Learns Her Future —

The next day all still seemed quiet in Men-nofer. Farther off, within the Great Eternal House which raised its shining cone towards the sky and glittered in tremendous heat, King Merenkere tried to tell if dawn had come, and continued his dreadful ordeal in the semi-darkness. The six priests of Set took turns at guard duty in the outer chamber, their knives ready on their knees. Four men woke, and two slept. Merenkere sat cross-legged on the litter in the inner chamber. He sat alone, waiting for some unknown form of death. The stone walls seemed to close in on him, the torchlight's flicker barely dispelled the heavy gloom. Here it was easy to remember Set and forget Osiris. Sometimes Merenkere was overcome with lassitude; at others he felt impotent mounting fury at the ease with which No-Hotep had entrapped him, and he would shake as Sadhi might have done. Then would come terror for Meri-Mekhmet and Ta-Thata, and the miserable certainty that by lack of foresight he had caused all this. It was a fearful place in which to entertain such thoughts. For the thousandth time he looked around him, acknowledged the impossibility of escape, and fought down a mounting, engulfing horror at his dark fate.

Inside the Palace all ran smoothly under the iron control of No-Hotep, who was preparing for the King's return to Men-nofer. He visited his hostages in turn, prostrating himself before Sinuhe as though he meant it, and terrifying him to near-imbecility by asking if he was prepared to take over entirely from his father? When he entered Ta-Thata's apartment he walked in on her familiarly and unannounced. She was determined to hold his gaze, and succeeded, although her knees knocked together beneath her pleated linen dress.

He smiled with genuine amusement. 'Very royal, my child – you'll make a good Queen, too good for Sinuhe. From your silence I take it that he isn't to your taste? Well, don't despair. He's not much of a husband for you, but you may do better, later. Come and sit down, I wish to talk with you.'

'Is the King my father still alive?'

No-Hotep raised his eyebrows. 'Do you think I would offend the gods by some impiety, Princess? Never – unless you anger me. So: come and sit down.' He advanced swiftly, scooped her up under one arm as though she were a kitten, and sat down holding her firmly on his knee. Ta-Thata kicked and struggled to escape. He drew back his hand and slapped her face so that her head rang and tears started to her eyes. 'Sit still! Remember your parents, and that I've warned you already not to anger me. Good – I'm glad you understand. Now, Ta-Thata: what do you think of the Princess Beltethazar?'

'I hate her.' Ta-Thata's fists clenched in fury. Her face had flushed dark red.

'Hate is a very big word – I'll tell you what you really think. She is beautiful, a great priestess and a great lady. She will care for you as though you were her daughter, and you'll love and obey her as a mother. If she requires it you will kiss the dust before her feet. Now put all this in your own words for me, Ta-Thata.'

She was mute, staring at the ground.

'Must I warn you yet again? It will be for the last time . . .'

When she had haltingly repeated the gist of No-Hotep's speech he said lightly, 'Good, that's better. Almost the end of a first lesson –' He twisted his right hand in her heavy hair to turn her face toward him as Sinuhe had once done with the indignant Su-Shunut. 'Yes, you'd like to hit me back, wouldn't you? It's most amusing. Sinuhe, poor boy, is a goose who thinks himself a phoenix – teaching you will be a pleasant change, you'll be a quicker and a more rewarding pupil.' He kissed her slowly and thoroughly, and then released her and stood up. If she had had a dagger she would have tried to kill him, whatever the result. He read it in her eyes, and smiled again. 'I have you cornered, pretty panther, so keep those royal claws sheathed. Any violent action against me – or against yourself – and the Queen will suffer for it. And don't fret – I shall not waste you long on Sinuhe.' The hangings fell into place, and he was gone. Ta-Thata stood staring after him, wiping her mouth compulsively with her hand. Isis, but this was worse than anything she could have imagined!

The hangings quivered again. She stiffened, trying to control her trembling. But it was Sadhi who crept in, looking over his shoulder as though expecting to be kicked. He ran to her and pressed her hand. They felt each other's shivering. There was little to communicate except their mutual fear. Contact, at least, was comforting.

Once more the hangings quivered. Sadhi and Ta-Thata jumped apart. A cloud of black fur advanced toward them. Ptahsuti was joined by Cefalu, who ran in tail erect and with a look of busy importance. Four ears and many whiskers signalled something or other which neither Sadhi nor Ta-Thata could understand, although they guessed at urgency.

'The Queen speaks Cat,' said Ptahsuti desperately. 'If only she were here!'

'Yes — a moment of true crisis, and undone for want of understanding! All these years in the Palace, and you taught Ta-Thata *nothing*?'

'I am the *Queen's* cat.' Ptahsuti's black cloud expanded with indignation. 'Is Ta-Thata's laziness my fault? We must make them understand —' and he ran at Sadhi, to grip him tellingly around the leg with his claws and try to encourage him toward the entrance. Sadhi drew back hurriedly, but didn't slap. He had grown kinder under Hekhti's teaching.

'Zsut! Is that the way?' asked Cefalu. 'Watch me.' He wound himself three times around Sadhi in a gentler manner, walked to the hangings, looked back, returned to Sadhi and pulled at him with a closed paw.

Now at last Ta-Thata understood. She wondered if Meri-Mekhmet could have sent Ptahsuti, and joyfully seized Sadhi's hand to tap out 'Follow!' as Hekhti had taught her. She saw light dawn in his frightened eyes. He smiled slantingly at her, and followed after the two erect tails into the corridor.

No-Hotep's guards outside the great double walls went to and fro at intervals. Crouched by the tamarisk inside the gardens Hekhti waited. Henmut was there as well to help him climb. They had risked much by coming, for it was broad daylight, and their entry had had to be well timed. They heard Sadhi coming through the bushes — his deafness made him indifferent to noise — and winced. The cats came into view first, crawling on their stomachs. Hekhti raised his finger to his lips, and Sadhi did the last stretch with an exaggerated stealth that cracked several twigs. He beamed when he saw his benefactor, flung his arms impulsively around him, and hugged him.

Hekhti dared not stay long. He hurriedly examined his small patient, and was relieved to find Sadhi's general condition still quite good, in spite of several cuts and bruises. Then he took a little piece of rolled-up papyrus from Henmut and placed it in Sadhi's hand, guiding him to hide it under the waistband of his diminutive kilt. On the child's wrist he solemnly tapped out the sign language for 'Ta-Thata' and 'give', after which he put a finger to his lips again to show that secrecy was needed. Sadhi nodded; he had understood. He smiled joyfully, and clutched at Hekhti's hand as though he would never let it go. Very reluctantly the architect turned him about and gave him a gentle push in the direction of the Palace. With equal reluctance Sadhi obeyed. The cats followed crouchingly, showing as they went one cloudy behind and one plush, gaunt, muscular one.

'Now, back over these walls,' murmured Hekhti to Henmut, 'as fast as we can go. And may Isis protect us from falling straight into the arms of No-Hotep's men!'

When Sadhi reached Ta-Thata's apartments once again he found the priestess Beltethazar talking in harsh tones to the Princess, who stood before her with bent head. Sadhi scuttled unobtrusively behind a chair, for he feared the gorgeously clad and unkind Beltethazar almost more than he feared No-Hotep; fortunately she didn't seem to notice him.

'– and furthermore it's not only manners that you lack, but true religion. This I shall attend to myself, for my great goddess is to be exalted here. Do you listen, little monkey?' She pinched Ta-Thata's arm.

'Yes, Priestess! I – I do not know why you are angry. I *am* listening.'

'You are listening insolently.'

'I – I truly did not mean to, Priestess, for –'

'Your ladies taught you nothing! Is it insolent to argue with me, or not?'

'Yes, Priestess – if you say so.'

'Another insolence! If? Did I *not* say so?' She cuffed Ta-Thata on the ear, in the casual manner of a lioness punishing a cub.

'Yes, Priestess.'

'That's better – but guard the expression of your left eye, and pay attention. The great priest No-Hotep, whom I hope you honour for all his kindness and care of you, is dismayed by your lack of training for your high office. The Royal Heir was always an apt and willing pupil, while you have just run wild, a spoiled daughter.' Here she cuffed Ta-Thata on the other ear for good measure. 'So the great No-Hotep himself will be your tutor in certain matters, as he condescendingly informs you now, through me. Do not annoy him, girl, or you annoy us both.' She started cuffing again, absentmindedly. Ta-Thata found it difficult to stay upright, and her ears began to buzz. 'Such is his zeal that he will give you your first instruction this very evening, in his own apartments. You shall hear later at what time you will be honoured. You understand?'

'Yes, Priestess,' whispered Ta-Thata, whose lips had gone very dry.

'Then understand too that his interest is caused purely by your royal divinity. Pride yourself on nothing, or you'll have me to reckon with!' Her features seemed to swell with jealous rage. She gave Ta-Thata one final, heavier cuff, and hurried from the room as though she couldn't trust herself to stay. Sadhi slipped from his hiding place, ran to

Ta-Thata, and thrust Hekhti's small roll of papyrus toward her. It was unusual for a Royal Princess to learn the hiero-glyphs, such matters were for scribes or learned men. Now, as Ta-Thata stared down unbelievingly at what she held, she praised Osiris that she had teased Hekhti till he had given in and shown her how to form the written language, and how to read it. Here was a message in his hand, proof not only that he lived but that he thought of her and Sadhi.

'Princess — the King and Queen are still alive. I must know when, where, and with fewest attendants No-Hotep may be found late this day. If your Highness can find out, write small on the back of this papyrus, and send Sadhi back to where he found me. Tell him "Hekhti" and "boy" and "tamarisk" and "wall" — then he will understand. Henmut will return there some while before nightfall and wait for him. Your Highness's loyal —' then it was signed with the black squiggles that were Hekhti's name. Ta-Thata gave a quickly suppressed squeal of pleasure and relief, and seized Sadhi's hands to dance excitedly with him about the room.

– and a Prince is Undeceived

Kalda of Shinar was in his tent, humming a little. It was a bright day – well, it was always bright, here – and he was thinking of Ta-Thata. He had his arms crossed upon his chest, and was wondering how it would feel to hold the Crook and Flail, when his bodyservant entered.

'Your Highness! A stranger asks audience of your Highness.'

'Send him away.'

'He's hard to move, your Highness – he is like a mountain. He says' – the bodyservant looked speculatively at his Prince, *could* the rumours about this odd expedition be true? – 'he comes from Court with a message from the priest No-Hotep, and with jewels for your Highness's approaching marriage.'

'Aha!' The Prince seemed to shine like the day itself. 'From No-Hotep ... We will see this fellow, with his jewels.'

Tahlevi was shown in, looking even more mountainous in a tent than he did outside it. The Prince's servants had searched him, but they were no match for one whose skilful hands could shift various defensive weapons around his body even while men searched his other side.

'Greetings, most gracious Highness! Greetings to my Prince, so soon to be my King.'

'You know that?' The Prince regarded him narrowly. 'We had not thought No-Hotep indiscreet.'

'Ah, your Highness, that priest is of all men the most discreet – on occasions could we say too discreet? – about his plans. Your Highness would care to see these necklets for the Princess Ta-Thata and yourself?'

'Not yet,' said the Prince, whose blunt soldier's wits had fastened on the phrase 'too discreet' and remained hovering there. 'What is No-Hotep too discreet about?'

'His discretion,' replied Tahlevi blandly, 'has prevented his informing your Highness that he means to mount the Throne himself. Your Highness will like the way I've matched carnelian with lapis, and –'

'What!'

'Your Highness prefers turquoise?'

'No-Hotep, man – No-Hotep! Means to mount the Throne *himself*?'

'Is it possible the thought never crossed your Highness's noble mind? I feared so. Your Highness has too open a nature to mistrust others.'

'He's to be my Vizier! My Chief Adviser!'

Tahlevi sorrowfully shook his head. 'My Prince, con-sider! No-Hotep's a young man – perhaps he found his way blocked by the good King Merenkere, who knows? For this reason he has killed the King –'

'Already?'

'So I think – he wishes to push matters on. Before he marries anyone with the Royal Princess he must likewise dispose of the Royal Heir. Many other people are already dead. This, to be made Vizier?' Tahlevi shook his head, and his eyes were warm with a great, deceptive kindness. 'Your Highness is very, very young.'

'He is devoted to the House of Shinar!'

'He is devoted to the Princess Beltethazar – your High-ness's loving sister.'

The Prince, most regrettably, spat.

'Quite so,' murmured Tahlevi. 'These fraternal relationships – But what is her place in all this? She will raise her goddess to high worship in the Two Lands. She will stand by No-Hotep when he mounts the Throne. Together he and she will rule – with the Princess Ta-Thata as their mouthpiece. Now, what of your Highness? Once soldiers are no longer needed – In some small unexpected skirmish, perhaps, your Highness is like to die.' He held carnelian against lapis and admired both. 'Or so I read it. Perhaps I am mistaken.'

The Prince stared at the ground. Often he found it hard to entertain more than one thought at a time. A second caused strenuous juggling, and a third could only enter if the first were discarded altogether.

'It rings true,' he growled at last, recalling his sister's scorn of him in childhood. 'True! What surprises me is that you know it, and bring your knowledge here. If *your* honesty's doubtful, friend –' and he drew a gesture across his throat.

'I would deserve it. But I wish only to serve your Highness.'

'Why? How have you served your King?'

Tahlevi sighed. 'I would not have troubled your Highness with my problems – yet now I must. King Merenkere is – was a good king, though in my view weak. Here No-Hotep's right: Kemi needs stronger, more warlike men. The King seemed to have little control over his Treasury, which – er – forgot to pay his jeweller. To prove my honesty toward your Highness I shall place myself in your Highness's hands by confiding a dark secret of my past: I was a common thief, a tomb robber. How the Treasury spies came to hear of it I cannot tell. But to say that good King Merenkere took advantage of my vulnerable situation is –'

'A fault indeed in a great sovereign!' exclaimed the

Prince. He shook his head, and Tahlevi shook his too. They stood and shook their heads like two old comrades.

'Well, we will trust you,' said the Prince at last. 'But have you any proof that No-Hotep will deal treacherously?'

'No. For someone I know in the Palace,' said Tahlevi delicately, 'came to me with tales of things – overheard. This is all I dare reveal, your Highness. He, like me, is someone who served the late King unwillingly. He too is devoted to the Princess Ta-Thata. The Royal Heir isn't worthy of her. No-Hotep has worked well, but should now be – set aside for a young, brilliant, charming, high-born soldier-King.' He stared at Kalda of Shinar, and his eyes kindled with what looked like admiration. 'And afterwards,' he added practically, 'I shall hope that your Majesty will patronize me as your Majesty's overworked, well-paid Court Jeweller.'

'Why, you're a scoundrel!' The Prince clapped him familiarly on the shoulder in a way that made the words a compliment. 'But count upon my gratitude. Now, first things first –' and he picked up his weapons to examine the blades. 'Let us go and dispatch this No-Hotep immediately.'

'My Prince!' Tahlevi raised his hands in horror. 'No rashness! That far-sighted man has some of your efficient captains eating from his hands. He has offered them advancement while keeping your Highness discreetly in the desert. Put the matter to the test by approaching him in the Palace, and you'll be dead before we may recite the names of Kemi's gods – much sooner.'

'Grrrr!'

'But if your Highness will deign to accept my humble advice, it's this : play a waiting game. For perhaps your Highness has more friends than those you know of – who can tell?' Tahlevi smiled sweetly and mysteriously into space. 'Yes – secret friends.'

'A waiting game?'

'Shall we say a little — withdrawn? As though ready — frankly — to be made a fool of? Perhaps your Highness would consider the wisdom of recalling those of your followers in the Palace whose loyalty is past doubt? Discreetly, and later today? Without allowing that meddling priest to hear of it.'

'It shall certainly be done! And afterwards, my ingenious friend?'

'Do not ask, my Prince.' Tahlevi leaned over the royal hands and kissed them. It was difficult for him to lean, but he achieved it. 'Only wait. If word comes from No-Hotep or the Priestess demanding your presence there, ignore it. And send no more soldiers, whatever their request. Say you're sick — yes, that there's grave sickness in the camp. Remain here, till a messenger comes to you bearing —' He held up a carved gold ring.

'And that will mean "Come now"?'

'Yes,' Tahlevi nodded thoughtfully. 'That is just it. I'll leave these valuable necklets with you, Highness, for I trust we shall see a happy outcome to these plans. One last word: could your Highness graciously provide your Highness's friends with three sets of Shinar's arms?'

He floundered into an obeisance, rose, and was gone. Outside the tent Kalda's men came running to supply the arms that he had asked for and load them on a donkey. As Tahlevi made ready to mount Anak he surreptitiously raised a corner of his robe to wipe his forehead free of sweat.

Moonwatch

The day drew towards evening. River, desert, buildings and tombs seemed to give off heat, doubling what was already in the atmosphere. Palm and vine leaf hung motionless. It was as though nature herself waited for something cataclysmic to take place.

With all his plans in train No-Hotep felt he could relax. He set Sinuhe some tasks, and when the boy begged to share them with his wife said sharply that he must earn the privilege by harder work. Then he visited Beltethazar, who was still furiously jealous.

'I am the only person who should have the right of entry to your apartments!' she said, stamping her foot.

'Peace,' he replied amiably, stroking her long black hair. 'You are right, as always. When I see the Princess it shall be in hers. Tell her to expect me when the moon rises –'

Yet it was neither of Beltethazar nor of Ta-Thata that he was thinking, but of Meri-Mekhmet who had always chosen to ignore him, had always looked away. Was I repulsive? he asked himself angrily. A mere humble youth with my way to make – Well, I was humble once! If I'm furiously ambitious, she has made me so – How I dislike her.

'– and of what are you thinking *now*?'

'Of the past. It is always a mistake to think about the past, it weakens one for dealing with the present! So – let us think of Sinuhe instead. He shall spend the night in his father's apartments – to greet him, as is fitting. It will frighten him, poor boy, but he must learn to carry out his duties !' His lips curled slightly.

'You have something else in mind.' She watched him narrowly.

'Perhaps !' He rose. 'I go now to discuss her daughter's future with the Queen. All this planning is most exhausting.'

'Well, you think of everything,' she said crossly.

'It is my duty – am I not to be Lord of the Two Lands, with your help? But it's also tiring – so I hope you'll not grudge me my relaxations after moonrise with my pretty, spoiled Princess.'

Merenkere, still alive in his own tomb, had passed beyond anything but resignation. Even thoughts of Meri-Mekhmet and Ta-Thata, and of his weakling son, were slipping from him now. Sometimes he remembered Osiris and realized in dull amazement that he would soon know if it were true, what men believed: that he would become Osiris when he died. The thought of Osiris was like a golden sun just beyond the threshold of his mind. But the real sun outside was gone. The night had dropped swiftly on the desert. Soon the darkness would be broken when a silver rim of moon rose above the far horizon.

Ta-Thata was staring bleakly from the window of her inner chamber. It seemed a long while since No-Hotep's message had reached her and she had sent Sadhi to find Henmut by the tamarisk. Almost immediately the guard on her apartments had been doubled, and no one allowed in to see her; so she could only guess if the meeting had been successful or if Hekhti's plan had thoroughly misfired. She watched the horizon and thought she could discern a faint milky glow paling the rich dark blue. She rubbed her cold hands together, and heard the heavy tramp of feet in the distant corridor. (Was the guard being changed already?) Then all was still.

Yes, the sky *was* lighter –

A clash of arms outside in the corridor as the guard saluted. Simultaneously the silver rim slid over the horizon. Ta-Thata turned her back on the window, and on her hopes of Hekhti too. She walked slowly into the outer chamber as No-Hotep entered from the opposite side, letting the hangings fall into place behind him.

'I hope you've been thinking of me, Ta-Thata – for State matters are a weary business.'

'You had no need to assume them, if you find them so.' She felt scarcely able to breathe, but sounded quite composed.

'I'm sure you were a very royal baby!' He began to laugh with what she described to herself as a horrible oily charm. 'Do you know, I didn't really want to marry you, it was just an obvious necessity for dynastic reasons? But I'm beginning to find you the most entertaining part of this upheaval. The Priestess mustn't know, of course.'

Ta-Thata dug her fingernails into her palms. *Marry No-Hotep!* She wondered if she was going to be sick. 'I am *Sinuhe's* wife.'

'I'd almost forgotten! Still, he isn't here, and you now share a Chief Royal Tutor with him. I've told the guard we're not to be disturbed. What are you afraid of, Ta-Thata?'

'Of nothing.'

'When I was a boy, in poverty and friendless, I was often terrified. But I learned to live with it, and so will you. I will even teach you to enjoy it, which is an art like any other.

Perhaps you really enjoyed this morning's lesson! Well – the King your father returns tonight by barge to Men-nofer, and your progress will be of some importance to him.'

She gave a small gasp, 'Oh! When may I see him?'

He walked across to her and, as she moved aside, sat down upon the couch, which had feet shaped like gold ox heads and was draped with heavy skins.

'Come here.'

She said again. 'When may I see him – please?'

'You may not, until you learn to respect your tutor. I told you to come here.'

She was staring straight above his head, with wide eyes. She said very slowly, 'But if I do come, you will not –' She dropped her eyes to his face, and smiled at him fully and gaily as though she liked him. 'No – you won't –' And as she spoke Hekhti rose to his full height behind the couch and brought down his clenched fist like a mallet on No-Hotep's head. A gasp issued from the priest's throat as he collapsed sideways on to the pile of skins and lay there in an untidy heap. Ta-Thata looked at Hekhti as though she couldn't believe in his existence.

'Are – are you going to kill him now?'

'Not just yet,' replied Hekhti, grimly surveying his handiwork. 'My Princess, are you all right?'

She said, almost inaudibly, 'Yes. But I thought you had –'

'Had failed? That lies still in the balance! Quick – call your guard. But softly.' He took hold of No-Hotep's wrists to turn him so that he lay stretched out on the couch.

'No, no – They'll kill you! They are soldiers from Shinar.'

'Not this pair! They're strange soldiers – mine. And if you look at what I'm wearing you'll see I'm now an officer in Shinar's army. No – don't start laughing, Princess, you're still in danger! Call your guard.'

She gave him a beaming look and ran to obey, but now that Hekhti was here she could no longer believe in danger. The men quickly gagged No-Hotep and chained his wrists and ankles together, then dumped him unceremoniously behind the couch before returning to their duty.

'Well – he has given them their orders.' Hekhti grinned as Henmut might have done, and sucked at a grazed knuckle. 'We are all three safe enough in here, for he is "not to be disturbed".'

'Oh, Hekhti! How did you get here?' She clutched suddenly at his arm to pull him down where No-Hotep had been sitting so short a time before. 'How did you get through the Palace?'

'I marched in, with a relief guard for your apartments, imploring Re himself – and Khepri! – to let us meet no one on the way who knew me, and counting that a headdress and martial swagger make any man anonymous to people who expect a guard to pass.' He smiled at himself. 'It's the first time I was ever a soldier, and do you know, Princess, that I long to intimidate people?'

'You don't intimidate me!' She pressed his arm fervently, and he looked away.

'The worthy jeweller Tahlevi – er, acquired our dress. My men were provided by Akhtat'nat, the desert commander who is loyal to my Sovereign, my lord. The men of Shinar who were to provide the guard tonight for your apartments now lie bound behind the bushes in the Palace gardens.'

Ta-Thata drew a deep, quivering breath. The words 'my Sovereign, my lord,' seemed to echo from another lifetime. 'Hekhti – is – is the King my father safe? Is he alive, or did No-Hotep lie to me?'

He looked grave. 'We hope that he is, Princess. And if everything goes well – pray to Osiris and all the gods that

it does! – then he will be back with you soon, the Queen
as well. But because we cannot leave your rooms until we
hear, we must be patient. We will have long to wait –
perhaps almost until dawn.'

'And – if it goes badly?' she asked timidly.

'Then we have all lost. But don't fear, death isn't always
terrible.'

'I'm not afraid – not so long as I'm with you. You've
been very, very clever, Hekhti. Did you hide there –'

'Just before No-Hotep came, yes.'

'And Sadhi – is he safe?'

'We must hope so. Henmut managed to see him back
almost to the Palace.' He looked at her white face and said
gently, 'When did you last eat?'

'I – I didn't want food.' She glanced over her shoulder,
but No-Hotep lay out of sight, silent behind the skins.

Hekhti's lips folded in on themselves, as they did when
he repressed his feelings. He said, 'There's fruit and wine
on that table, Princess. May I fetch some – since I am very
hungry now myself?'

They ate and drank, and presently Hekhti added, 'Now
we'll petition Isis and Osiris and all the gods for the safety
and well-being of the King and Queen.' And, afterwards,
'*Now* we'll have a game of draughts.'

'Do you think we should?' asked Ta-Thata anxiously.

'First petition the gods and then put your trust in them!
Come, Princess – nothing will be gained by worrying. I will
wager my set of arms from Shinar that I beat you. While
our friend No-Hotep lies behind this couch he'll be able to
hear me crown a king quicker than he could.'

'Hekhti –'

'Yes, Princess?'

'If it should – I mean, if anything were to – If you had
to – You would kill No-Hotep too?'

'I make you my most solemn promise,' said Hekhti between his teeth. 'Now : put your trust in Khepri who has always been your particular friend, and – since the white draughts are yours – it is your first move, Princess.'

Spears in the Desert

Reuben and Akhtat'nat, with the most slovenly-looking army that Kemi had ever produced – the men were still disguised – marched that night from Imhotep's tomb toward Merenkere's Great Eternal House. As they crossed the desert the moon rode high above them, pitilessly revealing whatever moved upon the plateau, and causing the experienced Army Commander concern over the tasks ahead. He muttered petitions to Sekhmet, She Who Dwells in the Desert Valley, for her help. Cefalu, who had insisted on coming too, and was lying across Reuben's knees high up on Anak's uncomfortable hump, twitched his whiskers thoughtfully. 'This man's need of lion-headed women makes me uneasy – it is irreligious. Can he be fitted to command?'

'He is a good man, Cefalu, devout according to his views.'

Cefalu blew doubtfully through his neat black nostrils.

'Besides,' continued Reuben, 'in spite of the difficulties attending surprise attack, I'm somehow heartened by a sense of light, such as one feels in the desert before dawn. Has the Lord my God yet led me through an adventure with no great ending?'

'True,' conceded Cefalu. 'But to assume great endings in advance is pride.' He closed his triangular lids and a bland expression spread across his small black mask. Anak gave a sardonic grunt.

They were half-way to their goal when a slight figure seemed to rise up out of the ground almost beneath the camel's legs.

'Ah, your scout!' Akhtat'nat gave a low rumble of laughter. 'He who will guide you to the inner chamber, my friend!'

'Welcome, Henmut.' Reuben made Anak kneel, and the boy scrambled up to join him. Then they set off again, behind ragged soldiers who had passed them at Akhtat'-nat's heels and were trudging forward into the night.

Near the Great Eternal House it was very still. The full moon, a silver platter in the sky, cast a hard cold light upon the sand. The sloping causeway shone whiter than by day, and the river itself was blanched still whiter. Hekhti's masterpiece towered over all. Around it, at intervals, small watch fires burned. A few soldiers sat by them, huddled in cloaks, silent or talking in low tones. The young Captain of No-Hotep's garrison had set sentries to patrol an invisible rectangular boundary that enclosed the buildings and stretch of land down to the water, otherwise most of his men were in the labour barracks, fast asleep. All had gone so smoothly that the mechanical tread of the four sentries seemed almost unnecessary. They looked out over a plateau where sand undulated in low dunes that showed a moonlit pattern of white, black, and grey. Only toward the Western Desert a shielding ring of palms and acacias cut off the view.

The watch fires burned lower. Men settled themselves in their cloaks to sleep. The sentries paced heavily through the sand, staring out with tired eyes across the rippling dunes and dreaming of relief. One of them paused a moment. Had he seen a little river of grains cascading downward from a sandy summit? He watched, but nothing further happened. A trick of the moonlight! Easy to imagine things after some time on duty ... He resumed his pacing.

Akhtat'nat's four picked men wriggled their way in between the dunes. They were as naked as the copper knives between their teeth. Crawl forward, stop, forward, stop. One unwary movement, and all would be spoiled –

Soon three of them were in position. They waited, counting silently as they had been instructed, while the fourth man slipped down behind the Temple toward the river bank. In the shadow of a statue plinth he crouched ready. He, too, was counting.

Four sentries moved along their beats. In perfect timing four knives rose behind them as they passed. Four blades flashed in the moonlight with a murderous copper glare.

There was no outcry, just gasping sounds quickly cut off. Then there was a listening silence. Almost immediately four sentries resumed their pacing. Three bodies lay spread-eagled behind the nearest dunes. One other had been rolled into the river. Men still slept peacefully as the watch fires flickered lower. Beyond the palm and acacia grove Akhtat'nat and Reuben, who had been monotonously counting too, looked at each other, stopped counting, and nodded grimly. It was time to put things to the test. All would depend on whose sentries were now waiting there.

Akhtat'nat turned to his men, making a forward gesture of his arm. In small, spread-out companies they moved in across the sand. Reuben, striding in the van, was tensely alert, waiting for the disaster of a sentry's shout. As he crossed the dunes they seemed like an endless sea.

The young Captain, who had been dozing by a fire, came to himself suddenly with a jerk. He looked at the moon, at his sleeping men, and down toward the river where the

King's barge should shortly be arriving. A little beyond him one sentry was pacing steadily, silhouetted against the moonlight. All seemed in order, yet –

He struggled to his feet and yawned. Perhaps one more inspection, although over-zealous, might be –

He plodded through the sand, still half asleep and rubbing at one eye. The sentry was now very near – And Isis! was the man mad, or –? The dunes were full of shadowy, advancing figures. The Captain raised his spear, his mouth opened to shout warning. But the sentry was on him, knife in hand, and he went down, floundering under the man's weight, and died, his bewildered gaze dimming before a stranger's face. Reuben, Akhtat'nat, and their men poured forward into the camp.

The fight was bloody. Soldiers leaped to their feet beside the watch fires and fell before they could draw their weapons. Others were quicker and fought ferociously. Their shouts and yells should have brought help pouring from the labour barracks, But Akhtat'nat had deployed his forces well and sent a party there to hold the entrance. Men fought to get out but were cut down as they came. The sand reddened, the clash of weapons made the night as noisy as before it had been silent. Deep within the royal tomb it was still silent, for the winding stone passages cut off all outer sound. And here again Akhtat'nat's plan succeeded : another small party of picked men had made straight for that entrance too, and held it against anyone who tried to get inside and warn the King's six guards.

Gradually the noise of fighting died. Reuben looked around him and saw only groups of prisoners and quiet forms huddled on the sand. Akhtat'nat was approaching with his right forearm dripping blood. Reuben stared down at his own knife and swayed a little. He, a man of peace and a musician, and for the first time – ! Dark drops were falling off the knife's blade. The sharp moonlight swirled before him suddenly in rags of icy mist.

Over in the palm grove Henmut huddled close by Anak's shoulder.

'All will be well,' pronounced Cefalu. But his tail had shuddered briskly at the screams, and he too pressed, as though absentmindedly, against Anak's woolly hide.

'You planned brilliantly, Akhtat'nat.' Reuben fought back his unusual sensations.

The hardened soldier grinned. He seemed indifferent to his wound. His little eyes raked the scene: the dead, the defeated prisoners, the blocked entrance of the labour barracks. 'Not a bad night's work, so far. Well, my friend, the next part lies with you.'

'It will be delicate.' Reuben's brain reeled at the thought of how delicate it would be.

'Yes. One false step, and they will kill the King. You want me with you?'

'Not a wounded man,' said Reuben sombrely.

'Ah, that!' Akhtat'nat shrugged. 'But it's my spear arm, and I'd be little use in crowded space. No – take the six men that I shall pick you, the best of my captains, and your young guide! See, here is Henmut.'

And there he was, a white and frightened Henmut who looked at something lying in the sand and was promptly sick.

Merenkere the King lay on his back staring at the stone slabs high above his head. He had lain thus a long while, his hands by his side or folded behind his neck. In the outer chamber four priestly guards watched, and two slept. Merenkere stared at the torch smoking in its holder upon the wall. The litter he lay on might well prove his death-bed, but he no longer cared. Let death come. What man could hold to belief in Re or Osiris, in himself as Osiris, while entombed alive? It was an eternity since he had watched Meri-Mekhmet leave.

He turned on one side and raised himself on an elbow. At this angle he couldn't see his guards through the narrow entrance. If he ran out suddenly among them they might kill him, and that would be an end and quickly finished, too.

He had one leg over the litter's side when he heard a very stealthy sound. His heart beat faster, for where – ? Not out there, beyond the entrance. He looked around him. His gaze fastened on the opposite wall. Something inside him gave a sick lurch, for one of the huge granite blocks was moving silently forward –

He crouched, waiting, his breath short, his pulse beating even quicker than before. If this were assassination let it come, but Isis! why this way, when his guards had only to fall on him . . .

A dim light flickered beyond the moving stone. There was a wider space now, and a man came climbing through it, carrying a knife. A man he knew, finger to his lips. The King's long, royal training in self-control made him able to suppress a cry, but his breath came shorter still. Could this be true – or was it delirium?

Akhtat'nat's seven warriors silently followed Reuben through the gap, leaving Henmut on the other side. Something small, black and furry slipped defiantly after them and dropped noiselessly to the ground.

Communication could only be made by gesture. Reuben motioned the King to roll over sideways and crouch down behind the litter. The seven warriors crept into position.

Reuben extinguished the torch and gave a loud, deliberate groan. The guards' chatter ceased. A nervous silence reigned.

The King, waiting in the dark, felt a small furry body press itself against him as though to say, 'Don't worry, I am here.'

The guards had realized that the inner chamber's light was out. What had gone wrong? Was the King – There was a sound of hesitant argument, then a torch flared at the entrance. The two first-comers were spitted as they came, and gave two wild screams of agony. The four other guards broke in terror, and ran, crying aloud that something supernatural was with the King. They ran as though Sekhmet herself pursued them, and as though all Kemi's outraged gods, guardians of that King whom they had profaned by their rebellion, were after them. They died somewhere between the outer chamber and the outer world, caught by two bands of men whose weapons came together on them like Sekhmet's teeth.

In the outer chamber itself Reuben picked up the fallen torch and returned to the King. Merenkere had pulled himself up onto the litter again, and was sitting with the backs of his hands pressed against his eyes.

'The Queen? The Princess?' he whispered; and then, 'My – son?'

'My lord the King, we believe them safe.'

There was little room for obeisance, and besides, the King wasn't looking. Reuben gazed about him at the dreadful stone chamber where his Sovereign had been so long entombed, and back again at the younger man's bowed form.

He stepped forward and put an arm comfortingly around Merenkere's shoulders. 'If all has gone to plan, the worst is now over. Forgive me, O Sovereign, my lord, for I should prostrate myself –'

'It is I, Reuben,' said the King in a hoarse and barely audible whisper, 'it is I who am prostrate –'

Return

The Royal Barge slid upstream just before dawn. There
was no sound except the rustle of waterbirds in the reeds
and the splash of the great oars. Merenkere sat amidships,
wrapped in a cloak of leopard skin. The sensation of out-
door air flowing past his face was almost unbelievable.
Now and then he wetted his lips, and looked about him
as though in a daze. Reuben, standing with Akhtat'nat
behind the Sovereign's chair and covertly regarding him,
wondered at his seeming resilience and hoped his frail
physique wouldn't suffer permanently from his ordeal.

A dark line of Men-nofer's buildings rose up against the
paling sky. 'Reuben, how many of No-Hotep's men will
await us on the quay?'

'O Sovereign, my lord, we're hoping that my lord the
King's return was planned at this time so he might pass
unnoticed through the city – in which case the soldiers
from that labour barracks might have been your Majesty's
sole guards.' Reuben glanced around him at the barge's
deck which was crowded with Akhtat'nat's men now kilted
and rearmed from the supplies of No-Hotep's garrison. His
lips curled. 'If more soldiers are sent, they will find
unexpected welcome.'

'Akhtat'nat.'

'My lord the King?'

'How many of your men were left to guard the prisoners
and wounded?'

'A dozen, O Sovereign, my lord.' Akhtat'nat smiled a grim smile. 'There were few left to guard – and they easily contained within the barracks.'

'When all is finished here, send back a physician.'

'O my Sovereign! For traitors? What mercy would those men have shown my lord the King?'

'It's not their mercy that's in question, but my Majesty's.'

Akhtat'nat made a despairing face at Reuben. He disapproved of sentiment toward prospective regicides. A nest of scorpions that needed cleaning out!

The King turned and looked at him, a faint smile curving his mouth. 'My good Akhtat'nat, to whom my Majesty owes so much – if the thoughts that are running in your head are as my Majesty suspects, dismiss them fast.'

'O Sovereign, my lord, they are dismissed,' replied Akhtat'nat meekly. For the moment, he added to himself. He felt paternal toward his King, god or no, and decided that in matters of clemency he required some guidance.

It was too early for much traffic on the waterways, and the great barge floated through a silent city. The King drew deep breaths of its particular smell of dung and dirt mixed with flower fragrance from wealthy people's gardens. There was no sinister reception party at the quayside, so the Sovereign's return to his capital was a simple matter of a litter escorted quickly through the streets by a force of men indistinguishable from those who held the Palace.

As the White Walls rose before them Reuben felt his stomach turn. His suspense reminded him of how he felt when he had strode across the sand toward the Great Eternal House, expecting to hear a sentry's challenge. *Surely* Hekhti had succeeded? – or No-Hotep, forewarned that action was afoot, would have had men waiting on the waterfront. *Or* – was ambush still to come? But the Palace fell back into the rightful Ruler's hands with little struggle and no outcry. Almost in silence No-Hotep's gains slid from him as two by two the guards were reached and over- powered and replaced by Akhtat'nat's men. Only in the long corridor, leading to where the Royal Bodyguard was still imprisoned, was there resistance which was quickly dealt with – and even there the clash of arms wasn't enough to rouse the Palace.

Merenkere glanced in the direction of the fighting, but his expression was remote, and all he said to Reuben was, 'The Queen?'

'O Sovereign, my lord, if your Majesty will deign to wait here –'

'No. My Majesty comes too.' The King started forward along an as yet unreconnoitred corridor. Reuben and Akhtat'nat almost ran to keep up with him, and Reuben committed sacrilege by clutching at his arm.

'My lord, my lord, it isn't safe!'

'If it's safe for the Queen, it's safe enough for –' Meren- kere quickened his pace. Then Akhtat'nat did a most daring thing. He seized his Sovereign – Kemi's great High Priest and God – by the shoulders to hold him back.

'Your Majesty : no.'

'*No?*' said the King, on a note of pure astonishment. 'Do you understand what you have said? Do you wish, man, to –'

'Die I will, your Majesty, if necessary –' Akhtat'nat still held the King, and even shook him slightly by mistake – 'but allow my Sovereign to go first down these corridors till they are clear of traitors, I will not!'

The King tried twice to speak, then turned in Akhtat'- nat's grip. His glare was royal, but the soldier had faced spears at closer quarters in his time. 'Your Majesty may have me killed later.'

Suddenly Merenkere gave his extremely sweet smile.

'You're a brave man, Akhtat'nat! But my Majesty never doubted it. There –' he freed himself from his soldier's grasp. 'Take your men and lead the way.' He stepped aside.

The Queen's guards were waiting for their dawn relief. When it came it was not quite what they had expected. They were disarmed and flung to the ground, and stared up in horrified amazement as their Sovereign passed. Beyond the hangings Tiya, the Queen's old nurse, came forward like a lioness aroused. She had been sitting with the sleepless Meri-Mekhmet all night, trying to calm her fears about Ta-Thata. The King's entrance was so swift and unexpected that she failed to recognize him. Then she gave an involuntary squeak, and flung herself prostrate to the floor.

'Oh, who – What is it *now?*' cried Meri-Mekhmet's voice tremulously from the inner room. Merenkere didn't reply. He simply stepped over Tiya's recumbent form, parted the second hangings, walked into Meri-Mekhmet's arms, and held her very close.

The Royal Heir had spent the night alone in his father's apartments. Ever since No-Hotep had left him there on the previous evening, Sinuhe's state had bordered on hysteria. He had sobbed out that it was the last place his father would expect to find him. In vain – the priest had merely raised his eyebrows, and replied, 'All customs have a beginning.' Then he had shown Sinuhe a goblet and the offering wine that he should present to Merenkere when the King arrived, and had forbidden the boy to drink any himself, since it was sacred to the gods.

The night had seemed endless. Up and down Sinuhe had paced, realizing that the torture of this meeting would be worse than anything that had yet happened. Towards dawn he lay in tears on the royal couch. He was sorry for himself, but even sorrier about the past and future that had been set in train by his ambition. Lately his remorse had steadily increased, along with terror. He now understood that Merenkere's affection had been the most stable thing in his own life, and without a father's support he himself was nothing. He thought shrinkingly of Meri-Mekhmet and Ta-Thata, and wondered what look he would see in the King's eyes when he came. He put his hands over his face, and saw blackness. His self-contempt wouldn't go away. He would have to live with it for ever.

It was all No-Hotep's fault, he tried to tell himself. If he was too clever for Father, how could I have understood him?

You had more opportunities to know, his self replied. But you thought only of glory, and the humbling of your sister.

I didn't want anything to happen, truly.

Truly?

O be quiet, he counselled himself desperately. I'm too weak . . . I don't want Father to die. I want him here, now. I can't bear him to come.

The tension was frightful. He raised his head, and from the colour of the sky saw that dawn had come. The only sound close at hand was the changing of the guard outside the apartments, and the twitter of a waking bird. Sinuhe was heavy-headed and dry-mouthed. He longed for water, but dared summon no one, in case a sign of wakefulness from him brought on the encounter that he dreaded. His gaze fell on the wine jar placed ready for the King. Water was what he wanted, but wine at least would moisten his dry lips – and a little might help him in this meeting with his father. He remembered that No-Hotep had forbidden him to touch it, and that in doing so he would incur the displeasure of the gods. But at that moment he would almost have welcomed their displeasure: any punishment might serve to ease his sense of guilt about the past.

It was the first time that Sinuhe had ever dared to disobey No-Hotep. He poured some wine shakily into the goblet. It was Delta wine, the best – pale and sparkling, with a sweet, raisiny scent. The night's chill had enhanced its flavour. When he had drunk, he wanted more, and readily poured out an entire goblet. After all, there was plenty for the King . . .

Sinuhe felt better suddenly, all his ugly thoughts dispelled. His vision cleared and he saw everything bright and clean and as though it stood before his astonished sight for the first time. Time itself seemed to include eternity, and nothing was really bad. It was all a dream, and somewhere in a cool and haunting garden was the warm reality he had looked for in self-glory and never known. The encounter with the King lost its terrors. Beyond, in the green distance, was a place where his father beckoned to him.

He gave a little gasp, and groped his way back toward the bed. Sleep was where he would find . . .

The goblet fell from his hand, rolled across the floor, and struck a chair. A splintering sound broke the heavy silence.

'The one unlooked-for ending,' said Hekhti sombrely. 'O Sovereign, my lord, your servant feels himself responsible.'

They stood now in the King's apartments. With the Queen and Ta-Thata they looked down at the body of Merenkere's only son. Sinuhe lay with his head turned slightly sideways, a faint smile upon his lips. Death lent his features stronger resemblance to his father's than they had ever held in life. The King put his hand gently on his son's, which was still warm. If they had come a little earlier –

Yet they hadn't known where they would find Sinuhe.

Meri-Mekhmet was wishing that her sadness for her husband and stepson weren't mixed with relief. She shifted her gaze to her daughter, and guessed that Ta-Thata, whose lips were pale and quivering, shared her feelings.

'This wasn't humanly foreseeable,' said the King. 'You are not responsible, Hekhti. I believe the wine was meant for my Majesty. See, there's only the one goblet, and why was my son left in here alone all night – just to greet me?' His fingers moved on the warm hand. 'Parricide,' he said. 'How hideous. And how clever. Who would ever have blamed No-Hotep for turning such a degenerate from the Throne?'

'Father, Sinuhe would never have given it to you knowingly!'

'No.' The King smiled mournfully. 'I do not think he would. I hope he didn't guess what he was drinking . . . He would have been very much afraid to see me . . .'

'He drank for courage, that was all!' Meri-Mekhmet put her arms around her husband.

'Let us hope so. And yet – What a thing for us always to remember. Poor child.' Now he could only think of Sinuhe as the frail child who had needed much protection when he was small, who had never caught up, in moral growth, with those about him.

'Your Majesty is not responsible, either.' It was daring of Hekhti to voice the words, but he had read his Sovereign's mind.

'No – No, perhaps not. So often, when humans try to forestall and foresee, the gods step in unannounced. And yet – Perhaps it's for the first time *I* now think myself a god, and know I should have prevented this.' He gave a thin, bitter smile, and bent to kiss Sinuhe's forehead. 'Send for the High Priests of Ptah and Sekhmet – if they still live – that they may watch by my son.'

The Restoration of Ma'at

It was still early when a messenger carrying Tahlevi's ring summoned the Prince of Shinar to the Palace, where he found Reuben waiting for him with Tahlevi outside the Throne Room.

'The Prince of Canaan, your Highness, who has the interests of Kemi very much at heart.'

'Ah yes.' Prince Kalda gave Reuben the glance of one who expects obeisance. 'You have dealt with that wicked man No-Hotep?'

'He is imprisoned, your Highness.' Reuben smiled.

'And the Princess Ta-Thata?'

'Awaits your Highness in the Throne Room.'

The Prince's chest expanded with the force of his emotion. He deserved much, and here it was! Yet he still paused. 'And my sister – Beltethazar?'

A faint shadow appeared on Tahlevi's blandly smiling features. 'Your Highness, she has disappeared.'

'Then look for her! She will be dangerous.'

'We're looking hard, your Highness, and –'

But Prince Kalda was already striding into the Throne Room. He wasted no time on admiring the exquisite designs of bee, plant and vulture, or the carved, delicate columns. He made straight for the two thrones at the room's far end, then halted, rocking slightly on his heels. He stared. A faint moan came from between his lips.

Ta-Thata was there, sitting on her mother's throne. She wore white linen, and Meri-Mekhmet's coronet of gold, carnelian, and lapis on her dark hair. She sat still and royally like a statue. But she was not alone.

King Merenkere's ordeal had left him pale and drawn, and his son's death had lent an alien grimness to his features. To Prince Kalda's horrified gaze he looked appallingly, obtrusively, threateningly Royal, while the Crook and Flail in his crossed hands expressed his attributes of Ruler-ship and Justice in the exact way they were meant to do. Young Kalda couldn't move nor speak. He could only stare at the uraeus above the King's forehead, at the Double Crown, at the loyal and now released Vizier standing behind the Sovereign; and then back again at those steady eyes, with their piercing and accusing gaze.

It was unheard-of for a young man in audience with Kemi's King to stand upright. Akhtat'nat and another officer stepped forward, and took Prince Kalda by the shoulders, and threw him to the ground in the correct position. Above his head he heard the Sovereign's titles called by a trumpeter; and, in the following great silence, the King's voice, tired and low, but vibrant with authority, 'Akhtat'nat – send to the Prince of Shinar's tents this message : let the men of Shinar lay down their arms and surrender them-selves to my Majesty without delay – lest their Prince be impaled outside the Palace gates before Re the Sun stands at his highest in the sky.'

'My Sovereign, my lord is instantly obeyed.'

'Wait, Akhtat'nat. If the Princess Beltethazar is in the desert camp, she shall be handed over.' The King rose, and the shadow of Crook and Flail seemed to grow enormous, reaching out to touch the Prince's shrinking form. 'Kalda, you have visited our Kingdom with lies, violence, and treachery. You planned to steal the Throne and the Royal

Heiress. You conspired with our enemies, and encompassed the death of the Royal Heir.'

At these last words Prince Kalda raised his head to utter a moan of dissent.

'Be silent,' said the King, on a thin note. His face was grey, and his hands trembled faintly from exhaustion, but he sounded royal as ever. 'Were you not Shinar's son, you should be killed. *Though* you're his son, you should be killed. But my Majesty thinks you a fool – the tool of other people. Your father Shinar will be delighted to hear of his son's exploits – if he doesn't know of them already?'

'O Sovereign, my lord – no!'

'It is well, then. Though entirely unbelievable! If he wants you back we will ransom you for half his kingdom. My Majesty would think him wise to leave you in one of Kemi's gaols for a long while. Perhaps even a fool will learn from humiliation and imprisonment. Remove him.'

Prince Kalda was seized by the heels and dragged backward by two of Akhtat'nat's muscular warriors. As the Throne Room sped away before his eyes the King and Ta-Thata looked smaller and smaller at the other end of it, until at last they merged into a haze of silver and gold and lapis, and bees and plants and other symbols that he had hoped to make his own.

So the forces of darkness that had temporarily invaded the Palace were defeated – or so it seemed; and the scribes recorded that this had been achieved 'by the King's Understanding and his Authoritative Utterance'.

'Though I feel myself a frail figure for such weighty and oblique pronouncements,' murmured the King to his Great Royal Wife, as they sat later in their daughter's apartments, 'which bear little relation to the truth. Reuben,

Akhtat'nat, Hekhti, Tahlevi, Henmut, Sadhi – and Cefalu!
And others – these were the true restorers of Ma'at. What
did the King do?'

Meri-Mekhmet took his hand. 'The King is you. It was
for Re, and for what *you* are, Merenkere, that they risked
so much. It's strange – our people may never know what
happened in the Palace!'

Merenkere gazed across at his daughter, who was standing with Hekhti and Sadhi by the indoor pool. Su-Shunut
and Keta kneeled beside them on the ground. 'Ta-Thata
will make Kemi a great queen. I will choose her tutors,
and her husband, more carefully than –' He stopped, and
sighed.

Ta-Thata hadn't heard what they were saying. She was
holding the small model barque that Sinuhe had nearly
spoiled. It had been restored in Tahlevi's workshop, and
she had decked it once more with flowers. Sadhi stroked
the bright enamelling with careful fingers. Once, he too
might have wished to destroy it. He smiled up at Hekhti,
who smiled gravely back. Ta-Thata's reflection leaned toward her in the pool as she placed the barque tenderly
upon the water. The protective goddesses, the small embalmed prone figure, the Canopic jars and wreaths of
cornflower and willow, floated across the still water as
though on the waters of the underworld.

'You're sailing it for Sinuhe, Princess?'

'You understand everything.' She watched the barque
on its smooth passage. 'Poor Sinuhe! I never thought
when I played with it last that next time I should be sailing
it for him.'

Hekhti sighed. He was not only very tired, but something incomprehensible weighed on his spirits. Perhaps
Ma'at was restored for the Two Lands, and yet inside him
was this sensation of being out of true.

'Hekhti? You're sad. You mustn't feel responsible for Sinuhe.'

Hekhti walked around the pool, Sadhi trotting at his heels, and scooped the barque out of the water. He held it in his hands so that light fell on one side and darkness on the other.

'You see this, Princess? Here are all men – half darkness and half light.' He turned the barque gently. 'Now one, now the other. The priests say that even shadows are a part of our own selves. In Sinuhe the darkness was often upper-most – and he was powerless against himself. He needed more help than others. His Majesty was too busy – but I, may the gods forgive me, disliked the Royal Heir.' He placed the barque once more upon the water. 'In omission, perhaps I'm more responsible than you would like to think.'

'You helped Sadhi. You cannot help everyone !'

'What a natural comforter you are, Princess.' He looked at her hard, and she reddened.

'Come and visit Khepri with me, Hekhti !' she said on impulse. 'We'll take Sadhi too, and leave Keta and Su-Shu-nut to wait upon their Majesties.'

In the sanctuary all looked as it had when Ta-Thata last met Hekhti there. Khepri lay carven and immense on his great block of alabaster. There was quiet, and a smell of incense.

'How can I explain to Sadhi that Khepri is called He Who Becomes the Rising Sun?' Ta-Thata guided Sadhi's hand to Khepri's nose, and made him pat it.

'There ! That wasn't irreverent, was it?'

Hekhti was staring into the burnished copper that hung upon the wall.

'Hekhti !'

'Princess ? Ah – Perhaps it was – Khepri's priests would say so, I don't know . . .'

'Did you see something in the copper ?' she asked insistently. 'Last time you saw the King's crown above my head, and I did, too. Although it was real, yet it was a true seeing. *Hekhti ?*'

He stared heavily at her. She was holding Sadhi by the hand, and Hekhti thought she had matured during the terror of the last days, and looked as lovely as Meri-Mekhmet. 'And if I did see anything just now, Princess,' he said slowly, 'it was not for you. No –' he corrected himself, 'it could be generally for everyone, besides myself.'

She gazed at him very hard, but saw his determination to say nothing more. 'What of Sadhi ?' she asked. 'What do you think could happen for Sadhi ?'

'Ah – Sadhi.' He took his patient's other hand, to examine it thoughtfully. 'He has good hands for a physician – a healer's hands. He would do well to follow me. But he couldn't acquire the knowledge unless he can be taught to hear and speak. Which is beyond my skill, or any man's.'

'We'll ask Khepri for help – He Who Becomes the Rising Sun!'

'The bright and morning star –'

'Is that another of his names ? I didn't know it.'

Hekhti shook his head. The look of trouble was back upon his face. 'Sadhi is my son now, as much as Reuben's. I would give anything to cure him fully. Now I leave him with you, Princess, for my work awaits me.'

'Do you know, Hekhti – ' he turned back to her – 'you're so wise! You would make a better ruler of the Two Lands than I shall. I wish they would marry me to you !'

He stared at her, startled. Her face was lit with laughter. She half meant her words, yet her feeling was unconsciously a child's love for its father. He caught his breath, and said

gently, 'That would never do – Princess.' He made formal
obeisance, and went.

Meanwhile, some way beyond the Palace, Cefalu was
sitting by a small artificial lake. He had come there to see
justice done. Others might be squeamish, but Cefalu was
not. King of all Waterfront Cats in Men-nofer as he was
since the battle with Khnum-Put, and a heavy fighter in
old days, he felt the ruthless laws of nature to be good and
true. Rumour had reached him via all sorts of obsequious
Palace cats that something was to be seen here this day.
So he sat and waited with an approving heart.

'I don't know why we're being honoured by a *cat*,' said
Hikupptah, King of the great Royal Crocodiles which lived
in the lake. He was very old and grand, and had done much
service for the King's grandfather and great-grandfather,
swallowing criminals every day. He had been named after
the city of Men-nofer itself, which men called Hikupptah,
or : House of the Ka of Ptah; and he felt all the glory and
responsibility of such a name.

'Yes – why is that cat sitting about, as though waiting
for something? There's little to see, these days.' His huge
length lay just below the surface. Only his nostrils, top
of his head, and hard, unwinking eyes showed where he
was. 'Our present Lord of Diadems is a wise man, and I
honour him as only a crocodile can, but he has one fault :
clemency. Clemency is no good. It doesn't feed crocodiles.
I've heard the waterfront cats talking, and they jeer as they
pass along the bank, saying, "There's no use for Hikupptah
any more, they ought to make him into something.
Hikupptah is getting soft." Soft I am not, but underfed I am.'
And he opened his ugly jaws and gnashed his teeth. 'When
the criminals came hurtling through the air, screaming as
they came, they gave me quite an appetite.'

'Wait,' said his mate, rubbing up alongside him in stealthy excitement. 'There's a sort of small procession coming!'

'Soldiers, commanded by – Akhtat'nat! I recognize him, a good tough commander. And someone bound. My dear mate, something tells me that the King is ignorant of – Come along.' He swam closer to the bank, fending off his descendants with his tail.

No-Hotep stood bound at the water's edge, and looked downward at his terrible approaching fate. This guardian of the Great House would swallow him up, and there would be an end of all his bright plans; his power, his Princess, his love for Beltethazar. Many and horrible faults he had, but he was brave. He managed to quell the shaking of his knees, though he felt cold all over with the chill of death. Now Hikupptah was just below him, cruising gently, and looking up at him with royal eyes full of ancient wisdom.

'If you want to say anything, say it now,' said Akhtat'nat.

No-Hotep could barely speak, but he managed, 'You've no right! The King himself hasn't yet condemned me. And he's discontinued this fearful end. He will punish you, when he finds out.'

'My shoulders are broad enough for punishment. What mercy did you show those children in the Great Eternal House? You caused the Royal Heir's death –'

'*He* wasn't meant to drink.'

'No – it was for our Sovereign, our lord, which is worse. Many good men are dead because of you. Will you jump, or shall we throw you?'

'Wait but a –'

'There's no escape,' said Akhtat'nat; but he waited.

No-Hotep looked toward the sun. All his life he had been looking away from it, or sideways. Darkness and Set had ruled his life, and now it was too late. When his heart was weighed against a feather in the Judgement, it must go badly with him. Yet he had been Set's priest, according to his lights, and perhaps Set would stand his friend. Briefly he stared about him, at the radiant daylight, and his heart was swamped with sorrow that he hadn't been a priest of Ptah, instead. He thought of the Royal Heir, whose affection he had gained and then misused – whom he had brought to death with not even one last look at the great sun.

'Free my legs,' he said almost soundlessly. 'I will jump.'

Akhtat'nat looked at the young man's face. No-Hotep was a despicable criminal; yet the fierce soldier's heart was touched by some sign of misery he saw there, different from the craven fear that might have been expected.

'Why, you're a brave fellow,' he said more kindly, 'whatever you have done. And it's true the King hates all unnecessary suffering –'

No-Hotep didn't seem to hear. He was gazing about him as one who sees the world for the first time. Akhtat'nat leaned across and struck him on the back of his head, and No-Hotep slumped unconscious in his bonds.

Hikupptah opened wider his great jaws.

Cefalu watched until he was sure that justice had been done. Then he unfurled his tail and walked delicately away.

'There was a lot of good somewhere in that young man,' said Hikupptah later to his mate. 'I can always tell. Some criminals are very sour, you could say their criminality was pervasive. A pity he used his dark side instead of his light. Still, it has not been wasted. I can feel he has done *me* good – right down to the bottom of my most majestic tail.'

The Cold Cup of Shinar

Hekhti returned to his own apartments. He was still haunted by a sense of uneasiness and discord. Unlike his great predecessor Imhotep he was neither Chief Ritualist nor Lector Priest; nevertheless, he was learned in the wisdom and secret doctrines that were the core of priestly teachings. The King's 'Authoritative Utterance' was a mere form of words. Once Ma'at had been upset by evil, restoration could only be confirmed through an appropriate act – a magic rite, sacrifice, or advent of a new king. Yet it was the coming king, the young heir, who had died. Even if this could be regarded as a sacrifice, it was an ambiguous one. Hekhti sensed that something more was required. And what he felt had been strangely enforced by the vision in the copper mirror.

He sat down upon his bed, and was overwhelmed by deep and terrible depression, such as he hadn't felt since Tak-te's daughter met her death. Fear seized him, as he wondered if this meant that Ta-Thata was still threatened. How his head ached, after the strains of the last few days! He poured himself some fruit juice from the jug that Amrat had left beside his bed, and drank a little. It was refreshing, and when he looked up everything seemed slightly brighter than before. Brightest of all was the look of triumph on Beltethazar's face. She stood opposite him, by the passage entrance, and smiled, and said, 'Quick or slow, it's always certain in effect! You've drunk little, but

you've drunk enough. Don't think you'll escape, though
you may live a short while yet.'

Hekhti looked from her to the jug of innocent-seeming
golden liquid. 'So – habit dull's a man's wits. Amrat has
always kept fruit juice by my bed.'

'Yes. The priest No –' her voice faltered – 'We learned
all the Palace habits, he and I.'

'Everyone has been searching for you,' he said normally.
At that time the only difference he could feel was the
strange brightness of vision. He couldn't yet realize the
shocking truth – three mouthfuls of a golden drink, and he
would die.

'People are so stupid! No one thought of looking between
your room and the gardens.'

Hekhti might not have heard her. He was still staring at
the jug, so little emptied.

'Shall I tell you how I saved myself?'

'I do not care. I care only that you should now be –'

He stood. There was a faint feeling of numbness in his
legs. Her hand touched his shoulder, pushing him back.

'Peace, my friend! Don't be so anxious – I've no wish
to live. No-Hotep will die, if he's not already dead. All
through you! Even he failed to understand what an enemy
he had raised up against us. I only call you "friend" because
we go into the dark together.' She raised the jug and refilled
the goblet to the brim, talking incessantly. 'Last night I
slept little, and at dawn looked from my window and saw
the King's return. Intuition told me that those soldiers
weren't No-Hotep's men. When I slipped down the corridor
to warn him, and saw those on duty outside Ta-Thata's
apartments, I knew we'd been tricked – for her guards last
night were to be my brother's men, and these had no look
of Shinar. If I'd gone there earlier –' Her fingers clenched

on the goblet. 'But it was too late, the King's men were already in the Palace! Or No-Hotep would still have won . . .'

She smiled fiercely at Hekhti, and drained the goblet. The swift brightness of vision came to her as she walked from him down the hidden passage. Outside, in the gardens, where the sun shone strongly on trees and flowers, she collapsed.

Hekhti had moved as though to follow her, but the creeping numbness was in his legs, and he sat again, letting the truth flood him till there was no room for disbelief. There was indeed little time left. Great physician though he was, he knew no antidote to this strange poison. He felt no anger against Beltethazar. It was as though somewhere a balance had had to be adjusted, and he must pay for it. He tried to clap his hands, but his fingers were clumsy, and now for the first time he felt afraid – would no one hear? But Amrat came hastily, pleased to see him there; and then, seeing his unusual pallor, quickly alarmed.

'The juice – is poisoned. Beltethazar – Let no one drink from standing jugs, or wine –' Hekhti gasped. He felt ill. 'Find – Princess Ta-Thata . . . she was in Khepri's – sanctuary. Ask her – come to – me, here.'

'Most noble Hekhti – poison! What antidote – ?' The boy dithered, terrified.

'None. There *is* – none. Fetch her. Warn –' Hekhti gasped again, and lowered himself backward on to the bed. He could feel the tingling in his arms that foretold numbness. '*Hurry* . . . above all, warn – the King!'

Amrat fled. It seemed a long while before she came. He saw her leaning over him, and the strange brightness of vision gave her a likeness to a goddess – to Hathor. His hands were stiff, his legs already paralysed, but, between gasps, he could still speak.

'Ta-Thata ... Princess. I'm sorry – you should – see me – die ...'

'Not Princess.' She clutched his hand. He could barely sense her touch, although he could feel her tears falling on his face.

He shut his eyes, and knew she was both herself and Tak-te's daughter.

'Hekhti – don't – don't die! We can't – *I cannot* – do without you –'

'But you must – it's necessary.' His mind, reeling under the gigantic pressure of eternity, sought pathetically for concepts, and words, 'All men – not just ... the King ... can become – Osiris.' He was conscious of despair. So little time, how could he tell what he knew, what he saw? 'Necessary –' he began again. Then, leaning closer, she thought he murmured, 'Sacri –' or was it 'Sadhi'? His face looked so still that she thought he had already died, till suddenly he said quite strongly, 'Take Sadhi to Imhotep's tomb and he –' Hekhti opened his eyes. They looked clear, but his mind seemed to be wandering. 'So very ... far ahead. Yet already – there. Outside ... outside time.'

'Oh, dearest Hekhti!' She leaned still closer, crying violently.

'The bright – and morning –' he said in a voice that barely whispered. Her lips touched his forehead, but he couldn't feel them. She heard a sound in his throat and his head arched backward, then tilted sideways.

The King arrived with Reuben just as Hekhti – his face pressed tight against Ta-Thata's shoulder – died.

The tragedy seemed unbelievable, when the evil shadowing the Two Lands had apparently subsided. It was as though Apep, having given up the Sun, had swallowed it again.

Ta-Thata was inconsolable. She wandered from one end of the Palace to the other, with Sadhi trailing behind her, sad and thin. He, too, pined for Hekhti. Sometimes they held hands and looked at each other, and their eyes filled with tears. Even when Ta-Thata sought comfort in Khepri's sanctuary, she could no longer find it. Huge and black and old, he kept his sphinx-like silence.

'When I was small, I thought you answered me,' she told him, and went away, restlessly. The Palace seemed very empty. She even missed Sinuhe's self-important chatter, and the liveliness of his tormenting presence.

'Everyone is gone,' she told Sadhi, who looked at her with uncomprehending eyes. She didn't know how to tap out what she meant upon his hand, and was too listless to try. 'I would have No-Hotep back, if I could have the others too.' She gave the little funeral barque to Henmut. When she had sailed it for Sinuhe, Hekhti had stood beside her – she couldn't bring herself to sail it now for him.

Thamar was very troubled by the children's misery, and apprehensive for her son. She, too, felt the magnitude of the disaster. With Phut she had moved back into the Palace, and she yearned for Reuben to bring in Joshu and the others from the desert. But her husband was closeted with the Sovereign and his Vizier, and seemed to have put thoughts of his family upon one side. The revolt was over, yet No-Hotep's ruthless stamping out of his opponents had left many gaps at Court, where new men had to be hurriedly initiated into high office, with all the stately ritual of tradition.

'What fearful things that misguided young man No-Hotep caused by his ambition!' she said to Su-Shunut and Keta, as they sat together in the gardens while Sadhi and Ta-Thata continued their restless wandering. 'Misguided' was as bad a term as Thamar could bring herself to use about anyone. 'And yet I'm almost sorry for him – if it weren't for Hekhti!' She sighed. 'Surely No-Hotep's death by crocodile is endless death, according to beliefs in Kemi? He couldn't be embalmed – where then is his chance of eternal life?'

Keta shook her head. 'I can't tell, Princess. But the Judgement would have been a dreadful thing for him, anyway, after what he did.' She looked round her, nervously, almost as though the dead priest's Ka might be watching her. A little snake slid across the grass. Keta hurriedly drew back her feet. 'The Ka can take up residence in one!' she whispered, and sighed with relief when the little snake wriggled into a hole.

'*I* shall take care to have myself embalmed,' announced Su-Shunut; then winced, thinking of Ket, her father, who had been killed in the revolt. 'But we don't really know all that the priests and High Priests truly believe, they've secret wisdom we don't have, and power too.'

'Yet *they* take good care to build themselves mastabas while they're still alive! Our Sovereign, our lord says that since his ordeal in the Great Eternal House he'll not rest there himself, but have a mastaba just like theirs – an ordinary plain white tomb.'

'The High Priests would object, and –' Su-Shunut was interrupted by Sadhi's arrival with Ta-Thata, who kneeled quickly on the ground before they could rise at her approach.

'You speak of tombs, Princess? Isn't that an omen? Look!' She held out her cupped hands. In them rested a small onyx figure, beautifully carved. 'Tahlevi gave it to me. Isn't he kind?'

'It is Hekhti!' exclaimed Thamar. 'Although –'

'Although not quite Hekhti. Yet I – and Tahlevi! – have seen him with just that expression of serene wisdom –

but as if he might laugh too.' She turned the figure round in her hands, and looked at it lovingly. 'Don't you know who it is? Imhotep.'

'I wonder where Tahlevi found it?' pondered Thamar. Statues of Kemi's great men were usually placed in their tombs.

'I don't know, but I shall put it in Hekhti's mastaba, so that Imhotep may watch over him – if I can bear to part with it. The King my father is to build him a fine one, close to Tak-te's and his daughter's. I can't believe Hekhti's dead.' She looked shyly at Thamar. 'When he was dying he kept talking of Osiris. Our country people believe that Osiris dwells in the corn – when he's trodden by the oxen, they call him "struck", but he still sprouts anew from the turned earth.'

'Why was it an omen, to speak of tombs, Princess?' asked Keta.

'Because when – when Hekhti – He told me to take Sadhi to Imhotep's tomb.' She raised her large brown eyes, which were so like Meri-Mekhmet's, and looked earnestly at Thamar. 'I couldn't bear to think of it before! Now I think we should ask the Prince of Canaan if he'll take Sadhi there – tonight.'

Reuben was with the Lord of the Two Lands, whose gruelling experiences and sorrows had left him frail but indomitable, and whose remarkable eyes could still flash in a way to shake men as Akhtat'nat was shaken now.

'Is my Majesty a child, that my Majesty's rulings against unnecessary suffering should be disobeyed? Who is he who gives judgement in the Two Lands – my Majesty, or Akhtat'nat?'

Akhtat'nat, from his position face downward on the floor, longed to answer, 'It *was* No-Hotep,' but replied with wise humility, 'It is my Sovereign, my lord – may he always be obeyed.'

Reuben hid a smile. How would the King deal with one to whom he owed so much, yet who had flouted him?

Merenkere bit his lip, aware that his soldier had avoided answering his first question. His own personal and savage loathing of No-Hotep had made him long to see the priest thrown to crocodiles – which was one reason why he would have forbidden it. By dealing promptly with the traitor, Akhtat'nat had paternally protected the child within the Sovereign. A child who had brought the Two Lands to the verge of disaster by too gentle rule. Kemi expected cruel treatment for its criminals, and would consider No-Hotep's ugly death a just reward.

'You knew my Majesty wouldn't countenance this thing?'

'O Sovereign, my lord, it's as your Majesty says.'

Akhtat'nat's meekness was like a goad.

Merenkere said very quietly, 'For your part in saving the Throne my Majesty appoints you to command over all my Majesty's armies. For on *that* score the Great House is eternally grateful to you, Akhtat'nat. This new command is yours in twelve moons' time. You may rise.'

Akhtat'nat kissed the King's feet, and rose, beaming.

'Those twelve moons you will spend under a different name in the hardest of hard labour on Monthly and Hourly Service for the priests of On. Now – you may go.'

Akhtat'nat blinked. He saluted after Kemi's fashion, then backed toward the entrance.

Merenkere grinned. 'It's a measure of my Majesty's trust in you that after your hard labour the Army will still be given to your charge – and my Majesty will look forward to your return, and not expect to be dethroned.'

'O Sovereign, my lord, your servant is deeply thankful.

Above all, thankful that your Majesty now knows whom he may trust. In the Temple of On the memory of the Sovereign's clemency will be as the sun's rays.'

'How was that last remark meant, Reuben?' asked the King, when Akhtat'nat had gone.

'O Sovereign, my lord, your servant could not say.'

'My Majesty feared so! Akhtat'nat thinks I'm Sadhi's age. Now – has my Court Musician nothing to ask of me?'

'Nothing, O Sovereign, my lord, except – may I now bring my other children to the Palace?'

'And Benoni! But the Palace is no happy place just now. Take them instead with Thamar to the house of Ay; and the Princess Ta-Thata shall stay there too till she recovers, and the mourning for the Royal Heir is over. I must do *something* for you and Thamar – what shall it be?'

'Perhaps your Majesty and the Queen would visit us in the water garden?'

'We'll think of something else, as well! You're always impossible – but we will come willingly, all the same.'

Shaking his head ruefully, and laughing at himself, Akhtat'nat strode down the corridors. 'What a man – what a God – what a King! I give him one quick, sharp lesson on how to deal with insubordination, and how fast he learns!'

Epilogue

The Star in the East

'This is a strange journey for you, my friend.'

'All my journeys are strange, Tahlevi!'

Beneath Reuben and Sadhi the vast bulk of M'tuska swayed to the delicate stepping of giant feet. Anak's expression was one of haughty resignation, for he carried Tahlevi's mighty weight above his hump. Henmut trotted on a furry donkey in the rear.

'And is this visit to Imhotep's tomb in keeping with the beliefs of your people, and their One True God? I don't ask to be difficult, my friend, I merely ask.'

Reuben had wondered about that question, himself. The animals moved through the dark as he considered it. Ahead of them, when the moon rose, they would see the tremendous, rising steps of King Zoser's Great Eternal House, built for him by Imhotep as King Merenkere's had been built by Hekhti.

'I know little of Imhotep, Tahlevi. When I was the King's slave the people venerated him as a demi-god. The scribes poured him libations before they worked, calling him father of medicine, the most famous of scribes. My eyes and ears were shut to the many gods of Kemi, so I didn't listen hard.'

'Indeed there are many! You were wise. But Imhotep – him I venerate myself. Besides, he has a fine, ingenious tomb.' Tahlevi cracked his fingers. 'I have still a few small keepsakes –' He glanced down at Henmut, now trotting beside him, and was silent.

'Keepsakes? So that's where the Princess Ta-Thata's little figurine –'

'Ahem! It was a pleasure to present it to the Princess. There was a look of our noble friend.' He wiped tears from his face with a stubby forefinger.

'I saw the resemblance, too. And it's because of Hekhti that we're here tonight. There, Tahlevi, is an answer to your question. Can it be irreligious to follow the dying wishes of so good a man?'

'I am not one to say what is irreligious, and what is not. As a man loves, so he is. I loved to steal – now I love to create. Hekhti loved to cure.'

They were silent. Presently Tahlevi resumed, 'As for the great Imhotep – may Isis reward him! – he was also Vizier, as you know, and Chief Ritualist. There was no limit to his knowledge, his wisdom and his power. He was more powerful than our good friend Hekhti, who had no wish for it.'

'Perhaps Hekhti died younger,' suggested Reuben.

'I don't know, being still a very ignorant man. But I do remember hearing that Imhotep wielded mysterious powers that put him far above the rest of us, Reuben. For all that,' said Tahlevi delicately, again forgetting his son's presence, 'his tomb was badly protected. I myself never received a revelation there, only fine ivory and gold.'

The moon had risen by the time they reached the necropolis, and illuminated Imhotep's giant masterpiece.

Tahlevi looked at it approvingly, as they turned their beasts down the pathway leading to where the greatest of Kemi's past great men lay at rest. Few people were about so late, except priests from the mortuary temples, or sick people brought by their families and friends. Camels they knew, but an elephant was a shock, almost a visitation, and they scattered at sight of M'tuska's bulky grandeur.

'Last time I was here, Akhtat'nat and I were much occupied with different thoughts !' Reuben made M'tuska kneel, took Sadhi in his arms, and slipped with him off the elephant's head.

'People are looking at us!' whispered Henmut.

'They're looking at M'tuska ! Reuben, you should have come in state with an escort, for here's a priest with a most scolding expression!'

But when Reuben had presented offerings of golden rings to the priest, and he had bitten one, he appeared mollified, and suggested that the whole party should follow him to the Vizier's actual resting place, away from the thronging sick and mendicants about the entrance.

Tahlevi's eyes sparkled, but Reuben courteously refused. 'We, too, are here as suppliants. Perhaps these sick and suffering poor have greater claim on Him who heals than has the King's friend with his golden rings and his privileges.' He sat down in the dust, and Tahlevi settled bulkily beside him. The two boys were restless after their long ride, and received stern looks from their respective fathers.

'What no ?' inquired Tahlevi.

'Pray ! Pray as you've never prayed before.'

'I never have. But I'll try – for how long ?'

'All night.' Reuben dropped his head in his hands and prayed, and the dismayed Tahlevi followed suit. Henmut stealthily wandered off, but Sadhi stayed close by his father. He was very puzzled by what was going on (Hekhti's sign language hadn't developed enough to include abstract ideas). He clutched one fold of Reuben's robe, and looked wonderingly about him. As the night wore on and his father neither moved nor raised his head, Sadhi found this very eerie, and wound himself closer into the robe. There were people near by. Sometimes a cough or moan broke the silence, or a mother hushed her crying child.

Sadhi looked upward at the stars and moon riding so far, far above him. He made patterns from them in his head, and designed animals and birds around them, drawing in the air with one raised finger. He thought of Hekhti drawing on a board. After a time he crept even closer to his father, and slept. Towards dawn he woke again, to see Henmut creeping back to lie beside Tahlevi. The two men still sat with their faces pressed into the palms of their hands. Sadhi shivered, and stared at the stars which were less dazzlingly bright than they had been – with one exception : a huge star, high in the East. Sadhi was fascinated and wondered why he hadn't noticed it before, for it burned in the sky with a tremendous light and power that contrasted with the weak, cold pallor of the setting moon. He couldn't look away.

Disturbed by his son's waking, Reuben raised his head. He had been so concentrated in prayer that the passing of the night had gone unnoticed by him, and by Tahlevi, who now shifted his bulk into a comfortable position, and stretched, and yawned gustily. Reuben held Sadhi against him, and looked dreamily at the sky, and at the giant star with its pulsating brilliance. It hung there like a cross of fire and, trained astronomer though he was, he didn't recognize it. For some while he watched it sleepily, then grew aware that the long night vigil had drained him of vitality. It was time to go.

They mounted their animals in silence, Tahlevi taking the sleepy Henmut up with him on Anak. The donkey trotted at their heels.

'Do you suppose –?' muttered Tahlevi, but left his question unfinished. He touched Henmut's shoulder with a protective hand.

Elephant, camel and donkey moved away from the necropolis. The great stepped tomb, containing its sleeping king,
now reared up behind them.

Reuben looked down at Sadhi. 'Son – are you awake?'
Sadhi's eyes were wide open, but he neither heard nor spoke.
A great lassitude came over Reuben. Why, after all, should
he be favoured, when so many people at Imhotep's tomb
would rouse uncured? No still small voice spoke to him
before the desert dawn. There was nothing but exhaustion
and depression of spirits; resignation for his child; a
renewal of sorrow for Hekhti, and for Sadhi's lost hopes
of help. As Tahlevi had asked the night before, he now
asked himself if they should have come.

He glanced about him at the desert, eerie with darkness since the moon had gone. He looked upward. The stars,
though paler still, were very clear – but the giant star, the
brightest, that one he had never seen before, had disappeared. Where it had stood, high in the East and pulsing
with light above the horizon, there only remained a scatter-
ing of small, unnoticeable stars. Reuben rubbed at his tired
eyes.

'Did you see an unusually brilliant star towards the East,
Tahlevi?'

'No, my friend – I did not look at stars. Ahhh! – how
my stomach rumbles, and I long for food!'

Was it an illusion? Reuben asked himself; and as he did
so, the dawn came. The sky flamed into colour, and the
sun leaped over the horizon as though someone had raised
it on a string. Reuben rode M'tuska forward, holding Sadhi
close against him. Deep within him, rising to consciousness
with the inevitability of sunrise, words formed themselves
into the phrase ' – for I have seen His star in the East . . .' and
mysteriously brought him a sense of comfort, in spite of
his afflicted child. But, as he neared Men-nofer, comfort

receded and depression regained its hold. He thought of
Thamar's hopeful waiting, and knew how her eager smile
would vanish as he spoke of failure. Tahlevi guessed his
thoughts.

'We're all tired. Let us eat, and rest a little, at my house –
before you take Sadhi to his mother. No one will know we
left Imhotep's tomb so early, and Thamar won't expect you
back till Re shines high above the city.'

Reuben gave a grateful nod.

Thamar had woken at first light, to find Phut curled up
beside her in the bed that had once been Meri-Mekhmet's.
She lay on her back and studied the doves and butterflies
painted on the ceiling, but her thoughts were all with Sadhi.
She would have gone with him, too, but there had been
Phut and the other children to look after, the cats, Benoni,
and the frail Court Chamberlain Ay who, since his recovery,
seemed equally dependent on her. Besides, Merenkere and
Meri-Mekhmet were coming to see their daughter after the
King's daily rituals were accomplished. So Thamar had had
to stay in order to receive the King and Queen, care for
everyone else, and see the cats were fed. This last was most
important, for Cefalu was upset and very quiet. To starve
him might have led to permanent estrangement.

She crept out of bed without waking Phut, pulled on her
linen dress, brushed her long hair, and then ran barefoot
into the water garden. It was very peaceful. The fountains
played against a vivid background of dawn sky, birds sang,
and there was an occasional plop! as one of the red fish
rose to the pool's surface. Thamar heard a slight sound, and
looked behind her. Cefalu had come too. He sat down with
his back ostentatiously toward her, and began to fidget with
his whiskers.

'I'm very sorry, Cefalu,' she said. Then added basely, 'But it was Reuben's decision, really.'

A derisive twitching of Cefalu's tail showed what he thought of such duplicity.

There was another sound behind her – the scuffling of small, determined feet. Phut had been awakened by some instinct that told him she was absent. He leaned heavily against her, to reach his arms up around her neck. Phut's arrival was followed by Benoni's. His tremendous coat, once cream-coloured, was now almost white, though still very thick. When he lay panting by the pool's rim it was as though someone had carelessly flung down a heap of woolly rugs. Next came Casper, who sat patting at the fish in an ineffectual manner; Thamar's two little girls, whimpering slightly till they reached her; and Joshu, gay, lithe, brown, more like Reuben every day, and ready even at this hour to do acrobatics round the pool. When Ta-Thata appeared, accompanied by Ay's bodyservant who said his master couldn't sleep, and had seen them from his window, and would shortly join them for fruit and milk and to salute the sun god, Re, Thamar gave up all hope of a short time to herself, and realized with rueful inner laughter that wherever she went a horde of demanding people immediately came too.

The morning wore on – and the lengthy stories of Ay's youth. Ta-Thata and Thamar escaped to change their dresses and arrange their hair before the King and Queen arrived. The children were shouting with pleasure at sight of a kingfisher sitting on a bulrush, when Merenkere and Meri-Mekhmet walked informally into the water garden. Meri-Mekhmet kissed her father, who with the stubbornness of age sat slyly where he was while everyone else prostrated themselves.

'They've not yet returned?' asked the King, addressing himself to Thamar.

'O Sovereign, my lord – no. We've been awaiting them some while.'

Merenkere looked down silently into the pool. If Sadhi had been cured, he thought, Reuben would have hurried back. Thamar watched him. Her heart sank. (But *I* have other sons.) He raised his head and looked at her. Each guessed what the other thought. He gave his gentle smile, and said, 'So. But life goes on. And in the meantime here's something unusual – Cefalu is ignoring me, and seems not to notice that his noble son Ptahsuti has arrived in the Queen's arms.'

'O Sovereign, my lord, Cefalu is ignoring everyone! He's much distressed. We – Reuben wouldn't take Casper – who has hurt a back paw – to Imhotep's tomb.'

'He would have assuredly got lost,' said the King with faint amusement. 'Which would have been distracting.'

Cefalu turned his head and gave Merenkere such a scathing look – half-closing his green eyes and laying back his ears – that he felt quite shaken.

'I wish he were my Majesty's Vizier! No one would dare revolt again.'

Benoni was much offended by the King's remark. A cat to be Vizier of the Two Lands! It was bad enough that they were honoured in the temples, where dogs went totally disregarded.

'Take Casper to the tomb of Meluseth,' he told Cefalu, giving the King a hurt look from his golden eyes. 'That Pearl of Wisdom would cure anyone!'

Cefalu put out a paw as though by accident, placed it on Benoni's tail, and extended his claws. Then he lay down with his back to everyone, and Casper was amazed to hear him say beneath his breath, 'She was the silliest cat in the

whole Palace.' He waited eagerly for more, but Cefalu had
gone to sleep. Like Benoni he dozed very frequently these
days, and often said the weather wasn't so hot as it used to
be, even here in Kemi.

'Let us go in,' said the King presently, 'or we shall be
roasted here!' He stood up and gave Meri-Mekhmet his
hand. For a moment they were reflected in the pool together,
as so often during their first meetings. She knew what he
was thinking when he said, 'Ta-Thata is wearing that little
coronet I gave you when you angrily rejected the thought
of being like a royal princess!'

'I cannot part her from it. She loves it, as I did.'

His hold tightened. 'We must find her someone charming
to give her coronets.'

'If she's like me, she will find him for herself.'

'Thank you, my first sister –' He kissed her ear, and led
her toward the house. As they went indoors, Meri-
Mekhmet said, 'Did you see – our kingfisher is back? Or
his descendant –'

'Yes, I saw. I wish Reuben would come, too, before our
duties call us. I fear that this –' He glanced at Thamar's
darkening eyes, and was silent.

Reuben did return, just as one of Ay's slaves was serving
the King with wine, and the party seating themselves on
couches and Ay's richest rugs. He propelled Sadhi into the
room ahead of him, one hand on the child's shoulder.

'Well, Reuben?' asked the King. And added, 'Don't prostrate yourself, it is too hot.'

Reuben's eyes met Thamar's, and he couldn't speak. He
gave a slight, almost imperceptible, shake of the head.
Failure was all the worse because – during that moment
of strange comfort on the journey home – he had allowed
himself to hope. Thamar summoned up all her courage, and
smiled at him as though she had expected nothing.

'Wine for the Prince of Canaan,' Meri-Mekhmet told Ay's slave. 'Reuben – we'll choose some priest or physician who will devote his life to developing Hekhti's work, and teaching Sadhi.'

'Your Majesty is always kind.' Reuben sat down at the King's bidding, and wiped a hand exhaustedly across his forehead. He kissed his little girls and Phut, and looking round him said, 'But where is Joshu?'

Ta-Thata and Joshu had lingered in the water garden with Cefalu, who slept.

'He's very tired.' Joshu stroked the short, black, furry coat from head to tail. 'The world will seem different when Cefalu's here no longer. I've known him all my life.'

'It's a strange world.' Ta-Thata regarded them thoughtfully. 'Don't you think so? People – and animals – are like kingfishers. They're in your life one moment, and the next : gone!'

Joshu propped his head on one elbow – he was lying full-length at the pool's edge – and regarded her in turn. 'I wish that I had known this Hekhti!'

'You knew I thought of him?' She looked surprised.

'I know a lot about you already – though we only met last night, Princess.'

'Ta-Thata.'

'I may call you Ta-Thata, then?'

'Yes, you may.' She shook forward her hair till her face was shadowed by it. Sudden constraint seized her, and a confusion that she hadn't known in her serene and childish love for Hekhti.

'Do all the girls in Kemi have such long lashes?'

'Why do you ask?' She didn't look up.

His voice teased her. 'Because it's inconvenient! They

cover your eyes. And your eyes are like an oryx's, they're enormous.'

It was an effort to look at him. She coloured, and said in a dignified way, 'I wish you wouldn't tease me! I thought you were sincere; just as your father's a sincere person.'

He played with her hand, and examined the rings on her long fingers. 'I'm rebuked! But you hardly know my father.'

'He has been several times to the King my father's Court. You look like him – Hekhti used to say that people who are alike in their bodies are alike in their minds, and –' she broke off, sighing. 'I wish Sadhi would come back cured! Then he could grow up and carry on with Hekhti's discovery – that's what Hekhti would have liked. He said Sadhi had a healer's hands.'

'This Hekhti! He's still in your mind. How am I to get him out?'

'You'll never do that! Why do you want to, anyway?'

'Don't you know? Look in the pool.'

She stood up gracefully, and Joshu jumped to his feet and stood beside her. He was a head taller, strong and compact. When he was fully grown he would have Reuben's breadth of shoulder. He already had Thamar's kind and bewitching smile, and her dark eyes. The expression in them, when he looked at Ta-Thata, was his own.

'Well – Princess? What do you see? There's a pretty picture for you : a great Sovereign's daughter, and a nobody who has developed sudden ambitions since last night.'

She tried to look composed. 'This ambition – it's because I am the Sovereign's daughter ?'

'What else could it possibly be – and you so sadly plain, my poor Princess !'

'I am *so* plain ?' She felt suddenly more lighthearted than she had since Hekhti's death.

'They haven't warned you?' The corners of his eyes crinkled. 'I suppose you're usually kept far from boys, and surrounded by ladies who would scream and wring their hands if they found a mere nobody kissing you. Isn't that so? Tell me, why do you wear that ridiculous little crown thing on your head?'

'It's not ridiculous. It is my mother's, and I love it. My father gave it to her beside this pool, when he – '

'When he fell in love with her? Take it off,' Joshu commanded, 'I want to look at it.'

Aware of feeling faintly disappointed, she took it off. He examined the jewels and gold wires intently. 'Yes, it's very pretty. Do you know, Ta-Thata, a sudden thought has struck me?'

'What is that?'

'Perhaps the King your father would sooner marry you to a nobody who had no army, than to someone like Kalda of Shinar.'

'Perhaps he would,' murmured Ta-Thata, finding it difficult to breathe.

'We're being watched by a kingfisher – he's wondering what I'm doing with this little coronet! Well, I'm going to put it on your hair, as the King your father did for the Queen your mother. Isn't that what happened?'

His brown hands skilfully rearranged the coronet. Ta-Thata smiled at him, and they looked into each other's eyes.

'She smiled at him, too –' Joshu put his hands upon her shoulders with an authority that, for all his youth, reminded her of Reuben's – 'and after that I think it very likely that the King your father kissed her . . .'

They came through the entrance into the long cool room where their parents were still sitting. Everyone looked up, and saw them standing there side by side. The King turned to Meri-Mekhmet and smiled a reminiscent smile. Reuben gazed at Thamar. Phut and the little girls jumped up and down. Sadhi, who hadn't seen his brother since leaving Canaan, came rushing excitedly to greet him. His lips moved as though they found it difficult.

'It's J – *Joshu* !' said Sadhi, with delight.

About the Author

Rosemary Harris is a Londoner, but spent her early years moving from place to place being slightly educated by a succession of governesses and different schools. Trained as a painter at the Chelsea School of Art, she later worked on picture restoring at the Courtauld Institute. She began writing very young, but only switched to it for a living when her first play nearly made the West End. 'My first stories were dictated when I was about four or five – the central figure was a greyhound called, oddly enough, Greyhound. He had endless adventures underground by the light of one naked light bulb suspended from a tunnel roof. After the stories were written down by someone else the illustrations were painstakingly done by me – I can still recall the matchless realism of that light bulb with thick black strokes all round it to represent the light. A shame my family didn't preserve this work – it might have made a fortune for Faber and me, with its eccentricity and Freudian overtones.'

Rosemary Harris's earliest books were for adults and included two thrillers; then in 1968 she published her first children's book, *The Moon in the Cloud*, which was awarded the Library Association's Carnegie Medal. Since then she has written for both adults and children, and has become well-known as a reteller of legends, illustrated by Errol Le Cain. 'Writing for children is more enjoyable, and I come back to it again and again because it gives more imaginative scope – children have a strong natural sense of theatre, and don't mind how much suspension of disbelief there is, provided the plot has a firm beginning, middle and end and is convincingly based on character; this is exactly like writing for the stage, my first love.

'As a profession, writing has its arduous side, and I would like at least six other lives (simultaneously) to do different things in. I like animals (but feel it's unfair to keep them in a Chelsea flat), music, photography, theatre, and seeing lots of people. (*People* don't really suffer in flats.) Too long in London, I start hankering for the country, and too long there I start hankering for London – and all summer, wherever I am, I hanker for the sea. I would like to have a garden again, I would like to ski, I would like seriously to study the guitar; there's the Tibetan exhibition at the British Museum and the Turners at the Tate, and my two desks are double-piled with papers, and in my next lifetime I'm going to lie on a hot beach all day (being really very lazy) and listen to all sorts of music played by someone else. Six lifetimes, did I say? One needs twenty-four!'

Also by Rosemary Harris

The Moon in the Cloud

Long ago, the Lord God stirred and grumbled,
'They're all bad down there, except the Noahs. I'll
have a flood.' But there was one other good and
deserving couple in Israel – Reuben and Thamar.
Even Noah, devoted as he was to the will of the Lord,
worried about them, and couldn't help thinking
it a little unfair that Ham, his own wayward and
selfish son, should be set above this gentle pair.
Ham, of course, thought it only right and
proper. And he said he could get both Reuben
and Thamar on to the Ark, when the time came. But
it wasn't his job to book places on the Ark –
and he forgot, as Noah never did, that the Lord
God was a watchful God.

The Shadow on the Sun

Thamar tries to discourage her husband, Reuben,
from returning to the land of Kemi, now that
the Flood has subsided. But they do return, and find
King Merenkere unhappily in love with Meri-
Mekhmet, his Court Chamberlain's proud and
beautiful daughter. When she rejects his love, the
King's benevolence turns to tyranny and his
aching heart leaves him prey to disease from the
rising Nile. Then a visitor arrives in Kemi – the evil-eyed
Prince of Punt. Why does he keep staring at
Meri-Mekhmet? His intentions are soon clear,
and Reuben finds himself on another great adventure
leading to a terrifying confrontation between
the forces of good and evil.

Up the Pier

Helen Cresswell

It might have been the homelessness that made
Carrie's eyes able to see the Pontifex family
when she began visiting the pier, noticing first the
oddly dressed boy and the dog who were there one
minute and invisible the next, and then the signs
that someone might be hiding in one of the sales
kiosks on the empty winter pier. After all,
George, Ellen and Kitchener Pontifex were homeless
too, though the problem with them was that they
had a perfectly good home waiting for them back in
1921 where they came from, but now they were
stuck in 1971 and having to camp out on
the pier . . .

The Mouth of the Night

Iris Macfarlane

'Before this,' said the storyteller, 'there was a king
and a queen and they had one son . . .' or maybe
it was a farmer or a fisherman, but they would be
certain to fall into fantastic adventures, for
these stories are folktales translated from Gaelic,
and that means richness, beauty and vivid
imagination.

   Here are tales of a prince who had to endure his shoes
full of water until he could find blackberries in
February, a boy apprenticed to a wizard, and
the labours set on the son of the King of the City of
Straw. Here also are the great giants, monsters,
princesses and every variety of enchantment, told with
the haunting and sometimes spine-chilling imagery
of the Highlands and Hebridean Islands.

   These are new translations of stories originally
collected by J. F. Campbell more than 120
years ago.

Heard About the Puffin Club?

... it's a way of finding out more about Puffin books
and authors, of winning prizes (in competitions),
sharing jokes, a secret code, and perhaps seeing
your name in print! When you join you get
a copy of our magazine, *Puffin Post*, sent to you four
times a year, a badge and a membership book.
For details of subscription and an application form,
send a stamped addressed envelope to:

The Puffin Club Dept A
Penguin Books Limited
Bath Road
Harmondsworth
Middlesex UB7 ODA

and if you live in Australia, please write to:

The Australian Puffin Club
Penguin Books Australia Limited
P.O. Box 257
Ringwood
Victoria 3134